JALAPENO CUPCAKE WENCH

Book One

The Amazing Gracie Trilogy

by

Carol Kilgore

For John,

the most Amazing man in the world

CHAPTER 1

Cold! *Cold!* Gracie Hofner looked down. *I can't believe I did that.* While reaching for her buzzing phone, she'd poured the remains of her water bottle, intended for her impatiens, over her bare feet. She pressed the button. "Hi, Nicky."

"Morning. I've got something you may want to see." The voice on Gracie's phone belonged to Nick Rivera, her partner.

Former partner. Their paths had been the same—patrol, homicide detectives, and then detectives in the San Antonio Regional Intelligence Center—SARIC. San Antonio Police Department all the way. Except unlike her, Nick had found his niche there.

In addition, they were friends. "Fun or work?"

"Nothing fun about murder, Gracie."

She went inside for a pad and pencil, greeted by the aroma of the coffee that had brewed while she jogged. "Are we cleared?"

"Negative. Double homicide. Missing family."

"If the family's missing, who's dead?"

"Hector and Therese Cantu. You ever heard of Cantu Electric?"

"Don't think so."

"Good reputation on the West Side. They've been around since my dad was a kid—started by Hector Cantu's father back in the fifties. The old commercial was like *Cantu can do.* Hector's son runs the business

5

now. Mr. Cantu's retired. Rephrase—now he's good and retired. He and his wife are the deceased."

She moved to the table and put her phone on speaker so she could take notes. "Who's missing?"

"The Cantus have three kids, two daughters and the son, all grown. Besides the electrician business, the son owns an upscale retail lighting store. High end only. Kim and I went in there after we bought our house. I couldn't afford a switchplate, much less a lamp or fixture. The son and his family are missing."

"How many?"

"Three. Husband, wife, daughter."

Daughter. Please, not a missing child. For a second, Gracie couldn't breathe. "What about his sisters?"

"Homicide's talked to both. One's married and lives out of town. Her family's all accounted for. The other's single, teaches at St. Mary's—ethics, philosophy. She's the one who found the bodies."

"How?" Gracie pulled some paper napkins from the stack and wiped her feet.

"She comes over for coffee every morning."

"That's a bitch." Gracie leaned back in the chair. "What makes you think Bastion would be interested?"

"A hunch. It stinks. This was a hit."

The planned kill plus missing family would've been what prompted Homicide to call in SARIC. Cartels and gangs used such tactics.

"We know who orders hits like this. The why must be something important." Nick's voice was tight. In Gracie's mind, he clenched and released the muscles in his jaw.

Nick was a good detective. His hunches usually amounted to something. Gracie couldn't help herself. She had to ask about the daughter. "How old is the girl?"

"Don't do this to yourself, Gracie." Better than anyone, Nick understood how she was.

"How old?"

"Six."

A knot formed in Gracie's stomach. Kids were the ones caught in the middle every time. "Let me run it by Jackson. I'll get back to you."

Gracie punched off and called her boss, Roland Jackson, Coordinated Solutions Director at The Bastion Group. Gracie was part of a small staff that reported directly to him.

He must've been holding the phone in his hand. "This better be good, Hofner."

"Morning, sir! I realize it's Saturday, but that's never stopped us before, right?"

"You're not on assignment."

"Not yet, but I just got a call from my former SAPD partner."

"Rivera?"

"Yes. Double murder, missing family members, including a little girl."

"Let's not talk about the girl yet. Why does he believe Bastion would be interested?"

"I asked him that same question. He said the deceased were an older couple, well-established in the community, and it looked like a hit. He also said it stinks. I trust his nose, sir."

"It's slow. I figured something was going to break. I'll call my contact over there, make sure this ticks enough of our boxes." He hung up before she could say anything else. Jackson knew how she was with kids, too.

After showering, she brushed her teeth and pulled appropriate clothing from her closet—buttery tailored slacks and a short-sleeve navy and white polka dot blouse. She had her hands on a pair of Nikes when Jackson called back.

"We're a go. Are you going to be all right about the girl if it doesn't go well?"

7

Gracie took a deep breath. "I'll handle it. But I'll do everything I can to make sure it does go well first."

"All right then. Get over there and let me know what's what as soon as possible."

CHAPTER 2

When Gracie disconnected from Jackson, she texted Nick to give him the news and get the address. His return text came while she was eating a slice of peanut butter toast. She finished eating, but ended up pouring half a cup of coffee down the sink.

So much for a free Saturday—and the vinca and lantana she wanted to buy and plant. Absently, she turned to dry her hands, but encountered the upper cabinet instead. "Ow!" She rubbed her fingers above her eyebrow. They came away with a red smear.

"Dammit." She grabbed the towel and pressed it to her head while she fished out her first aid kit. *This is gonna burn like a sonofabitch.* She squeezed some alcohol on a cotton ball and pressed it to the cut.

After the burn went away, she took the antibiotic cream and a bandage with her to the mirror in the hall. The cut was tiny. Last, she inspected her blouse and slacks. Blood free. She was good to go.

Fifteen minutes later, she parked her beat-up Jeep Cherokee at the curb behind a long line of police vehicles on San Antonio's West Side.

Her Jeep wasn't really beat-up, but it was ten years old, and the color of a slightly sun-bleached cow patty. Too ugly for anyone to want to steal, so that was always one less worry. She liked it because it let her blend into the night when that was important. It also had the biggest, baddest V-8 that would fit under the hood, giving her instant power when she needed it. And it had the coldest air conditioner in the state.

The neighborhood was filled with small mid-century frame houses with tidy yards. After clearing her entry with a patrol officer, she ducked under the crime scene tape and strode past the medical examiner's van backed into the driveway.

SAPD Sergeant Neva Salazar stood on the front porch. Gracie and Neva went back to Gracie's early days in Homicide. A confidant for sure, but also a mentor.

The week before, Gracie had gone to a surprise birthday party for Neva's fortieth. Gracie hadn't realized she was eight years younger than her friend— she'd guessed five, max. Neva didn't look forty, even though she'd been heading one of the homicide teams for three years.

Gracie stopped at her side. Neva pointed at the Band-Aid. "What happened?"

"I tried to make love to a kitchen cabinet."

"That's not what they mean by a woody, Hofner. Rivera told me you were coming before Gherkin did." *Gherkin* was what everyone called Lieutenant George Pickle, head of Homicide. Even the chief called him Gherkin. His wife, too.

"Who's leading it on your side?"

"Jones and O'Connor."

"May I go in?"

"Suit up first. Gear's over there." Neva inclined her head toward a chair near the door. "Don't mess with the cabinets."

Gracie donned the shower cap, booties, and gloves, pulling the shower cap to her eyebrows.

Nick met her between the living and dining rooms. "Hey, blondie. It's been a while since you've worked a homicide. You ready?"

He looked at her but wouldn't hold her gaze. This

was the first time they'd worked together since she'd left SARIC, but they met once a month or so just to reconnect. She hadn't forgot his tells. Something was up. "As ever. Let's go."

"They're in the kitchen." Nick turned and she followed him.

The living and dining rooms reminded Gracie of her grandmother's house, with seemingly unrelated pictures covering the walls and knickknacks sitting on every flat surface.

They entered the kitchen.

The bodies of Mr. and Mrs. Cantu leaned against each other at the kitchen table, fully clothed. Mr. Cantu's feet were clad in Spurs socks, and Mrs. Cantu's leopard-print flip flops complimented her bright red toenails. Coffee spilled across the table surface and onto the floor from Mrs. Cantu's overturned mug.

Together, even in death. Gracie took a moment to pack down the rush of sorrow that made her knees weak and threatened to overtake her. Murder scenes had been like that for her from the very first one. *Suck it up, Grace Elizabeth, and do your job.* Right now, it was business and nothing more. She could and would worry over the couple later. That was why she'd transferred out of homicide in the first place.

The investigator from the ME's office showed Gracie the bodies. A small caliber bullet hole centered each forehead, but it was behind the right ears that Gracie lingered. Each victim had been tapped two more times to ensure they didn't survive. The shooter had a plan long before he arrived.

Neva Salazar walked in. "Rivera, talk to me."

"They knew the killer. No jimmied doors or windows. Nothing broken. He shot them in the forehead first. Quick. Neither had time to react. The killings happened last night before they went to bed. Mrs. Cantu still had on lipstick, but it's not fresh as if she'd put it on this morning. And the coffee in the pot was cold when I got here at six-thirty. Plus, rigor's just beginning—the A/C was jacked down to sixty, so they've been dead since at least midnight. More like nine or ten."

"Hofner?"

"The first shot went to Mr. Cantu. He was the bigger threat. When he was shot, Mrs. Cantu jerked and spilled her coffee. Mr. Cantu's mug is upright. I think the killer sat or stood across from Mr. Cantu." Gracie pointed to the chair she meant. "His wound is right in the center. Mrs. Cantu's is a little off. The shooter fired before she completely faced him."

"That's it." Nick grinned. "Come back in here and show me up."

"What else?" Neva ignored Nick's comment and spoke to Gracie.

"Nick's right that they weren't threatened by the shooter. He had coffee, too. Or at least something to drink. In the kitchen—a friends and family place. Maybe there were cookies or something else sweet. Have the crime scene investigators check the trash—inside and out—and print all the plates, platters, saucers, and mugs that match the ones the Cantus used." Gracie waved toward the kitchen work area. "Use Bastion's investigators and labs if you need to. We're working for you—that means all of us, not just me."

Neva smiled. "The more, the merrier."

"Tell them not to forget spoons and forks. Glasses and liquid containers in the fridge. The tabletop and edges around the two vacant chairs. The shooter cleaned up evidence of himself sitting here, but maybe he didn't wear gloves when he did. And he damn sure wouldn't have worn gloves while sharing coffee with his targets. It's the little things."

Neva tapped her tablet. Nick paced, unable to

stand still, not looking in their direction. Something bothered him, but Gracie would wait until they were outside to find out what.

"Another thing. Check the coffee, both in the pantry and in the cups. The Cantus were older. If both regular and decaf are in the pantry, they need to check what's in the cups. If it's not decaf, chances are the deaths occurred earlier in the day."

Neva nodded as she tapped. "Anything in the rest of the house?"

Nick shook his head. "No."

"Yes," Gracie said. "Check for prints and bodily fluids in the bathroom. Toilet, vanity area, medicine cabinet, linen closet. Entire door and window area, wall above and floor around the toilet."

"You think he took a leak?"

"Maybe. I think he excused himself to use the bathroom and retrieved his gun while he was in there. If he didn't use a revolver, he probably flushed to mask the sound when he racked the slide. The autopsy will show the angle on the forehead bullets. He probably shot them from a standing position as soon as he returned."

"Now I remember how Gracie works." Nick walked around. "Have them check the TV remotes, too. A Spurs game was on last night. I remember someone saying that Mr. Cantu was hard of hearing, and I don't see any aids. The volume would've been raised, and that would've masked the sound of gunfire. Otherwise, someone would've called in on six shots unless he used a suppressor. Cantu may have turned it off, but if not, the shooter would've done so before he left."

"Good call, Nicky." Gracie had missed him and their brainstorming sessions. He was like her fourth brother, as if she didn't have enough sibs already.

"Will do." Neva tapped her tablet again. "Hofner,

any chance the missing son could have done this?"

"About as much chance as you falling off the edge of the earth. There's nothing personal about these killings."

"That's the consensus. Just looking for confirmation. The out-of-town daughter called me. I'm going to text you her number, Rivera. I told her you'd be calling and for her to tell you what she told me. After you talk to her, call me. I want you to hear the story from her before we decide on a plan. After we do, you can relay the total package to Hofner."

Neva handed Nick her card, with information handwritten on the back. "Here are the son's home and business addresses. Check out the home first."

CHAPTER 3

Gracie stopped Nick as they entered the dining room. "I want to look around in here and in the living room. Probably take some photos, too."

"Go for it."

A lace tablecloth draped the table. Gracie got on her knees and looked underneath. Clean. Same with the chairs. A buffet and a bar cart were the only other furniture pieces in the room. She pulled a yellow plastic swizzle stick from a plastic glass filled with shiny tropical birds and fish. She put it back.

The living room provided more choices—books, magazines, and doodads all over the place. "I'm taking shots of the bookcases, tables, and TV. Plus the remotes, if I see them out."

No response. She looked around. Nick stood on the porch taking off his gear. Gracie went back to work. Too many things to take in while he waited for her. He'd had hours to look at it all. When she finished, she took one last shot of the room from the front door to keep everything in perspective. In a homicide, anything at all could become important in closing the case.

Nick was talking to a patrol officer who left when Gracie joined him. She poked his arm. "Did you do a full check on all the furniture?"

She got the look—a probe clear to the soles of her feet by two deep brown eyes searching for her brain.

Nick was five-ten, and she was two inches shorter. They stood almost eyeball to eyeball, although she may have outweighed him by ten pounds, given her strong farm-girl bones and ample girly parts. One of which delighted in squirrelling away every single bite of anything sweet that passed between her lips.

"Do you think I forgot how to be a cop just because you left?" Nick placed his hands on his hips, daring her to give him any guff.

"Mea culpa."

He gave her a one-armed hug. "I forgot you're such a pain in the ass. Hard to forget the klutzy parts, though. I still have scars. Ready to go?"

They would always be partners—even though it wasn't official. Just like with Neva, Gracie and Nick had bonded through those early years of academy and patrol.

Nick stayed quiet on the way to his pickup. He opened the passenger door. "Get in. I want you to listen to this call, too."

Inside the truck, Gracie touched his hand. "Are you okay?"

"Yeah. I can't figure out why someone would want them dead. He never hurt anybody."

"Maybe one of them saw something they shouldn't have."

"People are fucking crazy." He hit the top of the steering wheel with the heel of his right hand.

Whatever bothered him was magnified by the murders. "That's old news. Something else is wrong with you."

"Nah. I'm just tired."

"Uh-uh." She shook her head. "We worked together too long. I knew the first time you wouldn't look at me back there. What's wrong?"

"Nothing."

"I'm the Queen of Nothing, so don't give me that.

What's wrong?"

"Kim and I had a fight. That's all."

"And you're waiting for her to call you? Ball's in your court, dude. That's what my dad told my brothers. Doesn't matter what you fought about. Or who had the last word. Or even if there's no way in the world she's right. You fight, it's your duty to be the bigger man. I consider you a brother, and my dad's not here, so I'm passing his orders on."

A puff of air escaped between his lips. "I've actually missed you, Hofner. Nobody's butted into my life since you left."

"Now I know why you really called me. We all need someone to butt in, especially when we think we don't." She flashed him a grin. "Back to business. Get the Cantu daughter on the horn, and let's see what she has to say."

Nick started the engine and turned on the air conditioning before putting up the windows. "I don't want anyone out there overhearing." He found the number and put the phone on speaker.

A female voice said, "Hello?"

"This is Detective Rivera, San Antonio Police. With me is Gracie Hofner. Who's speaking, please?"

"Carmen Leal. Carmen Cantu Leal. Sergeant Salazar said you'd be calling. Thank you."

"Sorry for your loss, ma'am. The sergeant said you have something to share with me."

"Is it all right to tell you with the other officer there?"

"Yes, ma'am. She's also involved with your parents' case. You're on speaker, and this call is being recorded."

"Okay. Victor—that's my brother—Victor's always reached for the brass ring, if you know what I mean."

The pain in her voice came through loud and clear.

"I do, but since this is a call, I'd appreciate your being more direct as to what you mean."

"I'll try." She made a little sound in her throat, not quite a sigh. "Growing up, Victor was like all the rest of us. But when he got older, he was all about show. He wanted the trendy clothes, a newer car. He started running with a faster crowd."

Gracie and Nick exchanged glances.

Carmen blew her nose. "I'm sorry. It hurts, you know?"

Nick stayed silent for a few moments to give Carmen a little space. "Just tell us what you can. It's hard to know what's important at this point. Take your time." Nick's voice was gentle. No one Gracie knew at the PD or Bastion was as good as Nick at getting witnesses to cooperate. He had a gift.

"We weren't wealthy, but somehow Dad and Mom managed to send all three of us to college. And we all graduated. Mom was so proud of that. She used to brag about us all the time. The priests told her she needed to quit." Carmen giggled.

"What's funny?"

"Mom got tired of hearing it and just stopped telling them about it at confession. She said it was her right and a privilege."

Gracie made a fish face to keep from laughing. Any woman with blazing red toenails and leopard print flip-flops wouldn't balk at holding out on a priest or two.

Nick chuckled. "Go on."

"Anyway, not long after Victor graduated, he tried to get Dad to sell the business, but Dad wouldn't hear of it. He kept on working, but when he was sixty-three, he had a mild heart attack and decided to retire. Victor had been working alongside him, and he took over. Dad made him promise not to raise prices to the regular customers or to anyone living on the

18

West Side. Victor didn't like it, but he promised."

"Did he keep the promise?"

"He did. Victor's degree was in business—he knew what he was doing. He advertised heavily in other areas of town and also pumped up the commercial part of the company. Cantu Electric took off."

"What happened then?"

"Victor got enough together to start San Antonio Lighting, and it's successful, too."

"How successful? Did he share any specifics with you?"

"No, but successful enough that he and Jessica—that's his wife— recently bought a big new house in Stone Oak."

Figures. Stone Oak was a pricey area in far north San Antonio. Some of the homes up there edged toward the million mark. A few were already there.

"He's doing good. What is it you think we should know?"

"Jessica called me last week."

"Is that odd?"

"No, we're close. It's odder that I haven't heard from her since then."

"What did she tell you?"

"Victor had been acting strange for a week or so, and she wondered if I knew what was going on."

"You and your brother were close, too?"

"Yes, we always have been. I'm the older sister. He's the middle child. Usually he'd tell me stuff before he told Mom, hoping he could figure a way to stay out of trouble. But he hadn't told me anything. I was going to give him a few days to see if he called, and then I planned on calling him. He called me the day after Jessica did."

Gracie could relate to that, being the youngest of five. Clearing things with an older sibling often helped to refine what she told her mother.

19

"He asked if it would be all right for Jessica and Maya—that's their daughter—to come stay with us for a few days. Maybe a week. I told him sure, but asked about school. He said he would make arrangements with Maya's teacher. My niece is in first grade, and while she's smart and likes school, she's still very young emotionally. Very tied to Mommy and Daddy."

While Carmen talked, Gracie's phone vibrated. She sent Jackson to voicemail. He wouldn't be thrilled, but he knew where she was. If it was urgent, he'd call back.

"Victor told me he was having trouble with someone and he'd feel better knowing Jessica and Maya were safe."

"Did he give you any additional information?"

"No. I asked if it was someone at work. He said he couldn't say, but he'd tell me later. I pressed, but all he said was that if anything happened to him, he wanted to make sure that I kept Jessica and Maya safe."

CHAPTER 4

Gracie fiddled with the air conditioning vents, aiming those on her side at her face, while Nick continued to jot details of the conversation as he wound up the call. Carmen and her family lived in Corpus Christi. She owned a small nursery. Her husband worked for the port. They had two teenage sons.

When he hung up, he slipped his phone into his shirt pocket before looking at Gracie. "Now you know as much as I do. What do you think?"

Gracie readjusted one of the vents. The smell of death hadn't been pronounced, but it still lingered. Probably in her mind more than in reality. "Most likely the shooter was male, and for sure he didn't just waltz in on a whim and decide to off them. Not a gang punk. The shots were precise, the bullets large enough to do the job without making a big mess."

Nick studied something unseen on the knee of his trousers, rubbing his thumb over and over the same spot. He wasn't picky. He was nervous. She'd give him a little while to remember how they always shared. If he didn't fill her in, she would ask. Keeping it inside could create a barrier between them as well as with his investigation. His head wouldn't be in it, and that was dangerous.

"The PD or Bastion can search databases and come up with a list of the usual suspects," Gracie said. "You know that drill. We haven't talked to the local daughter yet, but my money's on the son. There's some kind of involvement. We have to locate him, and not just because he has a young daughter. He's the key."

Nick nodded. "I agree about the son. And the shooter."

"I'm trying to figure out what makes the most sense. It doesn't feel like retaliation. Could be the son was being blackmailed and refused to pay."

"Blackmailed about what?" Nick turned in his seat and leaned against the door.

"Anything. Maybe the shooter learned he kept a girlfriend. Or a boyfriend."

"One of each." Nick moved again, and his elbow hit the horn.

He was edgy. Gracie wished he'd hurry up and tell her what was going on. "Could be. Maybe the son's a trafficker—people, drugs, guns, cash. The possibilities are endless. If that's the case, SARIC should be able to pick up on it easy enough."

Whatever the reason, the son had put his daughter at risk. That gave him a black mark in Gracie's book. "We can hope they find prints that shouldn't be here. Or DNA. And that whatever they find will match something in a database. Bastion can process everything faster, but I don't know if Gherkin will allow us to work it."

Nick's head popped up. "He's not completely onboard with you guys yet. Neva trusts you, but not all the other. Both people she doesn't know and how far Bastion can reach. She thinks Bastion's too much like Big Brother."

"She told me. We chatted the other day at her birthday party. I told her she should be happy Bastion exists—we're one of the things keeping Big Brother from taking over. Gherkin still thinks we're doing the same thing the department does. He doesn't get that we don't conduct official investigations."

"You do poke into ours from time to time."

"True, but we're nearly always looking for something different. No way to avoid that. I'm glad Jackson's contact sees us as we are."

"I realize you'll never come back to the job 'cause you won't give up your fancy phone. But don't you miss all this?"

Nick was right about not giving up her phone. It looked and operated like any other iPhone. But inside she had space for five separate encrypted lines, which was a real plus when she worked undercover. It also had special filters and construction that didn't allow for noise leakage beyond a few inches in either direction. Unless she used the speaker, those in the next seat couldn't hear anything from the person on the other end. She used her speaker a lot.

Gracie grinned. "I do miss it. A little. Not enough to come back. I like Bastion much better. Less routine, more broad-view thinking. Much less paperwork. Besides, I got tired of gang bangers spitting on me."

"Yeah, there is that."

An image popped into Gracie's mind. A little girl with dark hair playing with a doll. She sat in a woman's lap, but the woman's face was out of view. The vision in her head wasn't like an image her subconscious put together from clues, but more a comforting picture. Was she imagining Maya was safe? Or was it something sinister? Something to make her get on the ball? *What the hell?* Gracie wiped a hand down her face.

"Don't let the little girl eat you up, Gracie."

"I can't stop thinking about her. Maya. Now she doesn't have a grandma and grandpa. And it may be that the son and his family are already dead, too."

"Percentage?"

Over the years, she and Nick had developed

their own shorthand. He wanted to learn how likely she thought it was that Victor and his family were deceased. "Low. I think they're alive. Running or hiding." Maybe that's what the image in her head meant.

"Agree."

"If you find them, you'll have a better lead on who killed his parents. And why."

"It's going to be a bitch until something turns up. I hope it doesn't take long." He stared out the windshield, chewing the inside of his cheek. "One thing bothers me."

"What's that?"

"How would either of the Cantus know a hit man well enough to let him in?"

Gracie shrugged. "Could've been a hit woman."

"Still, though, the type of personalities involved."

"Sociopaths turn it on and off. You don't see what you're not looking for—that goes double for people like the Cantus. Could be an old friend or an old friend of one of their kids, even a neighbor. It's someone with a connection to the son or his wife, but that connection may be hidden."

"Yeah. Helps to brainstorm. I'm getting rid of frustrations. You're the only one I can do that with."

"Anytime. How come you still don't have a partner?"

"Three of us in the unit—all on our own. New blood's coming in next month. I'm sure we'll each get one of them." Nick blew out another whoosh of air. "I told you Kim and I had a fight."

Here comes the real talk. About damn time he remembered I don't bite. "Yeah."

"It wasn't a fight. Kim's having an affair."

"What?" Gracie had to nudge him to make him look at her. "You've got to be kidding."

He shook his head. "Not kidding."

24

"Did she tell you?"

"Hell no. Things have been off for a while." He barely opened his mouth.

Gracie waited him out. This had to be brutal for him. He'd fallen for Kim the first time he'd laid eyes on her, rookie year.

"I started following her."

"Oh, shit. Behave yourself, Nicky."

He nodded.

"Do you know the guy?"

Nick looked straight at her. "It's not a guy."

"No. Way." For one of the few times ever, Gracie had no more words.

"Way."

#

After goodbyes and a hug, Gracie walked back to her Jeep in a daze. Kim had been far from one of her besties, but Gracie had never picked up on any hint of her being anything other than straight. Or attracted to anyone other than Nick. She started the engine and aimed the air conditioning vents at her face. Nick waved as he drove past. It had been hard for him to tell her about Kim, but she was glad he had. Otherwise, her betrayal would've eaten a hole in his gut. Gracie didn't want to see him travel that road.

She turned off her favorite country radio station before calling Jackson. He hadn't left a message. "Sorry I couldn't answer. You called in the middle of an interview. What's up?"

"You tell me."

Gracie shared the facts of the Cantu case. It didn't take long. During the telling, a white van pulled up. The uniformed officer let it pass. On the side were the words Crime Scene Unit. This was the second group. Good. Neva was pulling out all the stops.

"What's your take? Do they need our expertise or

can they handle it? SAPD retains us, but they prefer keeping everything in-house."

"They're fully capable of handling it. Could we help? Of course. Should we? In this case, it would be beneficial, especially with searches, labs, that kind of thing. It's a perfect opportunity to show SAPD what we mean by surge dynamics. We can cut the time in half. Maybe even less. Our presence would give them a lot of bang for their buck."

"I'm composing my pitch while we talk."

"Hang on. The bodies are coming out now." Gracie kept silent as they loaded the first, then the second. How must it feel to know your parents were murdered? To know you'd never see or talk to them again, feel their arms around you, inhale their familiar scents? The medical investigator closed the door. Gracie heard the slam in her head, not through her ears. Final.

She shivered before taking a deep breath. "Okay. As we learn more, we'll gain a better idea. I'd like to go with Nick to talk to the daughter who found them. Nick's checking out the missing son right now."

"I'll clear it."

"Thank you. I took some photos of the living and dining rooms. Lots of dust catchers. Something may turn out to be important. Or maybe something is missing." Gracie's stomach growled. It was eleven-thirty, and her peanut butter toast was history.

"That's fine. We'll upload them to the file."

"The only other thing is the little girl. She's in first grade. Her aunt says she's still a Velcro kid with Mommy and Daddy. She's stuck in my head. I'm hoping her other aunt will give us some idea of where they've gone."

Gracie sank a little into a familiar sticky goo. All her life, she'd believed that she needed to look out for every kid who crossed her path. It was part of who she was.

"You'll hear from me as soon as I clear it about the interview. Get it done this weekend. I have an assignment for you."

Jackson's words brought her out of her funk. "What?"

"I'm heading to the office now. Meet me there at one."

CHAPTER 5

Slaton Enloe relaxed in his desk chair, his booted feet propped on the windowsill. Spread beyond the glass, as far as he could see, was the land that had been in his family for generations, since 1851—six years after Texas became a state. Patches of bluebonnets paraded their beauty in the April morning sun.

He spoke into his phone. "I'll tell you what, Governor. As long as you don't think the Lone Star is too far from Austin, consider the use of the ranch as my wedding gift to your daughter."

"You know I can't accept such a generous offer." The governor's words ended with a sigh.

"I'm not loaning it to you. I'm loaning it to your daughter. The Gathering Place, both patios, and the surrounding lawn will accommodate as many guests as you wish to invite. We only have five casitas, though. Most folks will need to make other arrangements for overnight."

The governor was silent, and Slate could almost hear the gears turning in the politician's head. Beyond the fence, Slate's favorite longhorn bull moved into view. El Rojo's awards filled a wall in the ranch office.

"How much is the normal rental?"

"Zero. The Gathering Place is for personal and family use only. Over the years, the family's loaned it to friends on occasion. There is a catering fee, though, if you hire my chuck wagon crew instead of your own caterer. Either way, there's ample space in the hall's kitchen. Because there's a precedent, you won't have political worries from either party." No matter the words spoken, Slate and the governor understood their true meaning.

Slate, like his father and grandfather before him, was careful to take care of both sides of the aisle in the State Capitol—from his own county, neighboring counties, and other counties up and down the Llano River, which flowed through the Lone Star Ranch and Cattle Company.

"When we were sure there was going to be a wedding, you were the only rancher I knew well enough to ask where to begin my search. Your generous response is a pleasant surprise. I accept your offer. On my daughter's behalf, of course."

Slate smiled. Marshall Anderson was nothing if not a shrewd politician, and Slate didn't doubt for a minute that the governor knew exactly what to do to achieve the result he wanted. "Of course."

"Since Dana was a little girl, she's had her heart set on a ranch wedding. She's already bought new custom boots to wear under a dress we're still haggling over. The damn thing costs more than I paid for my first new car."

"I understand. A woman's wedding is one of the most special days in her life."

"That's what her mother keeps telling me, but a man's got to draw the line somewhere. Know what I'm saying?"

"I do." That was the damned truth.

"Like this ranch thing. I don't understand what difference it makes, but my little girl wants a real working ranch, not one of the wedding rental places on a few acres that call themselves ranches. I told her I'd check around, but that she better pick one of those other places for a backup. She'll be happily surprised. As will her mother."

"Her mother's the important one."

Anderson laughed. "You got that right."

"I'm happy the Lone Star fits your needs. Tell your daughter's wedding planner to call my ranch manager to work out the details."

"Your hospitality is much appreciated."

"Like I said, Governor, my pleasure."

Slate hung up the ranch landline and lowered his feet to the floor. Plato lifted his head from his paws. The mutt had been a puppy when he showed up at the door to Slate's office one morning. He'd turned into the smartest dog Slate had ever owned.

"Did you pay attention, boy? We have the governor right where we want him. It's always good when someone owes you a favor, and it's especially good when it didn't cost you a dime to put him in that position."

CHAPTER 6

Gracie put her Jeep in gear and made a U-turn on the cramped street. On her way to meet Jackson, she made a slight detour to stop at Papito's Taco House for a soft chicken taco with guacamole. She ate fast, her thoughts centered on six-year-old Maya Cantu. Where she could be. Her current safety. And most of all, wondering if the first two were moot. Was she still alive?

As soon as she finished, she paid, pulled a mint from the bowl at the cashier's stand, and drove to Bastion's office near the airport. She arrived early and parked in her assigned space in the garage of a multi-story office building.

Other large tenants in the building included a bank, an insurance call center, and an energy company. Bastion occupied the top five floors plus a private helipad, but their name wasn't included on the stone marker at the front of the standard steel-frame-and-coated-windows building. Neither was it included on the list of tenants on the wall in the public lobby.

Gracie loved her work. Bastion gave her the freedom to do her job and offered her the opportunity to be part of a group dedicated to preventing some of the violence by getting into the trenches and working with at-risk populations. But here lately, even though Jackson said it had been slow, she'd been busy with one assignment after another.

Organizations, groups, and agencies worked with Bastion by paying a retainer to keep them on call as needed. Gracie hadn't had a weekend off in over a month, and she craved a chance to drive out to Fredericksburg to exchange a few hugs with her parents, hang with her sibs, and play with her nieces and nephews. She'd missed Easter, and was really hoping she could make it for Mother's Day next month.

The building had four public elevators in the main lobby, but only two of those extended to the parking level. She walked past them and entered a door that said *Authorized Personnel Only.* The wraparound desk inside was manned twenty-four/seven by one of any number of hunky former special ops guys. Their shifts were assigned randomly, and they had a monthly pool going for all kinds of things—who got the first shift, who got the last, who would have to switch because of a conflict, and so on.

Today the lucky volunteer was Saul Gallego. She smiled at her favorite hunk. "How's it going?"

"One more hour to go."

Gracie handed him her ID. Even though they knew each other, any number of things could go wrong. In the event either of them was in danger or under duress, there was also a crisis password that changed daily for all Bastion employees.

After he verified her ID, he handed it back to her. "Have a good one."

"You, too." Most of these guys were single and available. Only trouble was, they traveled all the time. They were in and out of the building like vacationing tourists.

The Bastion elevators were located at the other end of the space—four for quick access in either direction. She headed toward them and tripped over her own feet.

"Careful."

As if she had a chance with someone who had coordination in spades. "I'm good." Gracie punched the button, and the doors on her right opened. She entered and pressed the button for the floor next to the top.

The lowest Bastion floor held all the administrative offices. Accounting and payroll. Public and private liaisons—the sales and marketing people who designed the brochures and secured the contracts. Legal. That kind of stuff.

The next floor housed a small cafeteria, more like a grab-and-go, but it was staffed and could provide full dinners if necessary. On that same floor were a large meeting room and several dormitory style rooms for gathered personnel and those who needed to function on a couple of hours of sleep at a time until a critical project was complete. There were also showers, lockers, and a lounge space.

The cyber section occupied the middle floor of the Bastion complex. Part of their work was cybersecurity. Gracie had never been involved with that. She was more familiar with how their databases helped her. If an assignment included a computer or the cloud or social media, Bastion was involved, even though the only part Gracie had been concerned with so far was their search ability. One of the researchers could key in some obscure search term and receive mounds of data in return.

Jackson liked his agents to work smarter, not harder, and so he matched agents with cyber personnel whenever he could. It could cut hours to weeks off an active investigation. He also tasked them with not only thinking outside the box, but with forgetting a box even existed in the first place. Gracie loved the freedom.

All the big decisions were made on the top two floors. The top floor held the offices for all the partners, including Jackson's. She didn't know what else—she'd never been invited there.

The next to the top floor—Gracie's floor—held the secure safe rooms Bastion called the bunkers, along with Jackson's working office. Her space was one of a row of utilitarian cubes along a back hallway.

The bell dinged for her destination, and the doors slid open to an understated but elegant reception area. A dark charcoal gray wall faced the elevators with *The Bastion Group* spelled out in large aluminum block letters. Beneath the name, in smaller letters of the same style and material were the words *Integrity, Commitment,* and *Solutions,* separated by small centered dots.

Gracie was a proud Bastion agent. The receptionist greeted her by name. Like the elevator lobby, the hunks rotated through the reception areas on each floor on a monthly schedule. She didn't know this one but she enjoyed looking at him.

"Is he here?"

"He said for you to go on in. I'll buzz to let him know."

"Thanks."

Gracie continued through the space and took a few steps down the interior hall to Jackson's office. As she walked in, he took a bite out of a chocolate cookie. One of the three founding directors of Bastion and a former CIA officer, he was a totally unassuming man—until he had to be more.

"I hate that you can eat cookies and not gain an ounce," she said. "Look at you! A skinny thirteen year old could beat you up."

"She'd have to catch me first. I'm damned fast."

"Figures."

"Sit down. Have a cookie. What happened to your

34

head?"

Gracie sat on a black leather chair. "No cookie. I was in too big a hurry to meet Nick this morning and ran into a cabinet. It's okay."

"Take a cookie; it'll make your head better. Cookies are part of your new assignment."

"Are you going to pay for my gym membership?"

He held out a bakery box filled with a row of chocolate cookies, a row of lemon bars, and a row of sugar cookies. The sugar cookies were iced with white frosting and had something in the centers. That would give her a sugar high all by itself. "Take one of each. And a napkin. You'll work it off. Trust me."

She plucked the cookies and took a bite from the chocolate one. *Omigod! I've died and gone to heaven.* Deep dark chocolate, jalapeno, and not overly sweet. "I love this!"

Jackson put the box on his credenza and gave her a huge smile. "Told you."

She bit into the lemon one. *Ooh, tangy. Not lemon. A little salty.* "Margarita!"

His grin grew larger. "Try the next one."

"I'll be bouncing off your walls before I leave."

"I can handle it. Go on."

The cookie melted in her mouth into a sweet, milky flavor. She took another bite. "Is this a tres leches cookie?"

Jackson nodded. "Yes, ma'am."

"How do they even do this? Please don't tell me I'm going to be surrounded by these cookies every day."

"These and more. They come from a bakery in town, at Broadway and East Houston."

"That's near the Alamo. What's the name?" Gracie put the remainder of the tres leches in her mouth.

"Jalapeno Cupcake. You'll be there starting Monday. It's a storefront right near the corner. I'll give you a package with all the details before you leave. I sent everything to your tablet, too."

She nodded, still chewing, and wished she could enjoy the view out the large window. Relaxing would be nice, but they were talking about an op.

To reinforce her guilt, the wail of a siren floated up to them. Her immediate thoughts were always the same: Who needed help, and would it arrive in time.

Jackson's voice brought her back to the present. "The bakery's owned by Tessa Kyler. Been open about a year. Her background's in the package. She's a brand new mother, since Tuesday, and her brother's running the show until she can return."

"How many employees?"

"Besides Tessa, it varies between four and six. Right now there's her brother, Donovan Beck, and three others. You'll make it five."

"Please tell me I don't have to help bake." She made things all the time that didn't require exact measurements, but the thought of baking made her brain bounce around. Especially if it involved yeast. Way too regimented.

"No offense, but you might kill yourself in a kitchen."

"I'm a good cook, but baking's different."

"You'll work the counter. That way we're both happy."

"I can do that. Why are we running the op? What do I look for?"

"Our intel is that we're to watch for a delivery."

"What kind of delivery?" She wrapped the remains of the chocolate cookie and margarita bar in her napkin to be enjoyed later. *Keep that sugar high going all day, Gracie.*

"Unknown. All we know is there's to be a delivery to the Jalapeno Cupcake next week before the end of the day Saturday. It's important that we intercept."

"We don't know how it's coming?"

"Nope. We were told it would arrive before noon during business hours. Stay alert. The intel comes from a solid source. That's all I can tell you. Go over the material in the package. Learn the products well enough that the brother doesn't feel the need to let you go within the hour."

"Should be fun. What do I do when the delivery comes?"

"Leave it in place. Call in. We'll let you know at that point."

"What do I do after it arrives? Continue to show up?"

"We don't know that yet either. Plan on staying. Plan on making a quick exit. It's a loose op."

"I'll say."

"If I'm unavailable, use your own best judgment. I trust it."

CHAPTER 7

The package Jackson gave her was a three-inch black plastic accordion folder. Gracie tossed it onto the passenger seat for the twenty-minute ride home even though she looked forward to digging in. Folder or tablet. Usually one worked better for her than the other, depending on the information and her mood.

As she backed out, her phone rang. "Hofner."

"Gracie, you work too hard." It was her friend Ariana, who was beginning a week-long cruise. In Gracie's mind, Ariana shook her finger.

"You work as hard as I do. It's just not my turn to take a break. Are you on board yet?" Gracie pulled back into her spot.

"Yes! It's awesome. Next time, you're coming with me. I won't let you weasel out."

Gracie laughed. "I'll probably take you up on it. Have you met the man of your dreams yet?"

"No, but I started a list. And I brought my rose quartz necklace. If he's here, he's mine."

"Poor bastard."

"Lucky man, you mean."

They both laughed.

"We're getting ready to leave the dock. What do they call that?"

"I don't know—never been on a cruise."

"I forgot to ask you to water my ferns while I'm gone. And talk to them. They're Fiona and Isabella.

Izzie's temperamental. She's the one on the left."

Gracie smiled. Ariana talked to everything.

"Introduce yourself—they're expecting you. These are the plants in the big pots on my porch. They're drought tolerant, but the pots dry out quickly. I doused them good yesterday, so they'll be all right until Monday. They'll need water again on Thursday. Talk to them, but don't touch. They don't like that. Oh, and water them in the mornings."

Why would you touch a plant? "How much water?"

"How much do you put on those impatiens you have?"

"A glass every other day this time of year."

"Ferns are thirstier. Feel the soil when you get there. The hose is on the side of the house. Give it just a quarter turn, and count to about ten in a regular way for each plant. When you go back on Thursday, feel the soil again before you water. If it's wetter or drier, adjust. Then I'll get them back on schedule on the weekend."

"Good luck with me remembering how wet or dry something feels."

"You'll do fine. I wouldn't trust my babies to you if I didn't think so."

They hung up, and Gracie zipped home on the freeway. She liked driving on the surface streets, but local traffic was a bitch on Saturday afternoons. The twenty-minute drive to her street would've taken almost twice as long.

Rather, her aunt and uncle's street. Gracie had been barely past her rookie year with SAPD when her uncle's bank transferred them to London. They asked her to house sit on a semi-permanent basis, and Gracie readily agreed. The location of the small house was awesome—in the heart of the King William Historical District south of downtown. Plus, it felt like home.

That's when she met Ariana, the tenant in her aunt's garage apartment. Or had been until the end of March. They'd become instant friends.

When Ariana's grandparents died a year ago, her family agreed she should have their house near The Pearl, an old brewery now turning into its own little neighborhood, including a bookstore, a brew pub, a foodie heaven, shops, apartments. Even a hotel and farmer's market. The surrounding neighborhood benefited as well.

Ariana's family helped her renovate the old house, and finally it had been ready for her to move in. Her massage studio was in the front, with her living space in the back. It all looked fabulous. Even though Gracie already missed having Ariana just outside her back door, her friend's new home was perfect.

After Ariana moved, Gracie had both the inside and outside of the garage apartment cleaned and painted. Ariana came over to inspect and to do her own cleaning—ridding the space of her old energy so others would feel at home there. That was Ariana.

Gracie needed to find a new tenant, but she'd been dragging her feet—even though she knew Ariana wasn't moving back. Her aunt wanted her baby rented as soon as possible. She was an artist, and the space had been her studio before they learned they were moving. She had drawn the plans herself and overseen the construction. It wasn't quite paid for, and her aunt, like all the Hofners, didn't like owing anyone anything.

Gracie sighed. In truth, she envied Ariana with her new home, all hers. Also that she took time off for a cruise.

"No more pity party, Gracie." She didn't get these spells very often, and when she did, she talked and worked herself out of them as soon as she realized what was going on.

She dropped the folder and her phone on the patio, went inside, and changed into shorts and a tank. After fishing her tablet, pencil, and paper out of her bag, she got a bottle of water and headed to the patio. She set everything on the table before turning on the ceiling fan.

She started with the folder. More often than not, the old-school way got her juices flowing faster.

CHAPTER 8

Gracie worked in the order Jackson had loaded the paper file. He never did anything without a reason, and she respected that. Tessa and her baker were both award-winning pastry chefs. Her baker excelled on the sweet side of things while Tessa preferred making breads and savory items.

The more Gracie read the more she wanted to eat. She opened her water. It would have to do.

She read the menu. Sweets were the three flavors she'd sampled earlier—dark chocolate jalapeno, tres leches, and margarita—but the bakery offered a ton of options. Cookies, tarts, cream puffs, eclairs, and cupcakes. Plus a variety of savory items—jalapeno cheddar rolls and corn muffins, chili biscuits, chorizo quiche, pan verde, and crunchy jalapeno breadsticks with queso fresco dip.

That did it! She bounced up. In the kitchen, she grabbed a dill pickle, string cheese, and a bag of bagel chips.

Back in her chair, with food, she moved on to the staff details. The pastry chef was Webb Truitt. "Webb, old buddy, you look like a wrestler." He was from Sweetwater, west of Abilene. His background was on Gulf oil rigs. He must be good because they didn't tolerate bad grub out there. A couple of her uncles had worked on the rigs for a while. The pay had been exceptional.

Truitt's assistant was Maricelia Ortiz, an art school graduate learning a new skill. According to Bastion's intel, Tessa was teaching Maricelia how to bake while Maricelia was teaching Tessa advanced design techniques to use in pastry decorating.

The woman Bastion called a floater was Natalie Ferguson. She was attending culinary school at St. Philip's and was learning everything she could about working at a real bakery. She looked like Gracie's idea of a pastry chef—sort of like a smiling Pillsbury Doughgirl, complete with a dimple in her right cheek.

The counter girl Gracie would fill in for left a few weeks back and Tessa hadn't found a replacement before her baby arrived. It hadn't been a problem then, but being one person short—when that person was also a baker—meant they really needed an extra body to take up the slack with customers. Both Maricelia and Natalie would be spending most of their time in the back. Plus Fiesta was up and running.

Which brought up a whole other issue. Fiesta San Antonio had grown out of a parade in front of the Alamo more than a century ago. It honored the heroes of the battles of the Alamo and San Jacinto. Now it spanned ten days during the last half of April, with at least five parades and hundreds of varied events across the city. San Antonio partied hard for two straight weeks, and for a good cause. All the money raised at events went to local non-profit organizations.

Gracie loved Fiesta, but not working in the thick of it. The place would be hopping. She would need to hit the ground running.

She turned the page.

"Oh, wow." She feasted on the big chunk of eye candy that was Donovan Beck. "Ariana, you're going to be so jealous."

Dark hair, brown eyes, long lashes, handsome face. Gracie ran her tongue along her lips. "What's not to like about you, sweetie pie? I'm glad I saw your pic before seeing you in person. Otherwise I may have made a fool of myself."

She was staring at her new favorite hunk when her phone rang. "Hey, Nicky. You okay?"

"Yeah. Considering. Salazar just called. She said we're going to see Lupe Cantu tonight."

"Lupe. Is that the other sister?"

"Right. Guadalupe Amalia Cantu. By we, I mean you and me. Not Salazar."

"Excellent. I told Jackson I wanted to talk to her with you. I guess he got it blessed."

"Just like old times."

"You can apply to Bastion anytime. You know I'll vouch for you."

"That's your thing, Gracie. I need to stay here."

"I know, but I can't help wishing. What time? Do I meet you?"

"Actually, Salazar made the appointment for five-thirty at Miss Cantu's house. How about you meet me there. If you don't have plans for tonight, I'll follow you home and we can go over everything I've learned today."

"Works."

He gave her the address, almost across the street from St. Mary's and less than a mile from the Cantu home.

Gracie finished her first pass through the Jalapeno Cupcake package and made some notes. A little bakery not too far from her house was open seven days. It would provide a good, quick education. So in the morning, she'd drive over, pick a spot where she could see as much as possible and hang out for a while. She made a short list of other bakeries in the area, too. Just in case.

By the time she finished it was almost five o'clock. She changed clothes, brushed her hair, and put on some lipstick before heading out the door.

#

Holy Crap! How could I forget about Oyster Bake? A Fiesta tradition, it always took place on the first weekend of Fiesta on the campus of St. Mary's University. Traffic crawled.

Oyster Bake was fun, with lots of food and music and a small carnival. Fun if you had someone to go with. Someone was lacking in Gracie's life at the moment. *Who am I kidding? It's more like every once in a while someone's in my life. Until I chase him out for being a jerk.*

Fifteen minutes later, Gracie pulled up in front of Lupe's house. No sign of Nick—he must've hit traffic too.

A dark gray Prius sat in the driveway of a small, well-maintained frame bungalow with fresh white paint. Overgrown shrubbery fronted most of the houses on the street, but this one had been redone with small mounds of grassy-looking plants separated by red flowers. In the yard, mounds of multicolored flowers surrounded a small ornamental tree with dark maroon leaves.

Gracie had no idea what any of the plants or flowers were, but they looked pretty and she took a photo. In a way, it reminded her of Ariana's new place, with a mix of old and new. Except Ariana's looked larger.

Five minutes later, Nick pulled up behind her. He was on the phone. She gave him a minute, then got out and locked her Jeep. Before too long, he joined her on the street, frowning.

"What's the matter?"

"That was Kim."

"Oh?"

"She wanted me to know she's decided to file for a divorce."

"Shit."

"Nah, I'm happy she's doing it. Saves me the trouble. I won't even need to get a lawyer."

"I'd be careful about that, if I were you."

"Why? There's only the house to consider. Not even a dog to fight over. We decided to list the house next week before she goes to a lawyer. The sooner we're done, the better."

"There are hidden things you need to make sure of, Nicky. Your pension, savings. Anything you—"

"I'm a cop, Gracie. Kim spent all her money on clothes and makeup."

"Maybe. Maybe not. A lawyer can advise you."

He shook his head, still in denial.

"Not much left after we pay the bills. We have a small mutual fund. And a few thousand in savings."

"It adds up. Make sure you get your half. And if Kim does have a secret stash, you get half of that, too. Read the papers when you get them. Don't agree to her taking more, even if you think it doesn't amount to much."

He sighed but didn't say anything.

"One of my cousins is a lawyer in Fredericksburg. I'll ask him who's good here in SA and won't charge you out the ass. Might be wise, whether or not you think you need one."

"Sometimes you mess in my business in a good way. Why do you still drive that ugly piece of crap?"

"It runs great and the A/C will make you wish you had a parka, even in August. What more do I need?"

They walked up Lupe's driveway.

The front door flew open. A slim woman with long dark hair pulled into a ponytail shot onto the porch. "I just got a phone call!"

CHAPTER 9

Gracie and Nick raced to the porch. Lupe's hands shook and her hazel eyes roamed wild in her pale face. Gracie wrapped an arm around her shoulders, and Nick opened the screen door. He remained on the porch while Gracie led the woman inside. Gracie couldn't see him, but she knew he was searching the area.

She led Lupe to the sofa. "Sit."

Lupe hesitated.

Gracie sat, pulling the frightened woman down with her. She placed her hand over Lupe's before releasing her shoulder. The shaking had subsided, but Lupe's hands were icy. She sat with her back straight, feet together on the floor, shivering.

"Can I get you some coffee? A sweater?"

Lupe shook her head. "No. I'm so grateful you're here." She shivered again.

Gracie grabbed a throw from the back of the sofa and wrapped it around its owner. "You've had a shock. Just sit here a minute. Get warm. As soon as Nick comes in, we'll want to hear about the call. Plus he has some more questions for you. I'm Gracie, by the way."

Nick came through the door a minute later. Gracie caught his gaze and raised her eyebrows. He gave her a barely perceptible shake of his head.

After sitting in a chair next to the sofa, Nick pulled

out his notebook. "Miss Cantu, I'm Detective Rivera. We're sorry for your loss."

"Thank you. I'm Lupe. Please."

"You can call me Nick. I'm sure Gracie's already introduced herself."

Lupe nodded.

"Okay. Tell us about the phone call."

She clutched her hands. "It came on the landline, not my cell. Not many people call on that number. Mostly robocalls. I was only half-listening when I picked up. A man's voice said, 'Is this Lupe Cantu?' I asked who was calling."

"Good response."

"He said I was as rude as my brother."

Gracie pulled out her own notebook.

"That's when I started paying attention. I must've done something that showed my surprise because he sort of half-laughed. Then he said, 'Give him a message for me. Tell him if I don't hear from him by Wednesday night, you're next.' Then he hung up."

Gracie wrote fast. She was calling Jackson on the way home. This changed things. He could put someone else at the bakery. Nick was still writing. He'd get the call information, but it probably came from a burner phone.

They had been correct about the brother being involved in some way. It was an opening.

Nick looked up. "Do you have a gun, Lupe?"

"No. Dad had one, but I don't."

Gracie touched Lupe's arm. "What about your brother and his family. Do you know where they are?"

"No. I've called both their phones several times, but there's no answer. The call goes straight to voicemail. Carmen and I talked a few times today. Neither of us has a clue about anything. She plans to come up tomorrow afternoon and stay as long as she needs to. At least through the funeral."

"Did your brother or his wife say anything to you?"

A small smile played on Lupe's face for half a second before vanishing. "I'm always and eternally the baby sister."

"I totally get that. So am I. Go on."

"Carmen is his ally. Always has been. Always will be. I guess that's one of the reasons I was so close to Mom."

Nick leaned closer. "Tell me about the man on the phone. You're sure it was a man?"

"Yes. Definitely."

"How about an accent? Even a small one? Pronounce anything differently from what you usually hear?"

"No. He sounded just like everyone around here."

"Could you hear anything in the background? A noise? Voices?"

"Nothing."

Nick handed her his card. "Call me if you remember anything else. No matter the time or how insignificant you think it may be. Everything's important right now."

"I will. Thank you."

"I'm going to step onto the porch. Gracie wants to ask you some more questions."

Gracie waited until the door closed. "I have a lot of questions because I haven't talked to the detectives you spoke with this morning."

"That's okay. I don't have any plans, and it's kind of nice with someone else here. Especially after the phone call."

"I imagine Nick is lining up a patrol unit to sit outside until this is over. Maybe even an officer for inside with you."

Lupe bit down on her lips and gave a brief nod. She was trying hard to hold it together.

Gracie patted her knee. "Both of my grandfathers

and one grandmother are gone. All at separate times, and all so hard. I can't imagine what you're going through. And then that asswipe calls and threatens you. As if you needed more stress."

Lupe leaned back. "Yes! Exactly. Why is he destroying our lives? Mom and Dad never did anything bad to anyone. Ever."

There were as many answers to her questions as there were crimes committed every day. Bottom line: Most answers came down to greed. A lust for power, money, or sex—in all sorts of combinations. No matter the excuse the perpetrators gave.

Gracie patted Lupe's knee. "The more we learn, the quicker we'll have the answers for you."

"I feel so lost."

"I know." Gracie handed Lupe her card. "Call me. Like Nick said. Anytime. If you want to talk, cry, scream and yell. I don't care. We can even drink together over the phone, if that helps."

Lupe smiled. "I was thinking about a glass of wine later."

"We all are."

"I'm glad you're here to take my mind away from this disaster. I'm a one-glass wonder."

"Good to know. Let's get back to my questions. When you arrived at your parents' this morning, did you notice anything out of the ordinary?"

"The front door was locked. Dad's always up at the crack of dawn. He goes out through the front door for a walk, and he never locks it. When I got there this morning, it was locked for the night, including the storm door. I don't have a key for that one. Victor does, though. I thought maybe Dad was sick, so I went around to the back. Mom keeps keys to the back door there. Or I thought maybe she was in the kitchen cooking breakfast, but the blinds were still closed. I let myself in. That's when I saw them." Her voice broke on her last words.

Gracie wouldn't give her time to dwell on the image or her loss. "Close your eyes. Think back. Look at the kitchen, not at your parents. Was anything missing or out of place?"

Lupe closed her eyes. "I think I would've noticed. That house is as familiar as my hand."

"Keep your eyes closed. Look around."

"No, everything looks normal."

"What about the other rooms?"

"I left right away, directly through the back door. I called 911 from the driveway."

"Okay, open your eyes."

Gracie pulled out her phone. "I took some shots of the living room. I'd like you to look at them and tell me the same thing—if anything is missing or out of place."

After Gracie pulled up the photos, she handed Lupe the phone. She took her time looking at the pictures, sorrow on her face. She made a few swipes at her eyes and produced a few sniffles, but she held it together.

Lupe looked up. "Everything looks normal. Can you send me these? As soon as the police tell me I can go inside, I'll go over and look at everything through the whole house in person. I even know what's in their closets. Maybe this is a wakeup call that I need to get a life."

CHAPTER 10

For the first time, Lupe looked at Gracie's card. "What? You're not a police officer?"

"The Bastion Group is a security consulting firm. In the law enforcement arena, we work with several agencies when they need additional personnel or services. I'm a licensed peace officer, just like Detective Rivera, and a former SAPD officer."

"Do the two of you work together?"

"We used to be partners, but I'm working another aspect of this case. At this point, my primary interest is your niece." Which was true, but not the complete truth.

"I'll take you at your word."

Good thing 'cause that's all you're getting right now. "Thank you. I'll be here for you, too, anytime you need me. I mean that. Even after this mess is all said, done, and forgotten by most. You've lost a lot, and having someone nearby to talk and vent to who understands the magnitude can't be underrated."

When Lupe looked at her, tears had filled her eyes. "I keep thinking I'm holding it together, and then it falls apart." She pulled a tissue from a box on the end table and wiped away the moisture that threatened to overflow.

Gracie's heart broke for her a little bit. "That's understandable. The reason I asked to talk to you is for Jessica and Maya. But before we get to them, give me a quick overview of family dynamics. Were you, as a whole, chatterboxes or quick texters? Did you meet for Sunday dinner without fail, or barely all make it to Thanksgiving? Did you know each other's secrets, or not even know what movies they liked? That kind of thing."

"A mix. We're all close, but an outsider might not think so. I saw Mom—and usually Dad—every day. Sometimes more than once. Carmen and I text mostly. Sometimes several times a day, but we miss a day or two if one of us is busy."

"I get that."

"We always know what each other is doing. Sometimes, what we're having for dinner. I know stuff about Carmen's kids I don't think even her husband knows."

Gracie smiled.

"Victor's different. He and Carmen are close. She says she hears from both of us about the same. He and I talk or text every once in a while, but not regular or often. That said, if there's a problem, we're all there, and we're all in. Same for birthdays, weddings, funerals—" Her voice broke, but she recovered after a few moments. "Same for holidays. We're all together."

"I have a good picture. What about vacations or weekend trips? Did you ever take them together?"

"No. But if anyone was going anywhere, everyone knew. Even if it was overnight. If someone was out of town, everyone else knew where they went and how long they planned to be gone."

"How about Jessica and Maya? Were you close to them?"

"Closer to Maya than Jessica. She was always a little standoffish with me—because of Victor. He either ignores me or teases me, not much in between. So for her, I have lesser value."

Gracie was the little sister, too, but no one in her

family ignored her. At least not too much. Maybe because she'd always been in their faces about one thing or another, determined to be seen and heard. "Do you know any of Jessica's friends? Any at all, even their names."

"She talks about some. We don't share any."

"Will you make a list of the ones you know? Any phone numbers or addresses or workplaces would help, too."

Lupe didn't move for a few seconds. Then she nodded. "Sure. I'll be right back." She pushed herself off the sofa and shuffled to the kitchen, head down.

Gracie wished she could go back in time twenty-four hours and prevent the murder of this woman's parents. Since that wasn't possible, she wished she knew how to ease her suffering. But grieving was an individual process. It hurt.

In the kitchen, Lupe blew her nose. A moment later, she came back with a notebook and pencil and returned to sit next to Gracie. Without raising her head, Lupe started writing.

"How about Maya's friends?" Gracie asked.

"I probably know more of those than Jessica's."

"Keep Maya's separate, on another page, please. Also parents—plus any information you know about them. People talk, and Jessica may have said something unknowingly to one of them."

Lupe wrote for several minutes, referring to her phone along the way. "I think that's it. My classes are mornings and evenings. I often had Maya during the day. So I was the one doing play dates and birthday parties."

"I didn't know Jessica worked."

Nick entered through the front door and closed it quietly.

"Jessica works at keeping Victor happy. He's into being seen with the right people at the right places.

Along with that, he expects Jessica to keep herself, Maya, and the public areas of their home chic and wrinkle-free. It's a fulltime job."

"I can imagine." Gracie was getting a clearer picture of Victor Cantu, and she wasn't liking the image.

Nick returned to his chair.

Lupe handed the notebook to Gracie. "There are only a few blank sheets left. Take the whole thing, and you can add to it."

"Thanks. I have a couple more questions. First, do you have any idea where they may have gone? I know what you said earlier. I'm asking for a gut feel."

"No, still nothing. They go to all the *right* places. They host dinner parties and pool parties. They attend the same things at other homes. They attend social events. Victor likes to keep his name and face in front of movers and shakers."

"Is he planning to go into politics?"

"He hasn't said, and I haven't asked. Oh, they went on a cruise last year."

An image of Ariana sitting in a deck chair flashed in Gracie's head.

"Neither of them were overly impressed."

Ariana was impressed before the ship left the dock. Gracie hoped it continued. "What about weekend getaways, either separately or together? Or something special they did with Maya?"

"They sometimes did a winery tour with friends. Date nights from time to time. Mom or I would keep Maya. Jessica took her shopping and sometimes to her salon for a haircut. A movie every once in a while. That's all I know."

"Another gut feel question. Do you think they're all together or did they split up, with one taking Maya?"

Lupe held her head in her hands and massaged it with her fingertips before she answered. "I talked to Jessica yesterday. She asked me about keeping Maya for a few hours this afternoon while she cleaned her room. She said it was impossible with her there because she wanted to play with everything."

"I can understand that."

"Me, too. I told her I would. That's the last word from any of them. I believe that if it was at all possible, that they are all together. Despite Victor's faults, he loves his family. He's very protective of them. Because he is, he wouldn't hesitate to send Jessica and Maya elsewhere if he thought they would be in danger because of him."

Gracie and Nick exchanged another look.

"Because it was our parents who were murdered, my feeling is either someone is holding all three of them hostage or the reason for our parents' deaths has something to do with Victor. So if they're not hostages, Victor most likely sent them away."

Gracie gave her a one-armed hug. "I know voicing those thoughts was difficult. Thank you."

"I want to help. Jessica's family lives in the general El Paso area. All of them. I called her mother this morning and told her what happened. I did a bad thing."

"That's not bad, Lupe."

"No, not by calling her. I made her promise on Maya's life that she would let me know the instant she heard from Jessica or heard about her from anyone. She swore she would. I haven't heard from her, so I know Jessica hasn't contacted her, and she and Maya aren't out there. That means Jessica is really scared."

Or really dead. "Is there anything about either Jessica or Victor we need to know?"

"Doesn't matter what it is," Nick said. "Good or bad. We're not out to bust them, but if either of them are involved in an enterprise of some sort, knowing that could help us find them."

Lupe's head had snapped to Nick as he spoke. Gracie couldn't see her face, but she knew. One of them was involved with something. Most likely drugs.

Which meant cartel. Which fit the profile of the killings. But profiles were just guidelines. Sometimes people closed cases by matching the wrong person to the profile instead of following the evidence to find the right suspect. Gracie preferred using a profile as confirmation, not as proof.

Lupe dropped her head for a second before raising it and speaking. "Nothing that I know of."

But there was something, and Lupe knew what it was. Her eyes were flat, and she stared straight ahead.

Someone knocked on the door.

Nick stood. "I'll get that."

He returned in a few seconds, during which Lupe stayed silent.

"The officer is outside. He'll be here until someone from the next shift relieves him. If at any time of the day or night you don't see a patrol out front, you call me. If I can't answer, then you call 911. Check all your windows and doors. Make sure everything is locked. Keep the blinds drawn. I also advise keeping all your lights on day and night. That way you don't give away which room you're in. Stay inside. Let your sister run errands, go to the grocery. Okay?"

"I have to make funeral arrangements. I'm not letting this guy intimidate me."

"I'll see if I can get an officer to stay with you, accompany you."

"There will be a lot of people in and out. Several have called, some have brought food. Would either of you like some fried chicken to take home? There's a large variety to choose from."

"No, thanks. Don't let anyone in that you don't know. I'm going to push hard for an officer—I *will* call you and let you know. If I'm successful, I'll text you her photo. Don't let anyone but her and your sister in. I don't care what story they give you. If I haven't called you by noon on Tuesday, you call me. Sometimes the wheels turn slow, especially on weekends. I would volunteer myself, except the neighbors would talk."

Lupe's smile changed her face. She looked younger with the sadness stripped away.

"I understand. Thank you."

"Thanks for speaking with us, Lupe. Unless Gracie has more questions, we're done."

Gracie followed him to her feet. "Nope. I'm good."

Lupe stood up. "Thank you for coming. I have your cards. If I think of anything else, I'll call."

In the street, Gracie stopped Nick at her Jeep. "What do you think?"

"I believe everything she said until she clammed up. She knows something."

"True. We'll learn when the time is right."

"Agree. Now's not the time to push."

CHAPTER 11

Nick and Gracie sat on her patio, Nick at the picnic table and she in a swivel rocker left over from an old patio set. The patio had been added when the two-story garage was built. It ran the length of the house and was twelve feet wide. The cover tied into the roof, and two fat, lazy ceiling fans hung from its peak.

Gracie loved the patio. Her favorite thing about it was that it was screened all the way around, floor to ceiling. Small lights with clear globes hung in a random pattern. It was light, but not too light. And it had an old-fashioned screen door like the one that was on Oma's house, with a flip-down hook-and-eye latch. Its mate was at the door from the patio to the house—perfect for the few days in the year when air conditioning or heat wasn't necessary.

Nick had been quiet, but he downed his beer in no time flat. He set the empty on the picnic table and grabbed another from Gracie's cooler. "Can I sleep in your guest room tonight? I need to get drunk. Stinking, lousy, fucked-up drunk."

"Sure. Hand me your keys. And your Glock and your backup piece. And your knife. Put everything on the table."

Nick complied.

"Now give me anything else I don't know about."

"Gracie... would I hold out on you?"

"In a heartbeat. Put it out there."

Nick removed a second small revolver from a boot and another knife from his waistband.

"Is that it?"

"Yep."

"What about your spare key?"

"Oh, yeah." He pulled it from the compartment he had made into the side of all his boots and handed it to her.

"Give me your other boot and your socks. I'm going to lock everything up. Drink another beer. I don't stock anything stronger, except wine."

"Beer's good."

She walked over and latched the screen door before gathering Nick's belongings. When she came back, Nick had brought out her speaker, and Roger Creager was singing about Texas.

"Okay, big guy, everything's locked up. If you get out without me, you'll have to break a window. And walk barefoot. Let her rip." She raised her beer, and they clinked. She'd also turned down the guest bed and made sure the keyed deadbolt on the front door was locked.

This wasn't the first time they'd done this. Some cases were like that, and sometimes life was, too. Nick had returned the favor more than once for her. Partners. Always.

"Before things get too far along, fill me in. What did you learn that I need to know? What's your current take—besides Lupe knowing more than she's telling?"

"The employees are just that. First pass, no one knows anything. Victor treated everyone fairly. Not oppressive in any way. Worked as hard as he expected them to work. Everyone was in a state of shock."

"For real?"

"For now."

"Both places?"

"Yep." Nick stood with his beer and paced. "He

60

runs the electrical business out of a separate space carved out of the back side of the lighting company and rents the original building. The bookkeeper showed me the account. The original building is now rented by a cabinet maker. Victor set up a direct deposit into his dad's account for the full rental amount on the first of each month."

"Cool. First pass, sounds like his employees like him better than his sisters do."

"Yeah. They only see his boss side. So then I went to his home."

"Stone Oak, right?"

He nodded. "If you'd been along, we'd still be there."

"Why?"

He sat back down. "Downstairs looks like a magazine layout."

"So?"

"Not much food in the pantry or fridge. There are a couple of sets of matched plates and saucers and glasses. These are all in a separate cabinet. And silver, too. Real silver."

"Let me guess. Those items are for show and only for guests. What they use day-to-day is cheap stainless and old, chipped, and mismatched pieces with plastic glasses and cups."

"That's what I think. Salazar, too. I found those things in the dishwasher. And that's why we would've still been there. You'd have analyzed everything we saw, and before we left, you would've told me what he ate for breakfast three days ago."

Gracie shook her head, but there were a few grains of truth in what he said. Connecting the dots was her favorite part. She tossed a wadded-up paper towel at Nick's head. And missed. "It fits with what we learned from Lupe. Victor likes to be seen as the Big Man."

"I get it."

"What about upstairs?"

"Except for the little girl's room, it's chipped and mismatched, too. Clothes half-hanging in the closets, some on the floor. Drawers open. Makeup drawer looked like she'd scooped it out. The daughter's room isn't a magazine layout—you can see a little girl lives there and plays there—but it's close. Any little girl would love it."

Gracie was glad to hear that. Maya liked her room, but she would like taking an adventure with Mommy and Daddy, too.

"Her closet was cleaned out except for winter clothes. Drawers and shoes, too."

"Pink?"

"Her room?"

"Yeah." Gracie lifted the bottle to her lips and took a drink.

"With big yellow birds on the bedspread and curtains." Nick raised his arms and made what she thought were wing-like motions.

Gracie frowned. "You mean Big Bird?"

"No. More like a regular bird. Like a canary maybe, but like a cartoon. In goofy poses. Made me smile."

"That's because you're a big kid at heart."

"I've been a cop too long to be a kid, Gracie."

"Not where it counts. That heart of yours is the best there is."

"Whatever." He poured more beer down his throat. "Oh, she has the same bird made into a pillow on her bed."

"Cool. What about their cars?"

"Two. Only one is missing. They have a BMW and a Land Cruiser."

Of course they do.

"The Beamer's locked up tight. The Land Cruiser is gone."

"Maybe the three of them are together. And still

alive."

"Here's to hope." Nick raised his bottle in a mini-toast before putting it to his lips.

"Hope." They drank.

After a few seconds of silence, Gracie leaned forward, her forearms on the table. "I want to share something with you, too. Thanks to the threat against Lupe, I get to stay on this case."

"I'm sure Lupe's thrilled for you."

Gracie flipped him off. "But it's secondary. Monday, I'm UC, but in town and short-term, I hope. At least I don't have to pose as someone else. That's the only thing I hate about undercover assignments. Tomorrow's prep day for me. But even without the threat against Lupe, Bastion computers are working. Anyone and everyone who ever left a paper trail to any of the Cantu family, plus their contacts—all in the mixer. Bastion will be sending files to SAPD ranking possible suspects from most to least likely."

"Doesn't mean our guy is on the list."

"We know that. All of us. But it provides the best starting point for Jones and O'Connor to look deeper."

"So are you UC twenty-four/seven?"

"No. I'll be free mid-afternoon, and I'm starting with Lupe's list. If that little girl's still in SA, I *will* find her. This shooter won't stop with Lupe."

"I agree. I'll text you any updates."

They continued talking, safe from mosquitos and other night feeders. Safe in their twilight cocoon, the conversation ventured down so many paths, Gracie lost count. The empty bottle collection grew, plates of snacks emptied, and music went from Texas country to metal to Tejano to Buffett and back to country.

Nick sang along from time to time and vented about the case, Kim, the job, and life in general.

"Who's in your life now, Gracie?"

"Nobody." She drained her beer.

"Smart." Nick gave her an exaggerated nod. "That's the only way to fly. Independent as hell. And liking it that way. That's why I like you, Grace Lizboos Hoffer."

Gracie shook her head at his slurred speech. Sometimes she liked being the way he described her. Most of the time she wondered if she'd ever find a man she could love. Really love. Not just be hot for. "You're a drunk sonofabitch."

"Yes, ma'am. And that's the way I like that, too." Another big nod.

He drank two or three bottles for every one she did. At midnight she switched to water. She was, after all, the designated watcher and protector.

About two-thirty, Nick was weaving in his chair. She didn't want him to pass out and fall to the concrete.

"Come on, Nicky. Time for you to lie down before you fall off that chair and hit your head."

"Nah. One more."

"One more needs to be water. Come in the kitchen."

He got up and went inside. She took a few seconds to turn off the patio lights and lock the keyed deadbolt on the back door. When she turned around, Nick wasn't anywhere to be seen. She went straight to the guest room. He sprawled across the bed, arms and legs everywhere.

"Nick?"

He answered with a snore—and a fart.

CHAPTER 12

The sun had been up about an hour, and it sparkled on the bright blue water. Slaton Enloe was on the river trail atop his favorite mare, Arabella, when his phone rang. He pulled it from his shirt pocket. "You have news?"

"Finally. He's made contact and estimates two or three days. I told him to check in every day."

"Keep on his ass." A mockingbird started singing somewhere above Slate's head.

"Yes, sir."

"Make sure he knows, in no uncertain terms, that there will be zero tolerance for failure." He had too much invested for this to go south now. If more people needed to die, so be it.

"Of course."

"Zero. I hold you as the responsible party."

"Yes, sir. I understand. Absolutely."

Slate pushed the end call button and returned the phone to his pocket. His phone held more than one line. Each had its own uses. Courtney would come unglued if she knew. But she would never find out.

"Come on, Arabella. Let's finish our tour before we go back and make breakfast for you and the girls."

Slate had enjoyed his morning ride. Seeing the river, his own land in every direction he looked, helped him organize his thoughts. The game had just begun. It was going to be a busy week.

CHAPTER 13

After a cup of coffee and getting dressed, Gracie checked on Nick. It was nine o'clock, and he was still asleep. No surprise there.

She loaded all the beer bottles back into the box and set them outside the patio. This afternoon, she'd call her neighbor. Josie made things from them—candles, ornaments, hummingbird feeders, all kinds of things, and sold them at festivals and flea markets.

Back inside, she took Nick's things out of her lockbox and left them on the floor just outside the guestroom, along with a note, before she left for the bakery. She got a later start than planned, but maybe the Sunday morning rush would be over.

In her dreams.

The line strung out the door, but it moved fast. At the counter, she ordered a gooey cinnamon roll that would pack at least six inches on her hips and a small coffee. She took her breakfast to one of the three bistro tables along the wall.

This bakery was more for Gracie's local neighborhood. The Jalapeno Cupcake was for tourists and downtown office workers. But this one would still give her a feel for how things worked. The counter person hopped everywhere. Jackson had been right when he said she didn't need to worry about cookie calories.

The rush slacked off as she ate, although people

still entered the shop. By the time she finished her coffee, the clerk was wiping down and re-stocking product. Gracie could only see a portion of the kitchen, mostly shelves and one tall rolling rack with shelves for about ten trays.

At the second bakery on her list, she ordered another coffee and a half-order of churro bites. This one offered a better view of the kitchen. Ovens and racks. Shelves. And two large work surfaces. Three people, all busy. Being a baker looked like hard work.

Nick's truck was gone when she got home. She went in, grabbed Lupe's notebook and returned to her Jeep. Four hours later she pulled into her driveway, no closer to finding Maya Cantu than the day before.

Gracie needed to figure out what she was missing. She also needed to finish memorizing the Jalapeno Cupcake menu and go to bed early. Her six-thirty check-in time at the bakery would arrive way too soon.

But first she had to call Lupe to see if she stood a chance of finessing her into spilling the secret she kept hidden the day before. She got Lupe's voicemail and left a message, hoping Lupe's sister, Carmen, had arrived and they decided to ignore the phone.

At ten, she turned off the lights and climbed into bed. Lupe hadn't returned her call, so after she finished her shift at the bakery, she'd go by for a pop-in visit.

She'd just dozed off when her phone rang. It was ten-fifteen. "Hey, Nick. How'd you feel this morning?"

"Been better. Been a damn sight worse, too, so I'll take it. Had to work, so no time for feeling bad. Thanks for being my watcher. Ready for your undercover gig tomorrow?"

"Yeah. Early start. I just turned off the light."

"I debated about whether to call and decided the chances were greater you'd kick my butt if I didn't than if I did."

Gracie smiled at his truth. "You have news?"

"Maybe. A cabbie called in that he'd dropped a woman and girl at the end of a strip center in Balcones Heights. Everything in the center was closed. He wasn't sure if they were the missing mother and daughter, but the situation disturbed him."

Gracie jumped up and grabbed Lupe's notebook. "Damn. No addresses here in that area. Could have been a meeting point, though."

"A two-alarm just came in for that center."

"Shit! I'm getting dressed."

"No. I got this. You sleep. You have a new gig tomorrow. I'll call you if they find the woman and girl. Otherwise I'll text you details tomorrow. I promise."

"I trust you Nicky. Thanks. By the way, you made the right decision by calling me."

She was wide awake. After tossing and turning for five minutes, she got up, poured a glass of milk, and settled down for a few rousing games of Solitaire.

CHAPTER 14

Gracie didn't sleep worth a damn. It was still dark outside when she put on makeup and tried to pull her hair into a bun. A little concealer covered the cut. Her hair was... her hair. The bun looked messy, but it would do. Her sister could've made it look better— Trinka had more patience.

For this assignment, Gracie wanted to look young and fresh. She dressed in a pair of hot pink capris, a pink and turquoise over blouse, and pink Converse sneakers. Maybe she was channeling Maya's love of pink. That's what Ariana would say. Her concealed hip hugger holster held her Glock, a spare magazine, an extra set of keys, her Bastion credit card and ID, and her folding knife.

Last, she added a pair of small watermelon tourmaline earrings Ariana had given her for Christmas one year. She said they would ground her and make her less anxious. Not that Gracie really believed any of that hogwash.

She took time to eat a bowl of instant oatmeal so she wouldn't be starving when she got to the bakery and became surrounded by goodies. Today would be the most important day. She had to sell herself. This case would be no different from the hundreds of other undercover assignments in the past. She'd be friendly, chatty, and ask questions. The most important part was to listen to the responses and pay attention to body language.

On the drive into town, she went over her cover story. She'd be using her real name, so that wouldn't trip her up. But anything else could. She took a deep breath. The first day of a new job always made her antsy. Plus, Nick still hadn't contacted her.

She parked in the lot Jackson had recommended. Before she got out, she texted Nick. When she reached the bakery a block later, he still hadn't responded. The shop lights were on, but the door was locked. As instructed, she knocked on the glass. Her phone read six-twenty-five.

The king of all hunky males came out from the back. The photo didn't do Donovan Beck justice. He was a ramped-up Channing Tatum—like a Channing Tatum with everything awesome about the original boosted a hundred percent. Maybe a thousand percent. Gracie had never seen such a good-looking guy in person.

That doesn't mean he's not a turd, Gracie.

On his way across the shop, he smiled and waved. A towel hung over his shoulder. Turd or not, Gracie hoped she wasn't drooling.

He opened the door. "Are you Gracie?"

The aroma of sweet chocolate saturated the air. She inhaled her sugar fix for the day. "I am." She held out her hand.

He held his up. "Flour. I'm Donovan Beck. Come on in." He relocked the door and wiped off the flour with the towel. "I don't know anything about baking, but I can help to measure ingredients. Today I'm making a mess with flour duty."

"I'm not a neat cook, either."

He led her behind the counter. "Put your purse in that bottom drawer over in the corner. No one is back here except us."

"Thanks." She deposited her bag.

70

"Follow me to the kitchen. I'll wash up and introduce you before we get to work out here."

Webb and Maricelia were working and not paying attention to her or Donovan. Natalie was absent. Gracie was in the perfect position for the job she was here to perform—the lowest in the pecking order. No one would notice anything she did.

Donovan finished washing his hands and introduced her to everyone. "Natalie is the other member of our little family. She's normally here at six, but this morning she had a Fiesta breakfast project for school. She'll be here by seven."

Maricelia was shy and reserved. Webb was talkative but absorbed in his work.

After a few minutes, Donovan said, "Okay, then. Back to work. Gracie, when items are ready to go in the cases, the trays are put on these racks by the door. Now we need everything, but during the day, you'll need to look for what you need. They try to keep the most popular items within easy reach."

"Will I be the sole person responsible for keeping the case filled?"

"No, we're fluid. If we're slammed out here, yell back that you need margarita muffins or whatever. Sometimes Natalie or Maricelia will come up to see where we are so they know what to work on next based on their inventory. And I go back and forth, too, just not when there's a line."

"You work the register, correct?"

"I do. Tessa insisted on that. I take a couple of breaks, and Maricelia runs it then. As she does for Tessa." He stopped. "My sister. She's the owner, and a new mommy."

"Boy? Girl?"

"Prettiest little girl in the world. Emily April Kyler."

"Aww, I love her name."

Donovan held out an apron. "Put this on, then

grab a tray and come on out front." He pulled out a tray and headed for the shop.

Gracie unfolded the apron. It was bright blue and on it was a big chocolate cupcake with chocolate frosting. On top sat a fat red jalapeno. She smiled as she aproned up and followed Donovan's actions, hoping she didn't drop her tray and spill cupcakes all over the floor.

Back in the retail part of the bakery, Donovan showed her how the cases worked. Tags on the back edge of the shelves with the item name, and when to refill as the supply dwindled. The spaces without an item name were for overflow and any specialty items that Webb may have made that day.

With two of them working they finished stocking in about fifteen minutes. Then he opened the drawers behind them and showed her the location of the bags used for regular orders and various sizes of boxes for larger orders.

"This is a lot to remember when people start coming in."

Donovan smiled. "I'll be right here to help."

"Good. On my own, I might have a meltdown."

"You're doing great. It was only a few weeks ago that Tessa showed me. I didn't know anything about running a shop. Every morning, that feeling comes back until the first customer comes in."

"You're a pro now."

"Not according to Tessa."

She laughed. "I have siblings. I get it."

"Right. Anyway, the coffeemaker is over there. We're not one of the big boys on the block, but we have great coffee. Regular and decaf. They pay, you give them the cup. Keep an eye on the gauge. Coffee packages are in the basket at the bottom of the coffee table. No separate filter needed"

Two wicker baskets sat on the bottom shelf. Each

bore a tag—one *Regular,* one *Decaf.*

"Either of us can make it. Water is piped in. All we need to do is dump the brewed grounds into the trash can at the end of the table, put in a fresh coffee bag, and press the button."

"How many do you make a day?"

"Three regular. Two decaf. Give or take. Each brew makes thirty-six cups. If we're swamped and need coffee, yell for Natalie to make it. That happens at least once every morning."

"Got it."

"Questions?"

"Plenty once I get started, I'm sure, but none right now."

"Okay, then. It's almost seven. What do you say we get adventurous and open five minutes early?"

CHAPTER 15

Natalie-with-the-dimple arrived about two minutes later. The first customer, right after. Energetic, chatty, and eager to learn, Natalie was the perfect Jackie-of-all-trades.

Gracie got a short break at nine-thirty. She took off her apron and retrieved her bag. "I'll be back in fifteen."

On the sidewalk, she checked her phone. *Yes!* A text from Nick. They had no luck with finding the taxi fare, but he had received a tip from one of his CIs and wanted Gracie to call him.

Not always, but often, confidential informants were the sleaze of the earth, trading information for leniency or cash. Gracie had learned early in her career how valuable they were to closing cases. By her second full year on patrol, she'd amassed a good beginning of a solid list from all parts of society. A lot of work, but a necessary part of the job.

She pulled a bottle of water from her bag and downed half of it before calling Nick back. It felt good to walk in the morning sun.

Nick finally picked up. "Get my text?"

"That's why I'm calling."

"When we hang up, I'm going to text you a name and an address. My contact says this is her sister."

"Whose sister?"

"Sorry. I'm driving. Some jackass just cut in front

of me. Let me start over."

"Please."

"My contact, a woman, gave me the name and address I'm sending to you. My contact says this name, another woman, is her sister."

"Your contact's sister?" A group of schoolgirls with confetti in their hair passed, giggling and goofing off. Confetti-filled eggs called *cascarones* were a Fiesta tradition.

"Yes. My contact says her sister knows Jessica Cantu. That they're good friends, but nobody knows."

Gracie's head drooped. One of those. "But it's something we can check, even if we rule it out."

"Any lead is better than none. I figured it's better woman-to-woman than for me to question her. What time do you get off?"

"I agree. Twelve-thirty. I'll grab a bite and head over. I'm six-thirty to twelve-thirty through Saturday, unless the reason I'm here happens sooner. So I have a full day's worth of free time every day to look for them."

When Gracie returned, she went to the restroom, down a small hall near the door. In the hall, she noticed a second door. After leaving the restroom, she stopped at the second door and turned the knob.

Inside was a small walk-in closet. On the shelves were paper items, both for the front and back of the bakery. She snapped a photo so she could check every day to see if perhaps the delivery would be located here.

People started leaving not long after she got back. Webb left first, at ten. After he left, Donovan took a short break. The traffic had slacked way off, and Maricelia handled the register for the few customers who came in before he returned. She left next, followed by Natalie at noon.

Gracie and Donovan remained. Standing next to

him in the quiet bakery, she grew increasingly aware of him as a man. That couldn't happen while she worked, but it would be a short job. "Is it all right if I go in the back and see what it looks like all cleaned up and without bakers running around?"

"Sure. Now's a good time before the after-lunch rush begins."

She stepped through the open doorway. The lights were off, but plenty of light filled the space. For the first time she realized the area had several windows. One looked out onto the street, and two short, wide windows near the ceiling faced the alley.

The front door opened and two female voices floated back. One giggled. They flirted with Donovan, and he flirted back.

No place to hide anything in here. The only door that didn't belong to an oven or a refrigerator was the door to the alley. The room was larger than the retail space in the front, but she hadn't thought so that morning.

The women left and Gracie returned to the retail floor. "I decided to hang out in the kitchen so those two could have you to themselves."

Donovan ducked his head. "They come in here a couple times a week. Their lunch break."

Gracie bit her lips to hide a smile. Donovan was embarrassed. She needed to change the subject. "So what do you do when you're not working here to help your sister?" Of course she knew the answer. He was a fraud investigator for the Texas Department of Insurance.

"I'm in the insurance business."

Why didn't he tell her the full story? Was he working a case? Or maybe he thought it was more impressive if she thought he ran an agency instead of having a job with the State of Texas.

#

After leaving the bakery, Gracie drove to Ariana's to give Fiona and Isabella a drink. She found the hose on the side of the house and turned the spigot like Ariana said. The hot rubber burned her palm, so she lifted the tail of her blouse and wrapped it around the hose for a little protection, doubling the end of the hose back and squeezing it to keep the water from flowing.

She pulled the hose with her to the front and opened her fist. Hot water gushed out, and Gracie sprayed it over Ariana's tiny lawn. It took a minute for the water to cool. When it did, she climbed the three steps to the porch.

"Okay, girlfriends, I'm here for happy hour. Drink up. You're first, Isabella, since you're the moody one."

After the prescribed watering, Gracie returned the hose to the side yard and turned off the water. Out of habit, she walked around the house checking for anything amiss. She returned to the front porch and checked the front door.

"You girls behave. I don't want to come back and find any little ferns around and have to explain to your mama what happened while she was gone. I'll be back on Thursday. *Hasta la vista!*"

Ariana had told her about a little taqueria a couple of blocks away. Gracie was almost there when her phone rang. "Hi, Mom."

"Hi, sweetie. Can you come home this weekend? Your dad decided he wants to barbecue, and he wants everyone here."

"I'm on assignment. It's supposed to be done by Saturday, but you know how these things go." Her dad's barbecue was the best, so she hoped Jackson was right about Saturday.

"I do, and so does your dad. You stay and catch the bad guys if you have to. I'll take care of your dad."

"Such kinky talk, Mom." Gracie smiled.

"I just may do that, too, Miss Smartie Pants. Let me know as soon as you know one way or the other, okay?"

"Sure thing. Love you. Tell Dad, too." Her mom and dad sometimes acted like newlyweds. Gracie could only dream how their kind of love must be.

After she finished eating, she checked the address on the map. It was near the medical center, so there would be traffic. In her car, she called Jackson. "How's it going?"

"I'm up to my eyeballs in paper. Are you bringing me a cupcake?"

"No. I'm done for the day. Too bad you aren't."

"Rub it in. You're a bigger workaholic than I am. Are you looking for the Cantu girl?"

"You know all my secrets. Nick got a lead, and I'm off to check it out." She gave him the address.

"Tell me about the bakery."

"Any delivery will be noticed—if it comes while I'm there. If they hide it at the shop, the only places are a large trash can or a small storage closet. Everything else is open shelving or already full drawers."

Jackson was silent.

"You still there?"

"I don't like it."

"You're not alone. I'm only there for six hours. The baker gets there at four. The owner's brother leaves between two and three. So that's several hours someone else is there when I'm not."

"I get the feeling we were given busy work, and I don't know why."

"There is one thing."

"And that is?"

"The brother."

"What about him?"

"I asked him what he did when he wasn't being a helpful brother, and his response was that he was in

the insurance business."
    "Huh."

CHAPTER 16

The address turned out to be a consignment and resale shop. Gracie stepped inside and smiled. This place rocked. Bright and cheery, lots of customers, and filled with items she could've sworn she'd just seen at the mall. She spotted a large planter with a fantastic price for her patio. Plus it was lightweight. She carried it with her to the counter, which stretched in front of the far wall. Two women stood in line.

"May I help you with that?"

Gracie turned at the sound of the voice. A tiny gray-haired lady stood at Gracie's elbow. Her name tag read *Sheila*. Sheila could fit inside the planter, and Gracie would have no trouble carrying both. "Thanks, I'm good. I'm going to check out. Do you know where Rachel is?"

"She's in the back. I'll go get her for you."

Sheila scooted off before Gracie could say a word. At the counter, she asked if she could set the pot there while she continued to shop.

As she was asking, Rachel appeared, identified by her name tag. Taller than Gracie, she stood at least five-ten, with curly strawberry blonde hair, freckles, and green eyes. "It's fine." She pushed it behind the counter.

"Thanks, I could've done that."

"I move things all day long. Second nature. I'm Rachel."

"Gracie." She led Rachel toward the center of the room, away from customers and staff. "Is there someplace we can talk for a few minutes? It's about Jessica."

Rachel's head snapped up. "Cantu?"

"Yes."

"Follow me." Rachel's long stride got them to the back and out the door into the narrow parking area behind the building in no time flat. Two wooden benches sat there, several yards apart, each under an awning attached to the building. Rachel stopped at the first one. "This one is smoke-free. Sometimes we all need to get out of there for a few minutes."

"Most of us feel that way at one time or another." Gracie got her bearings. They were in an open alley anchored by large trash bins at each end. A wooden fence ran along the other side of the space, separating it from a residential neighborhood.

"Is Jessica okay? I've been worried sick about her since the news of her in-laws. No one answers when I call—like her phone is turned off. That's not like her at all. How did you learn about me?"

"I can't divulge that information."

"Are you police? I assume..."

Gracie handed her a card. "Mostly undercover work." She laid her phone on her thigh. If Lupe called, she needed to answer.

Jessica glanced at Gracie's card before sticking it in the pocket of her slacks. "Since you know we're friends, I see no point in trying to cover it up. It was Jessica's idea, anyway."

"Tell me about that."

"She started coming in here about six years ago—pregnant with Maya and looking for nursery furniture. We're about the same age and struck up a conversation. I'd just been through a baby a couple of years earlier, so I shared what had worked for me.

I also told her I was out and about a lot and would keep my eyes open for anything I thought she'd like."

"Jessica appreciated that idea?"

"Oh, yes. She was still working back then, and her husband put in long hours, too. She needed all the help she could get."

Gracie picked up her phone. "Before we go further, will you give me your phone number, please. That way I can text you if I need anything else." She'd expected this to be a false lead, and it was turning into anything but.

"Sure." She gave Gracie the number.

"Thanks. Okay, go on."

From one of the neighboring backyards, a dog barked. Gracie looked up. A squirrel landed on the top of a fence and ran along the boards. The dog was quiet. He'd done his job.

"After she found the furniture pieces, I kept looking for other items. Lamps, wall hangings, that kind of thing. Jessica was explicit that she didn't want any clothing or sheets or blankets. Nothing fabric. All of that would be new."

First baby. Gracie got that. She had a trough full of nieces and nephews.

"So one day not long before Maya arrived, Jessica asked if we ever got designer clothing. For her. I asked what she meant by designer. Like Liz Claiborne or like Prada. Levels, you know?"

Gracie laughed. "I'm guessing she wasn't looking for Old Navy."

Rachel shook her head. "Not Gucci, either, but well above Liz Claiborne. Specifically, nothing older than three years. Preferably two years or newer."

Gracie's head spun. Her sister would love something like that. A blouse. It would make a great birthday gift, and Trinka's birthday was in June. "Do you have things like that here?"

"Not often. Some other shops in town do, but they get snapped right up. I gave Jessica the names."

Gracie's hopes fell. She would never drive all over the city to shop for something that may or may not be there.

"I like Jessica. Even though she was too proud to share details, I got a good glimpse of her life. I told her I'd keep an eye out, like I did for the baby furniture. I really did want to help."

"She needed help. I'm sure she was appreciative."

Rachel nodded. "This is my shop. It used to be my mom's. After you've been in this business for a while, you build relationships with other shop owners. We all know who keeps what type of merchandise. Some of us will send regular customers elsewhere if we've just seen something we know they would like. Like I did with Jessica for clothing. Or we'll buy it ourselves to resell here. Not all of us. There are a few sellers who would rather cut off a foot than loose one single penny to another dealer."

"I'm sure Jessica was happy you weren't one of those." A huge grackle landed a few feet away, searching for crumbs. Just as she was. *Good luck, buddy. We're all looking for something.*

"Over the years, we grew closer. Sometimes we'd meet for lunch. Maya used to call me Rash-ee when she was still learning to talk. I went to their new house a couple of times. Jessica wanted me to see the spaces she needed pieces for so that if I saw something, I'd know if it would fit."

"Did she furnish and decorate the whole house through you? I heard it was amazing."

"Not the major pieces, but tables, accent pieces, accessories, some of the art. Things like that."

This was all good information, but Rachel still hadn't told her the important stuff. "You were such a great help to her. I'd love to have someone like you to shop for me—if I had major things to shop for, that is."

"Shopping's my job. I love making the deal."

She'd try a more direct approach. "Did Jessica have a lot of money to spend?"

"Compared to the average shoppers I see, yes. But that's like comparing Chanel to the Gap. We're back to levels again."

We're getting closer. "Not sure I follow. Can you explain, please?"

"Jessica shopped for champagne with beer money."

Bingo!

Rachel shook her head. "Her husband... I never met the man, but I didn't need to. Jessica loves him. I know why she married him, but I don't know how she loves him enough to stay with him."

Gracie took Rachel's hand. "Why? Is he abusive to her? To Maya?"

"No, not at all. Not in the way you mean. According to Jessica, he dotes on Maya. And Maya is always telling me about her daddy and things they do together."

"We humans are a strange lot." The grackle flew away, as if saying it wanted nothing to do with strange humans.

"Yes, there's that." Rachel sighed. "Here's the thing. Jessica gets a monthly allowance. It's a nice sum, more than a lot of people have to support a whole family. But she's expected to make that money go twice as far as most people could extend it."

"Fill me in." Gracie pulled out her notebook.

"Their house is huge. More than four thousand square feet. Large rooms. She's not allowed to hire a cleaning service because Victor doesn't want a stranger touching his things. And the downstairs area has to be spotless. Every day."

"The man's insane."

"Exactly. You and I and Jessica know how impossible that is, especially with a child and shopping, cooking, laundry. Jessica figured out early on how to make it look the way he wanted without doing all the work. I lied about only being over there a couple of times. I go over every Monday morning, except for today. She cleans down, and she pays me to clean the bathrooms upstairs, change their sheets, and run the vacuum."

"I take it Victor isn't aware of this arrangement."

"Oh, hell no. She dusts up there every so often and does a little bit of other cleanup along. She said she told Victor with massive maintenance downstairs, there was no way she could keep the upstairs clean, much less immaculate, and she wasn't even going to try."

"He was okay with that?"

"Apparently. Jessica said as long as she cleaned good one day a week, she could keep the downstairs living space looking fresh with only about thirty minutes a day. Longer after people were over, though."

"Let's get back to the money. Tell me about that."

"Out of her allowance, she pays me a few dollars for those Monday visits. She also pays for her hair, makeup, nails, and clothes. Victor wants her to wear only current styles of clothing and accessories. Makeup every day. He's not a fan of the natural look."

Gracie touched her bun, or what was left of it. Not much. The minimal makeup she wore was only for the job. Victor wouldn't approve at all.

"When her things got older, she'd bring them to me to sell for her. The same for Maya—a new wardrobe for her a couple of times a year. A lot of clothes for each of them. Jessica purchased as much as she could through me, but nothing could look worn. Even with that, she was careful to buy about half of Maya's things new and two or three new things for herself each season. Plus she continually changed accessories for the house to keep it from looking stale."

"All that shopping would make me lose my mind. I wouldn't remember what was old and what was new. Jessica must have a degree in money and time management."

"I think she has a degree in some kind of history. She made a checklist. Unless she found something she couldn't resist purchasing or bear to say goodbye to, she would change one or two items in each of the downstairs rooms every month. Or add one or two. So she always had a mix of old and new. The house looked completely different from one January to the next. Plus she stores items specific to each season. If Victor so much as hinted he didn't like something or was tired of a piece or tired of a color or style, she removed it before he came home the next day."

Gracie's phone beeped, and she sent Nick's call to voicemail. "My sister would know how all that adds up. I don't buy much, so I don't know. I do know dollars don't go very far, even with pre-owned items."

"You're right. Jessica spent the majority of her time each day shopping. Victor liked to see something he hadn't seen on them about once a week. Plus she had to purchase food, cleaning supplies, and general toiletries out of her allowance. Victor purchases his own clothing and foots the bills for all their parties and get-togethers."

"Jessica must've been tired."

"Exhausted. All the time."

"You said earlier that she wanted to keep your friendship secret?"

"Yes. It didn't bother me. Well, it did irk me a little at the beginning, but it was a little thing. She didn't want anyone thinking she purchased things from a resale shop. That's why she turned down things that would have been out of their reach new so that no one would think they were used. Unless it was antique. She always tried to keep at least one antique piece in each room."

"What did Victor think of her resale shopping?"

"Oh, he didn't know about that, either. That's why she didn't want anyone thinking she didn't purchase everything new. For Victor, all the things were a status symbol. Jessica said if Victor found out where she really shopped, he'd go berserk."

CHAPTER 17

Before Gracie left Rachel, she asked if she had any ideas where Jessica would go if she wanted to hide.

"It's obvious she didn't come to me. She's a member of Holy Cross Parish. Maybe she asked for sanctuary there. She also knows the layout of every mall in town. It's possible she could elude security at night and sleep there, then mingle the next day. Food's available. Restrooms. A mall would be my top guess."

Gracie could never cover all the malls on her own. Bastion could, though, by running facial recognition on the security tapes and putting a few agents in each. Jackson would have to get approval, but with a little girl's life at risk, it should be a no-brainer.

"What about military bases? Does she have any friends in that area?"

"None that I know of. But she did tell me her cousin would be in town for a conference. I forget which hotel. But one of the ones at the Riverwalk. I don't recall the dates. Sorry."

"What kind of conference?"

"He's an optometrist, so I guess something to do with that."

"Did she mention her cousin's name?"

"Not that I remember. They were hoping to meet for lunch."

"You've helped me a lot, Rachel. Thank you. I'm

going to find them. Maybe not today, but soon."

"I know you will. I feel it."

Ariana would've said that.

#

Back in her Jeep with the air conditioning on, Gracie checked her voicemail. She'd worked up a sweat just sitting in the shade outside, and it was a long time until real summer heat arrived. Nick's message asked her to call him. He didn't answer. She hung up. He'd see that she called. Next, she called Jackson and shared the information Rachel had given her.

"I'll get the ball rolling for the mall security tapes. It shouldn't be a problem. We'll get people in place today and tomorrow."

"Good. How about the optometry convention?"

"Hang on, I'll have to find that out." Less than a minute later, Jackson came back on the line. "It's at the Marriott Rivercenter, but it doesn't start until tomorrow."

"Damn it. Every time I start rolling, I come to a screeching halt."

"Take a breath. I'm pulling up a map. If she's thinking that tomorrow she'll be home free, maybe her cousin is arriving tonight even, then she's going to be close by. Ah-ha! I was right."

"What? I can't see what you're doing."

"This is the hotel that's directly connected to Rivercenter."

"That's where she is. Has to be. But she and Maya won't be easy to find."

"What's the cousin's name?"

"Don't know. Don't know if it's male or female. Most likely he or she lives in El Paso, though."

"Let me get back to you."

Gracie hung up and texted Nick. *I have news, too.* Followed by a raspberry emoticon. Two cars pulled in while she sat there, so she needed to leave to free up a parking space. She headed toward Lupe's. After she got out of the medical center traffic, she pulled through Sonic for a limeade.

One car was ahead of her, obviously ordering burgers, fries, and shakes for an entire Little League Team plus parents. Of course Nick wouldn't call now. His call would come as soon as she entered heavy traffic, as if he watched to mess with her.

The car ahead finally got their order and pulled away. Gracie pulled up, bills in hand. No one worked the window. She stared straight ahead. *Unbelievable.* She could've been at Lupe's by now.

The window opened, and a perky princess confirmed her order and took her money. She looked back at the street. "Webb Truitt!" She'd recognize the Jalapeno Cupcake baker anywhere, with his stocky build and super short hair. And there he was, walking down the sidewalk on the other side of the street in front of her. Did he ever look pissed!

CHAPTER 18

The limeade arrived, and Gracie pulled forward. At the sidewalk, she stopped and looked for Webb but didn't see him. She looked back at the way he'd come and saw the service department of a car dealership. That explained his attitude. Nobody liked having car trouble.

After waiting for the traffic to clear, she turned left. She'd turn left again in a block, so she didn't have much of a chance to see Webb again. But she did—walking up to a Mexican restaurant. Car trouble and hungry. Not a good combination.

She finished the limeade halfway to Lupe's. A block later, Nick called. "About time."

"Gang-on-gang shooting off Rigsby. Messy as hell."

"Better you than me, brother."

"Say it like you care."

Gracie laughed. "You know I love you. What's up?"

"I talked with Salazar this morning. She said Bastion came through like a champ. Jones and O'Connor have good leads."

"Tell me."

"She wants you to call her. I don't know. I'm back in SARIC. You have her cell?"

"I do." She passed the St. Mary's University School of Law. "Shit."

"What?"

"I forgot to call my cousin to get lawyer names for you. I promise I will do that tonight."

"No sweat. I told you, I don't think I'll need one."

"You're going to have one. End of discussion."

"You are one stubborn German woman."

"Don't forget it."

"Yes, ma'am. You said you had news, too?"

"Oh, yeah. I don't know where Victor is, but I'm almost at Lupe's now. I've learned a ton about Jessica. And about Jessica and Victor as a couple."

"Not surprised."

"Your CI lead panned out."

"Good to know."

"I just drove up to Lupe's. The patrol is here, but there are no cars in Lupe's driveway. Call in and let him know who I am and that he needs to talk to me. I'll hold."

The two minutes it took felt like an hour.

"Okay, he should be motioning to you about now."

"He's getting out. Young. Thanks. I'll talk with you later."

Gracie got out and walked to the patrol officer. She stuck out her hand. "Gracie Hofner."

"Alan Scott."

"What's the deal with Lupe? Is she here? Her sister?"

"No, ma'am. I only know about her. I haven't seen a sister."

What the fuck?

"What about a female officer inside?"

"Yes, ma'am. The officer is with Lupe now. They went to the grocery store."

"Can you contact her?"

"Yes."

"Tell her to get them back here ASAP."

"She's not going to like that."

"I don't give a rat's ass what she likes. Lupe

Cantu's life is at stake, and she doesn't need to be running around town showing her face. Are you sure you haven't seen her sister?"

"No sign of a sister, ma'am. I came on at two."

"I'm going to knock on the door while you call. Maybe she's inside."

Gracie stormed to the porch. *Idiots.* She knocked.

"Who's there?"

Gracie's head jerked up. "Gracie Hofner. Lupe?"

The door opened. An older replica of Lupe stood inside. "Come in."

Gracie felt as if she'd barely caught herself from falling down Alice's rabbit hole. This must be Carmen. Whoever she was, she closed the door behind Gracie and locked it.

"I'm Carmen. Lupe and Erin went to buy food. And wine. And Pepto."

Gracie counted to ten and hoped she wouldn't sound angry. "Why didn't you go?"

"Something didn't agree with me last night." The color drained from Carmen's face, and she ran down the hall. "'Scuse me."

Gracie waited, trying to let go of her frustration. She paced, did a few squats. It was a bad situation without a right choice. Leaving Lupe here may have been safer or placed her in greater danger. Sometimes there just wasn't a good option.

A few minutes later, Carmen returned. "Sorry. I'm getting better, but the surprise attacks still happen." She sat in the first chair she came to.

"What did you eat?"

"Chicken, potato salad, tamales, cookies. I'm a stress eater. Some kind of sandwich. All I've been able to taste and smell since about two this morning is grease. We threw away all the food people brought."

"Are you able to keep anything down? You want to be careful not to dehydrate."

"Since a couple of hours ago. But it's not all out of my system yet. I'm hoping soon, but I still feel it churning."

"Can I get you anything?"

"A new body."

Gracie laughed. "Wish I could conjure up one of those for myself."

A door opened at the back of the house. Gracie stepped in that direction, her hand on the Glock at her hip. Two women stood there carrying four reusable shopping bags each. Gracie didn't recognize either. "Lupe?"

"Me." The woman nearest her set her bags on the table and pulled off her curly wig and sunglasses. Lupe started putting things away. "People brought food, but we tossed it. Did you talk to Carmen?"

"I did. Did you know everyone who brought food?"

Lupe nodded. "My friends. Neighbors here and at Mom's mostly. Some of their friends that I know, too."

"Did you eat?"

"No. I drank some wine and then some milk later. I wasn't hungry."

"Okay." Sounded like accidental food poisoning. Gracie turned to the other woman. "Erin?"

"Erin Montgomery. SARIC. I've heard about you." Erin pulled her badge ID out from under her shirt. "I'm dying for a salad. Never thought I'd say those words."

"I'm glad you disguised her since you had to go out. Better than leaving her here."

"I've got a whole bag full of shit in there." She waved toward the other side of the house. "I can make myself look like her if I have to. That's the one thing I know how to do." She pulled off a plain-Jane brown wig and pointed at her head, topped by short hair the color of apricots with blue tips. "They pulled me out of that assignment and sent me here."

Lupe sat a container of dishwasher pouches on the counter. "I love her hair. She was working undercover. Doesn't that sound exciting?"

Gracie and Erin exchanged a look.

"Oh, I guess not for y'all—you do it all the time."

"No problem, sweetie." Erin gave Lupe a big hug. "Sometimes it is exciting. And fun. Other times, I say a lot of prayers before and after. Most of the time, it's just another day. I said a few prayers on the one they pulled me from, but plenty of adrenaline flowed as well."

Other than being about the same size, Erin looked nothing like Lupe. She had green eyes, fair skin, light eyebrows, and her nose was a different shape. "Must've been some wild happenings where you were. I'm glad they pulled you. You're exactly who they need here."

"Wild's not the half of it. They should finish it in a day or two."

Gracie helped empty bags. "Good. You like SARIC?"

"Love it. Came over about a year ago from Street Crimes. Mostly I work UC."

"That's what I did. But I nearly always went as myself. Still do. Acting's not in my repertoire."

"You have a better understanding of why people do weird shit, though. You get right to the root. That's what I've heard anyway."

"We all have our strengths. I like to figure out the why and put the pieces together from the people side." Gracie no longer doubted Erin's decision to go out. She had a sound head on her shoulders.

"You should've applied to the FBI to be a profiler."

Gracie shook her head. "Not my thing. At all. I like to be out, thinking on the fly. Not sitting behind a desk creating a chart."

"Pleasure to meet you. I'm assuming you want to

chat with Lupe."

"I do. Where are all the cars?"

"Lupe's is back out front. Carmen's is in the neighbor's garage. Mine is at the curb diagonally across the street."

"Okay." Gracie drew her bottom lip between her teeth. "Listen, I know I'm not officially involved here. This is your case. But I'm busting my butt trying to find the missing mother and daughter. I have some solid leads, and that's why I need to talk to Lupe. Also, I'm relieved to see she's in good hands here."

"SAPD's finest. You know that." Erin grinned and turned to empty the dishwasher.

"I do now." Gracie turned to Lupe. "I'm going in the living room with Carmen. Come on in as soon as you're finished in here."

CHAPTER 19

Gracie sat in the chair Nick had sat in on Saturday. Her stomach growled.

Carmen rubbed her middle. "Your stomach sounds like mine, except in a good way."

"You'll be starving tomorrow. I need to ask you a couple of questions. But if nature calls while we're talking, just go."

"You bet I will. Ask away. It's good to put a face to your name after Saturday's phone call."

"Same here. First, do you have a gun?"

"Erin asked already. Yes, I do. And a carry permit. I often work by myself, and I'm used to carrying it. My little nursery is in a semi-rural location by our house. I'm often the only person within a half-mile or so. I get a lot of real customers, but I also get a fair share of transients looking for day work. And some unsavory types checking to see if I'm a pushover. I'm a good shot and a fair judge of character. I won't hesitate to pull the trigger if necessary, but I'm not a hothead. I have no problem with Erin taking the lead."

Extraordinary circumstances call for extraordinary measures. The phrase popped into Gracie's head. She didn't remember who said those words, or something similar, but they fit the situation. It was Erin's call to make about leaving the gun in Carmen's possession. "Erin made the right decision. How are you and Lupe holding up?"

"Fair. We have each other to hold onto. It's easier to realize Dad's gone than Mom. His health problems. Mom was active and full of energy."

"I understand. I'll make this as painless as possible." Gracie pulled out her notebook. "Have you ever heard Jessica talk about a cousin who's an optometrist?"

"Hmmm. Not that I recall. But she easily could have, and I don't remember. I have teenagers, and honestly, I've learned to tune people out if they go on for a while."

"You must know my mother."

Carmen laughed. "You'll understand one day."

Gracie doubted that. Her role was the crazy aunt beloved by all the kids. The cards dealt to her didn't include marriage. "What about a woman named Rachel?"

"I've heard her talk about Rachel. Maya used to call her Rash-ee. Jessica and Rachel are shopping buddies, that's all I know."

"That's all right. What was Jessica's maiden name?"

"Bernal."

Gracie wrote in her book. "Do you know any other names in her family?"

"Oh, gosh." Carmen rubbed her forehead. "Let me think. I met one of her aunts and some cousins when they moved into their new house."

"Okay, what did I miss?" Lupe flopped on the sofa next to Carmen.

Side by side, no one would doubt Lupe and Carmen were sisters. They moved alike, their heads were shaped alike, and they inclined them in the same way. *Very different from Trinka and me. Trinka's a delicate orchid. I'm a thorny cactus.*

Carmen turned to Lupe. "Gracie asked if we know any names in Jessica's family, especially a cousin who's an optometrist."

"You'd be the one with that knowledge." Lupe shook her head. "You know how they treat me. Pat my head and tell me to go out and play."

Gracie bit her lip to keep from laughing. She needed to teach Lupe how to make the most of being the baby.

"Uh-oh." Carmen jumped up.

Gracie followed her quick progress up the hall as she leaned forward. "Lupe, I need you to help me."

"I'll do all I can."

"I may ask for more than that."

"I don't understand."

Gracie stood up. "Nick and I know that you know more about what's happening than what you've shared."

"No!" Lupe sprung to her feet.

"Sit."

Lupe bent double as she sat, her head touching her knees.

Gracie pressed on. "It's okay. You're frightened. Your parents were murdered in their own kitchen. Anyone would be afraid."

"It's not just that."

"What is it?"

"It's Victor."

"What do you mean, *it's Victor?*"

Lupe didn't say anything.

Gracie sat beside her. "Tell me, Lupe. You can help save lives. The more we know, the more we can help."

Lupe stayed silent.

Gracie stood again. "We're going to find out whatever it is you're hiding. The longer it takes us, the more auxiliary information we'll learn. If you did pot one time in tenth grade, the police will find out. That's just how this investigation thing works. Don't you think it's better to tell us so we can all be on the same page?"

"Tell her, Lupe. Or I will." Carmen walked toward them. "It doesn't matter now. Finding Mom and Dad's killer is more important. So are Victor, Jessica, and Maya. It's what Mom would want. Dad, too."

Lupe raised up. Tears flowed down her cheeks. She ran to Carmen, and they hugged. Carmen rubbed her sister's back and let her cry.

Part of Gracie felt like a heel. She moved her gaze away from the two women and noticed Erin standing in the kitchen doorway. Erin gave her a nod and a thumbs up. The cop in Gracie returned the nod. Sometimes the two parts of her didn't get along.

CHAPTER 20

After several seconds, Gracie stepped over to Erin. "You need to be in on this. Listen from over here, or come in the living room with us—your choice." She kept her voice low.

"Do you have a recorder?" Erin's voice matched Gracie's.

"Not on me. Just my phone. I don't know how long that goes."

"I have one. Let me get it, and then I'll be in. We need to get this down in case it turns into something."

"I agree. We'll wait." Gracie went back to the living room.

Carmen and Lupe sat next to each other on the sofa holding hands.

"Erin will be joining us in just a minute. She's getting her recorder. It's important that what you tell us is as complete and truthful as you can make it. Like I said, the more facts we know, the more likely it is we can find Victor and his family and identify and apprehend the person who killed your parents."

Erin returned.

"Before you start that," Carmen sat forward, still holding Lupe's hand, "what happens if something of what we tell you will result in an arrest of Lupe or me? Or Victor? Shouldn't we have a lawyer here?"

"I got this." Gracie glanced at Erin before looking from one sister to the other. "Like I've said before, I'm a licensed law enforcement officer. Just like Erin. If anything I tell you differs from her instructions on this case, she will tell you what that is. Does everyone agree so far?"

Three heads nodded.

"Here are the things I'm interested in. Finding Jessica and Maya. Number One. A big Number One. Keeping the two of you safe. Finding Victor. Finding who murdered your parents. In that order. I think Erin has the same marching orders, but likely in a different order."

"Yes, my order is different. Lupe is first. And now Carmen. Followed by the shooter. Then finding the family."

Lupe smiled at her. They were already bonding. That meant Erin was doing a solid job.

Gracie stood up. "I don't care about anything else you've done unless it's a person-on-person crime."

"Same for me." Erin raised her hand.

"Unless you've assaulted someone, done a hit-and-run, committed a robbery, something like that, anything else you tell me will be ignored by me. If you have, then you better get a lawyer, as far as I'm concerned. Erin?"

Erin was quiet for a few seconds. "Yeah, I'm good with that. And I've decided I'm ditching this recorder." She got up and walked down the hall, returning empty-handed a few seconds later. "Let's pinkie swear."

#

After the pinkie swear ceremony, they all sat back down, except Gracie.

She wished she had an inkling of what she and Erin were about to hear. The urge to move was strong, but she compensated by stretching her arms and shoulders. "Okay, Carmen, just talk with me and tell us the story."

Carmen nodded. "Have either of you heard of *La*

Luz?"

"No." Erin shook her head.

"Like *the light*?" Gracie raised her eyebrows.

"Yes."

"No." The feeling to move had passed, and Gracie returned to her seat.

Carmen smiled. "Good. I would be more worried if you had. Victor is *La Luz*. And our father before him. And his father, and his father, and his. Five generations of Cantu men beginning with Papa Arturo."

"What does *La Luz* do?"

"The Cantu family has lived in South Texas since the 1700s—before there was a Texas or even a United States. When the area still belonged to Spain, and later, Mexico. We Cantus are a large family. We have cousins who live all around the world."

Gracie leaned back. Carmen was a storyteller, and this one was off to a good start. She was setting the stage for what she had to say.

"In the days of my great-great-grandfather, the borders were open. Family members visited for births, christenings, birthdays, weddings. Deaths." Carmen made the sign of the cross. "They arrived from every direction. Our great-great-grandfather and his family traveled in every direction as well."

Gracie closed her eyes to keep the mental images in her head.

"This was during the days of Pancho Villa. With the fighting, it wasn't safe for people to travel near either side of the border."

"Rather like today with the cartels."

"Somewhat. Yet the Cantus were a festive group, and they continued one life celebration after another. As a young boy, my great-great grandfather played among those ridges and canyons with his cousins. Along both sides of the Rio Grande. He knew the trails, both human and animal. He knew the places to hide and never be found. He knew many ways to reach one place from another."

As Carmen spoke, she no longer looked from one of them to another. Her gaze was focused on a landscape only she could see. Her words took on a cadence different from her regular speech. She was reciting a story she'd been told many times over, much as Gracie could tell Hansel and Gretel. Or Cinderella.

"Over the years, Papa Arturo learned the art of evasion, and how to live off the land. He used his skills to safely move his family and other Cantu families back and forth to one celebration or another, successfully eluding Pancho Villa's revolutionaries, General Pershing's army, and any other *bandidos* out to rob those on a journey." Carmen took a sip from a bottle of water she stuffed between the cushion and arm of the sofa.

The picture was coming together. Gracie didn't want to interrupt before it was complete.

"Soon, America was involved in the First World War. General Pershing and his army were sent away to fight. A few years later, Pancho Villa was killed. Even so, some violence persisted. Because it did, Papa Arturo continued to escort family members through the region. It was at this time that he began carrying a flashlight." Carmen stood. "Be right back. Go ahead, Lupe."

Lupe watched her sister, then turned to face Erin and Gracie. "When they would meet, he always told them to look for the light. He carried a shiny metal flashlight. In the day, he would hold it to reflect the sun's rays. At night, he would shine it at the appointed time. Our aunts, uncles, and cousins began to call him La Luz."

CHAPTER 21

Despite Carmen's instruction to Lupe to keep telling the story of La Luz, Lupe bounded to her feet. "I need water. And a snack."

After Lupe left the room, Erin turned to Gracie. "What do you think?"

Gracie liked Erin, but she didn't know her well enough to share her thoughts. If ever there was a time for generics, this was it. "Too early. Could be the obvious. Or could be a hundred and eighty out from that."

Erin nodded. "Most of the cases that fall into my lap are the not-obvious ones. Just so you know."

Gracie may have nodded at Erin's words, but she wasn't sure. As Erin talked, Gracie grew cold from the inside out. Her skin tingled, and she felt as if the house was about to fall in and crush her. The words *Get Out!* flashed in her brain. "I have to make a call. I'm going out back. Don't let them start without me."

"You got it."

The feeling she needed to leave came out of the blue, sudden and overwhelming. She had no idea why. In the kitchen she told Lupe she'd be right back before fleeing through the door. What was going on?

In the backyard she walked straight to a glider swing sitting under a tree. She pulled out her phone in case Erin was watching. If it was Erin out here, Gracie would watch. She sat down and pushed the swing with her foot.

Nick didn't answer her call. She hung up. Ariana would say she had the heebie-jeebies. Gracie didn't know what to do. She needed to run, but she couldn't do that now. Instead, she closed her eyes and tried to calm herself.

Her phone rang, and she jumped. It was Nick.

"Hey, thanks for calling me back." She meant that more than he could know.

"Did you talk to Lupe?"

"We're doing that now."

"Okay. Why did you call me?"

Now she felt silly. "No reason."

"Gracie..."

"I don't know what happened, Nicky. I had to get out of there."

"Anxiety?"

"No. Maybe. I don't know. Nothing like that has ever happened to me before."

"You've been hanging out with your freaky tenant too long."

"Ariana's not freaky. And she's not my aunt's tenant any longer."

"She talks to a ghost. That makes her freaky in my book."

"Yeah, well, it works for her. She says Zoe is a spirit." A ladybug crawled up to the arm of the swing, looked at her, and moved on.

"Maybe she can ask her ghost what's going on so you'll know."

"She's on a cruise."

"What happened inside when you wanted out?"

"Erin Montgomery's the live-in."

"I know her. Not well."

"Carmen is here." A burst of breeze came up, and Gracie shivered.

"Right."

"She's got a stomach thing—death food from the neighbors. Getting better."

"Ugh."

"The sisters agreed to tell us what Lupe held back on Saturday. Carmen's been giving us background. She had to visit the loo again. Lupe went to the kitchen. I was talking to Erin, and the feeling hit like a punch in the gut. I said I had to make a phone call and came out to the backyard."

"Did you pick up on something hinky off Montgomery?"

"I don't think so. Didn't feel that way."

"How are you now?"

"Better. Still jumpy when I think about going back inside, though." Gracie got off the swing and started around the perimeter of the yard.

"I need to hang up in a minute. Are you going to be all right?"

The walking helped. Not as good as running, but better than sitting. "I'll be fine. Talking helped."

"Good. Call me after." And he hung up.

Gracie kept the phone to her ear and continued walking for several minutes. Long enough that she made three full circuits of Lupe's backyard before putting her phone back in her pocket and heading toward the door.

On the way, she took in a few deep breaths. By the time she reached the door, she felt okay. Not great, but okay.

Back inside, Gracie still felt all right. Whatever bothered her had gone.

Erin stood in the kitchen and moved toward Gracie. "Everything okay?"

"Yeah. Another case. You know how that is."

Erin nodded.

"Let's go finish up." Back in the living room, Gracie looked at Carmen. "Are you ready to go ahead?"

"Yes."

Gracie watched the sisters. "We've learned how your great-great-grandfather guided your family on their journeys, and how he came to be known as La Luz. Now it's time for you to bring us current."

Carmen nodded. "Papa Arturo continued his mission until the start of the Second World War. He couldn't see as well as he once did. The families were growing, and he no longer recognized everyone. Over the years, he'd taught his oldest son every trail, cave, and secret that he knew. Soon his oldest son joined the Army."

Some of Gracie's older relatives had fought in that war, too. She was thankful they'd all returned home safely, even though she never knew some of them. She wished the same for Carmen's.

"By the time Papa Pablo returned from the war, Papa Arturo could no longer make the journey. He rode with Papa Pablo a few times until it was time to leave the car and continue on foot. After those trips, Papa Arturo was assured Pablo remembered the routes and the hiding places.

"Grandpa Joe was now a teenager. Papa Pablo took him on every journey. Grandpa Joe was a quick learner and adventurous. He found new trails and new places to rest that wouldn't be easily discovered."

"It gives a new meaning to family business." Lupe was finally talking. "Even though there's never been a business. Just family looking out for each other. On the other side of the Rio Grande, descendants of Papa Arturo's brother, Oscar, have done the same."

"I grew up with Dad being the most current La Luz. He started taking Victor after his tenth birthday. From that point until Victor started college, they'd go out just to practice a few times a year. When Dad had his heart attack, Victor took the title on his own."

Carmen grew silent. Lupe as well.

Gracie sat forward. "Is that it?"

"What do you mean?" Lupe stared at her. "We just told you that Victor brings people across the border illegally. Isn't that enough?"

Gracie shrugged. "I don't know about Erin, but I'm not interested in that. What I care about is finding your niece. What she's interested in is learning who killed your parents."

She glanced at Erin. Her face remained impassive.

"However, if you think someone sought Victor and/or your father out because of La Luz and that had something to do with the murder of your mom and dad, then I'm interested."

Erin stayed silent. Smart woman. Smart cop, too.

CHAPTER 22

Without a word, the sisters turned to one another. Gracie knew what was happening. She and Trinka did the same thing. Whole conversations, important decisions, all occurring within the space of a single look.

Lupe stood up. "Okay. We do think La Luz had something to do with their murders. But we don't know what. Carmen said she told you about Jessica's call. And then talking to Victor."

"Right."

"When I said Jessica and Victor treat me like I'm ten, I didn't lie to you. I don't know anything. I saw Maya earlier last week, and she didn't share anything with me either. Whatever happened, Victor and Jessica were careful to keep it from her."

"How about you, Carmen?" Gracie would get to the bottom of this if she had to stay here all night.

"In recent years, because of cartels and drones and the Border Patrol, it's been more difficult for our family in Mexico to travel. The Caballo Canyon area is desolate. The terrain is treacherous. That's the main reason it was chosen to begin with."

"What about checkpoints?"

"Victor says he never worries about them. I don't know if he has prior knowledge or pays someone off or provides the people with correct identification. He didn't elaborate, and I didn't ask. I realize now that was a mistake."

Gracie nodded. "Go ahead."

"For our cousins in Mexico, staying in their towns and villages is dangerous enough. Earlier Dad, and now Victor, have brought a few to Texas to stay until the danger passes. But because of the danger, most travel to our country is being done through official points, even though the travel time is much longer and the process more involved. It's safer. Period. But word of La Luz has traveled. Victor's approached several times a week by people he doesn't know."

The storyteller had arrived again. "Does he hire himself out?"

"No. He always refuses."

"Are you sure?"

"He says that with most, he just says he has no idea about La Luz, but if they keep on and say something that indicates they know it's him, that he tells them that he only works with family and won't do it for anyone else. Or he says he no longer does it. Not even with family. I have no reason not to believe him."

Gracie leaned back and crossed her arms. "I'm not buying this *family only* scenario." She didn't doubt that it began as family only. Today? Not so much.

Erin looked at the floor.

Carmen jumped up. "It's true! Even back in Papa Arturo's time, there were people who smuggled others out of Mexico for money. But our family has never done that. The Cantus go back and forth, with the exception of a few families during troubling times. There are more crossing points now, but the tradition continues from the time when only a few existed."

Erin raised her head. "How does Victor avoid surveillance planes? Drones? They're used up and down the border these days."

"I don't know. You'll have to ask him that when he

comes back."

"We will." Someone would get to the bottom of that. Jammers were illegal, but that didn't mean Victor didn't have one. "How do you contact him out there?"

"We don't. He carries a satellite phone and keeps it off. It's for his emergency use only."

Figures. Probably not many cell towers out there anyway. Wherever there *is.* "Where is this place, anyway? It's a long border."

"I've never been there."

"That's not what I asked."

"Past Marfa, that's all I know. He's made fewer and fewer trips the last couple of years."

"Wait a minute." Gracie cocked her head. "You said *when he comes back.* You know more than you're telling us. We just learned of La Luz. You're telling us now Victor's on another La Luz venture. With no hesitation. You just laid it out there."

"No. That's not what I meant. I—"

"Carmen?" Lupe faced her sister. "Is it true? Has Victor gone to Caballo Canyon? Does that have to do with Mom and Dad?"

CHAPTER 23

Gracie's phone vibrated. She didn't recognize the number and sent the call straight to her voicemail. Her attention snapped back to Carmen.

During the few seconds Gracie had taken with the call, worry lines had crowded onto Carmen's face. She still hadn't answered her sister. All eyes were on her, and she sat a little straighter.

"Victor did tell me more than I've told you. But mostly I've put a story together in my mind that may or may not be true."

Now we're getting somewhere. "First tell us what he told you. No more cover-ups."

Carmen nodded. "A man called. Victor thought it was a setup, so he blew him off. He called back several times. Each time, he told Victor a little bit more about things he shouldn't know."

"Like what?"

"Like Lupe's name and where she lives and works"

Lupe's eyes flashed in anger. "Oh, fine! No one thought I should be aware of someone spying on me? Or thought my knowing may be a good idea so I can protect myself?"

You go, girl. Give her hell.

"We tried to protect you."

"A little late for that." Lupe walked to the blind-covered window. A second later, she snapped back to face them. "When is everyone going to realize I'm no longer a child? I'm an adult. I have a doctorate, for God's sake. I can think and form my own opinions. Give me some credit!"

Erin was quick to lead Lupe to the kitchen. She needed time to cool off, and Erin would see to it that she did.

Gracie turned to Carmen. She didn't want to lose momentum. "What else did the caller know?"

"Where Maya goes to school. Her teacher's name. The salon where Jessica gets her hair and nails done. That Dad had been La Luz before Victor. He knew where Mom and Dad lived. He knew Dad went for a walk every morning and Mom went to confession every Saturday afternoon. He talked about Mom and said she'd promised to teach him how to make tamales."

It was Gracie's turn to stand up and pace so she wouldn't unload on Carmen. *What the fucking hell! Some people didn't get it.* Why wouldn't Victor believe threats to his family weren't serious?

She turned back to Carmen. "Had your mom said anything to you about teaching someone how to make tamales?"

Carmen shook her head.

"Lupe!" Gracie raised her voice.

The younger sister walked back and sat down, followed by Erin, who gave Gracie a quick nod.

Gracie raised her eyebrows in return and then faced Lupe. Her jaws were clenched, and she didn't look at her sister. But she was participating. The two would make up soon. "Did your mom say anything to you about teaching someone how to make tamales?"

"I don't know. She could have, but she was always making something for somebody. Or teaching them how to make things the traditional way. She thought people were forgetting the important things. I didn't know everyone she talked about."

"What about a new acquaintance for either your

mom or dad? Someone they'd met within the last several months who they would ask over or who maybe had been over before?"

Both women shook their heads.

"They had an active social life with a lot of friends," Lupe said. "I really only knew a few other than neighbors and some from church. Dad has—had—a lot of friends I don't know."

Gracie looked at Carmen. "How long had these phone calls been going on?"

Carmen just sat there. Gracie half-expected her to bolt for the bathroom, but she took a big breath. Another. "Since right after the first of the year."

Lupe bounded up. "Since January! January, Carmen. Really? You and Victor are just as guilty as whoever killed them." She ran down the hall.

Erin followed her. In seconds, both were out of sight. The house was silent.

Gracie turned back to Carmen. She looked as if she'd lost her last friend. Maybe she had. Gracie had learned long ago that under stress, people do and say things they would never dream of doing or saying otherwise. Sometimes they dug themselves into a hole so deep, they believed the only way out was to keep digging.

"She'll be okay," Gracie said. "So will Victor. And Jessica. And Maya. But it's up to you. I understand how this is a family thing no one ever dreamed would become public. But it has. You and Victor have done a good job of keeping Lupe out of the picture, but you're going to need to square things with her."

Carmen nodded.

"It's always easier to make the right decisions looking back after you have all the information. In real time, it's often harder than a teenage boy on Saturday night."

"I could tell you things about that." Carmen smiled

and rolled her shoulders, relaxing a little.

"Not necessary. I have three brothers. Wait right here. I need to talk to Erin for a minute."

One of the bedroom doors was closed. Gracie knocked and opened the door at the same time, a trick she'd learned from her mother that used to drive her straight up the wall. But it had taught her to react faster than a bouncing bunny.

She poked her head around the door. Lupe sat on her bed, head in her hands. Erin leaned against the wall. "Talk to you for a minute, Erin?"

"Sure."

Gracie pulled her into the bathroom and left the door open. "Listen, I know this game is going on in your ballpark."

"Let me stop you. I think you're going to ask me to hold off notifying the homicide detectives."

"Yes."

"I'm SARIC, not Homicide. Too much is at stake for us right now to go full throttle down the murder road. Homicide looks at things differently than we do. If SARIC can follow the trail, we may be able to get closer to the origin of some of our most pressing problems, most of which end up in Homicide's lap."

"I knew I liked you."

"As long as I don't hold back from my team and my sergeant, I'm good. My sergeant will see the wisdom. The killer will always be there. We're after his boss, and his, too."

Gracie patted Erin's shoulder. "I'm going to phone my director as soon as I leave. When you report, just ask them to get in touch with Roland Jackson at Bastion. He'll have all the information we learned here." Gracie jerked her thumb upward. "Let them make the final call."

Erin bobbed her head. "Good plan. Let's stay in touch." She fished out a card from her jeans pocket and handed it to Gracie.

"Works for me. My cards are out there." She inclined her head toward the living room.

"Next time." Erin returned to Lupe, and Gracie went back to the living room.

Carmen glanced up from her hands. "I suppose you need to know what else I know."

Finally. "That would be good."

"The man who found Victor wanted him to go to Chihuahua and bring back two packages."

"Drugs?" It didn't sound like drugs.

"If Victor knew, he didn't tell me. But I don't think he knew."

"What's your take? Did he go or is he in hiding?"

"He believed the man was full of hot air. Then. But after he learned about Mom and Dad, I think he went to do what was demanded of him. But not before making sure Jessica and Maya were safe and wouldn't be found. They were the only people he loved more than himself. I know he's scared out of his mind. Not for himself but for Jessica and Maya. He doesn't know about Lupe. She's the caller's trump card."

CHAPTER 24

On the way out of Lupe's, Gracie nodded to the patrol watchdog and walked to her Jeep. She started the engine and, hoping the Jeep would cool off quickly, called Bastion, punching in the extension for Research. When they picked up, she gave them the number of her previous caller. "Who does it belong to?"

"That number belongs to a Donovan James Beck."

"Donovan Beck. I know him. Thanks."

The hunk. Wow! Who knew? She grinned. Life in the personal column ticked up a notch. She put the Jeep in gear and drove off. "I'll call you as soon as I get home, Mr. Cutie."

Her next call was to Jackson's cell. He picked up right away. "I finally got the scoop on Victor Cantu."

"Not our case on that end, Hofner."

"I told you I would find Jessica and her daughter."

"Did you? Find them, I mean."

"Not yet. But I did learn a lot. So did a SARIC detective. So you need to get with them. She's holding off so you'll have the information first."

Gracie filled him in on what the Cantu sisters had told her and Erin.

"Good work. I suppose you're going to spend your evening looking for the mother and daughter."

"Not all my evening. I'm going home to eat a sandwich and make a couple of phone calls. Then I'm going to two places—Holy Cross Church in Stone Oak and a burned-out strip center in Balcones Heights."

"Why the strip center?"

"It burned last night. Before it did, a cabby reported dropping off a woman and little girl at that location. I'm going to see if there's a repeat tonight"

"Watch your back. Not the best place to be."

"Aware. If I don't find them, I'm coming home and going to bed. I have a job tomorrow. Remember?"

"I'm glad you didn't forget."

#

Gracie washed up, opened a bottle of water, and made herself a ham and cheese sandwich. She topped it with lettuce and tomato and forked the last dill pickle from the jar. "Protein, dairy, veggies, carbs. Looks balanced to me." She flipped the television on to a news channel to see what she'd missed during the day.

When she finished, she put her plate in the dishwasher and took the rest of her water with her to the recliner. She put her feet up and returned Donovan Beck's phone call.

"Hello, Gracie."

She smiled. His unseen voice made her warm inside. Not that it was different from his working voice. Well, except maybe a little huskier and more intimate.

"Hi, yourself, Donovan Beck."

"How did you know it was me? I didn't leave a message."

"When you said, 'Hello, Gracie.'" Her mother would roll her eyes right across the floor like two tiny bowling balls if she knew how easily some lies flowed off Gracie's tongue. "I recognized your voice. It's hard to miss."

"I called to check in about how you liked your first day."

119

"Fun. I had a great time." She paused. "I hope I did okay, that you're not calling to fire me."

"Oh, no. You did great. I didn't know what to expect. You showed up with some initiative and a lot of enthusiasm. I was happy."

"I love staying busy and meeting new people."

"It shows. I told my sister about you, and she wanted to know if you'd be interested in staying on—assuming the two of you get along, of course."

So much for Mr. Hunk being attracted to me in a personal, I-want-to-ravage-your-body, way. Damn it.

"She said if you are, you can go ahead and fill out the application and forms so that all the paperwork and the physical are done before she comes back full time."

What can I tell him? "It's a great place, but I have to say no. Please tell her how much I appreciate her offer. And thank you, too, for considering me. But I..." *what the hell am I*—"I'm going to work for a consulting firm next month." *Whew! Not totally a full-blown lie, either.* Bastion's guidelines were to stick as close to the truth as possible in such situations.

"We'll miss you."

Did he say we?

"What sort of consulting?"

Would he never stop? He asked more questions than she did. "International. I'll be able to use my degree."

"Great. What's it in?"

"I have a master's in Bicultural Studies. My bachelor's is in Psychology." She conveniently omitted the other half of her double major in Criminal Justice.

Donovan laughed. Maybe roared was the more proper term.

"What's so funny?"

"You're a brainchild, and I taught you how to sell cupcakes." He laughed again. When he calmed himself

120

enough to talk, he said, "Wait until I tell Tessa. She's going to be all over me for being such a blockhead."

"That's what sisters do. We're usually good at it."

"You have a brother?"

"Three. And a sister."

"Big family. It's just Tessa and me in ours. Are you from here?"

"Fredericksburg. You?"

"Austin. I still live there, at least part of the time. I travel. When I'm here, I stay with Tessa. They bought a house big enough for a football team. Emily's the first, and she doesn't begin to fill it up."

"When you said you were in the insurance business, I thought you were an agent with an office in a strip center."

"At times that sounds pretty good. I'm an investigator."

Well, there's part of the truth. "Investigation sounds more interesting than sales and service."

"Unless I'm selling cupcakes." Gracie heard the smile in his voice. He was flirting.

"As long as you aren't investigating your sister."

"That would bite. Tessa would never need investigating, but if she did, someone else would handle that case."

You bet your ass they would.

"Well, I guess I better go and break the news to her. See you in the morning."

Gracie stared at her phone. She wasn't sure what to think. Not about the job offer, but about the flirting. Maybe he was as awkward with it as she was, but she didn't think so. He was too good looking and comfortable in his skin. She didn't think he would be intimidated by her degrees either since he'd laughed about those and at himself. Maybe he didn't want to get involved with anyone because of his job, since he still hadn't told her the full extent of it.

She hadn't told the full truth either, but she had a reason. She wondered what his reason was.

CHAPTER 25

The map on her phone showed a large area with several buildings at Holy Cross Parish. Gracie hoped one of them was the rectory. After she got on the road, she called Neva Salazar.

"Hang on, Gracie."

"Hanging." She was just passing the exit for the zoo when Neva returned.

"I'm back. Sorry about that—I needed to finish up a call on the other line. Gherkin said you're helping look for the son's wife and daughter."

"On it right now, in fact."

"We talked to the child's teacher today. She told us that Maya had been talking a lot in the last week or so about going to the Alamo."

"Had she been there?"

"Everybody in SA's been there, Hofner. Even Maya. The teacher said Maya was excited because they were going to go to all the missions and spend the night at the Alamo."

"With her parents?"

"That's the impression the teacher got. We sent a couple of patrol units to check all of them, but they didn't find anything. Others made sure the Alamo was secure at closing. They're not inside."

"Maybe it's some kind of group tour coming up."

"We're checking on that tomorrow. I thought you should know in case the missions were on your list."

"They weren't, but that doesn't mean anything. Just because they didn't find them today doesn't mean they're not around them someplace. I'll work on that and let Jackson know." Especially since they could leave through one of the back entrances to the Alamo and spend fewer than thirty seconds on the narrow streets before entering Rivercenter. Much less if they went through the lobby of the Crockett Hotel.

"Sounds good. Roland Jackson is on his toes about keeping SAPD informed. I like that. Bastion is extremely responsive to our needs."

"Told you."

"Only a million times. Maybe more. I like taking things slow. Remember, I just had a birthday. I'm old."

Gracie laughed. "Right. At the moment, I'm checking on another lead in a different part of town. If I find her tonight, I'll text you. If not, I'll work on this tomorrow afternoon. I'm on a morning assignment this week, but Jackson will be aware. He's a daddy, so he has a high interest in finding Maya, too."

"Best I can ask for. Thanks."

"Appreciate your staying in touch. You have my cell number now. Don't lose it."

Neva was laughing when she hung up.

Next, Gracie called Jackson.

"Make it quick. I have a bowl of pasta waiting."

"Yum. Can you send Sabrina over to cook for me?" Roland Jackson's wife was a private chef and did most of the cooking at their house.

"She's got a gig tonight. I made this all by myself. Fill me in."

"Don't forget to clean up." Gracie brought him up to date with Neva's information.

"I'll get with SARIC and station some folks out by each of the missions tomorrow. SAPD can't free up enough officers to cover all of them at the same time.

We'll get the four in the park, the Alamo, and San Fernando Cathedral, too. Just in case."

"Thank you, sir. Maybe someone near the Rivercenter entrance to the Marriott, too. They need to watch for an adult and child. Jessica is slender. She may dress them both as male. I don't know. So give them their pictures. They'll have to get up close and blend in, because that's what Jessica will be trying to do. Lots of people out with Fiesta."

"You let me worry about that. Call me if you find them tonight."

#

Gracie made a wrong turn and had to go around the block in the middle of a busy Stone Oak shopping area. On the second pass, she found the church and pulled into the parking lot. The third building she came to was the rectory. A white Acura was parked out front.

The website said the parish had three priests. She hadn't written down their names and couldn't remember the order. She remembered them as TEX— Fathers Timothy, Eduardo, and Xavier. She hoped one of them was home.

Not that she expected any of them to say Jessica was with them. Gracie wouldn't tell, and she certainly wasn't a priest. If she wouldn't confess, she didn't expect them to.

No, she came to give them information.

On the way up the walk, she saw the camera above the door. Good to know they were careful. She rang the bell. And waited.

A young man came to the door in shorts and a tee. "May I help you?"

He didn't look like a priest, but you never knew. She handed him her card. "I'm Gracie. I'd like to talk to a priest, please. It's important—possibly a matter of life or death." She watched his face. He might be

125

young, but he didn't give anything away. Maybe he was a priest.

"If you'll call the parish office tomorrow and make an appointment, one of the priests will be happy to talk to you."

She'd expected as much and had come prepared. "Tomorrow could be too late."

He actually raised one eyebrow. She'd tried to do that ever since she was a little girl and had never been able to master it.

"I'm not kidding. I need to speak to a priest. I'm a member of St. Mary's Parish in Fredericksburg. My whole family is. You can call Father Leo over there. He won't know why I'm here to talk to you, but he'll vouch for me and tell you I'm not evil or crazy."

The man's mouth drew into a line. "Stay here. I'll be right back."

The door opened again before anyone would've had time to make a phone call. An older, priestly looking man came out. He wore shorts and a tee, too, but Gracie knew without a doubt he was a priest.

He closed the door behind him. "I'm Father Tim. How may I help you, Ms. Hofner?"

"Thank you for seeing me, sir. I'll be happy to make a donation to your parish tomorrow." And she would.

"Not necessary, but always appreciated. Father Eddie is calling St. Mary's now. Leonardo Saenz is an old friend of mine. You sure he'll say you're on the up and up?"

Gracie grinned. "Clever. It's Leonard Karl, and you know it. Yes, he will. He'll probably say I'm a persistent pain in the ass and you were smart to deal with me early or you'd have to put up with me nagging you until you did."

Father Tim laughed and shrugged. "My own failed attempt at Sam Spade. I hope I'm a better man of God than private detective."

The door opened and Father Eddie poked his head out. "Leo said to tell both of you hello. He said he expects Ms. Hofner at confession the next time she's in town so he can hear what this is all about." The door closed.

So the younger guy is a priest after all. I must be getting old.

"All right, then," Father Tim said. "It's a pleasure to meet you, Gracie Hofner. How may I help?"

"Two members of your parish are missing—Jessica Cantu and her daughter, Maya. They've been unaccounted for since Saturday morning."

"I read about Victor's parents in the paper and prayed for their immortal souls." He made the sign of the cross in an offhand manner, almost without thinking. "I have not seen Victor, Jessica, or their daughter."

Perhaps he told the truth. Or maybe Father Eddie stashed them in the Parish Office and Father Tim just hadn't been over there. Truth came in varying degrees.

"I work for a law enforcement consultant firm. We're working with the police on this case." Gracie reached in her bag and pulled out a manila envelope. The clasp was closed, but the envelope remained unsealed. She'd left the contents available in case the priest was telling the truth about Jessica but knew how to reach her. "In the event you see or hear from Jessica, will you please give her this?"

The envelope contained a note from Gracie explaining what she'd told the priest and her card along with a couple of details about Carmen and Lupe plus a mention of Caballo Canyon and Chihuahua. She asked Jessica to call her, and she promised to keep them safe.

If Jessica was here, or elsewhere under Father

Tim's protection, she was at about a four or five on a one-to-ten safety scale. The Bastion bunkers would keep her at a solid ten, but Gracie couldn't tell her that. She hoped the small amount of knowledge she shared would frighten Jessica enough to contact her.

Father Tim took the envelope from her. "Of course."

"Thank you, sir. We believe her life, and perhaps Maya's as well, may be in danger."

Father Tim ran his fingers along the envelope's edge. "What about her husband? I have heard from others that he, too, is missing."

"My focus is on Jessica and Maya." She could tell only bits and pieces of the truth, too.

CHAPTER 26

On her way home from leaving the envelope for Jessica, Gracie called Trinka.

"Hey, sis. What's up?"

"I need Ben's number."

"Our cousin Ben?"

"Yeah. He's the only Ben I know. You got a Ben on the side you didn't tell me about?"

"Ha-ha. You want his home or cell number?"

"Text me his cell after I hang up and give me his home now. I need a name from him for a friend."

Fredericksburg was so small, Gracie knew the area and prefix already, so she only had to memorize the last four digits. She called as soon as she hung up.

Ben's wife answered. They chatted for a couple of minutes before Ben came on.

"Gracie! Good to hear from you. If your mom didn't tell you, the girls really loved the birthday money you sent."

"Girls always like money. Ask Missy."

"No need for that. I got the picture early on. Whatcha need?"

"A name. A really good friend—my former partner at SAPD—is getting a divorce. His name is Nick Rivera. Nicholas. His wife left him."

"Ouch. Sorry to hear that."

"Not a loss. Believe me. Even though he's not

seeing it quite that way yet."

"I understand."

"He planned to not get a lawyer, but I told him he had to have one."

"You need a referral."

"Yes. But more. Not just somebody. I want Nick's lawyer to be someone you know. And somebody who will give him a family rate. He's a cop. You know we don't have spare attorney cash."

"I can do that."

"Nick's willing to give her whatever she wants. No kids, but some property, his pension. He needs someone who's not afraid to move the fight so that Nick has the advantage. She has nothing of her own, or so he believes."

"But you don't believe that."

"I believe it could go either way. The attorney needs a good investigator so they learn all the facts. Not just the stated facts. Understand?"

"Yeah, I get what you mean. I know someone who will go deep and still read between the lines after she's found everything. Sound like what you're looking for?"

"Exactly. I also believe—especially with Nicky being a law enforcement officer—that the right judge is important. So your referral needs to be law enforcement friendly, too."

"She is. I actually have a couple of people in mind—both are like what you're looking for. Let me talk to them tomorrow. You'll hear from me by the end of the day."

"Great. Thank you. I owe you one."

"I won't forget."

True, for sure. She and Ben had traded favors off and on since they were kids. Not much as adults, though. They hadn't even talked in a couple of years. She frowned, trying to remember. *Oh, yeah—Mom and Dad's Fourth of July party.* She frowned again,

130

counting on her fingers. That had been four years ago. Everybody was too damn busy these days.

Only one more place to visit before she could go home and shower. She exited the freeway into the Balcones Heights neighborhood. It didn't take her long to find the strip center that had burned. This was the time of night the cabbie had dropped his fare. Gracie wanted to hang for a bit to see if tonight would be a repeat.

Her phone beeped with a text.

From Ben.

I decided to call tonight. My first pick. She's top dollar pro-bono. Plus, she'll reimburse your friend for filing and service fees and court costs. She's owed me a couple of big favors for a while and is happy to pay them off. I know you understand that.

Her phone beeped again.

A name, address, and phone number.

Gracie recognized the attorney's name—Rayann Dailey. Ben made a perfect choice.

She texted back: *Don't make me pay that steep a price. I'm family.*

Ben's text followed two seconds later: *You know me, cuz* followed by a smiley and a bag of cash.

That was the thing. She did know him. But he'd never failed her, and that's what counted.

A pickup turned onto the street while Gracie waited. The single occupant turned out to be a bulky bald man. He pulled into the apartment complex driveway and continued out of sight.

Gracie returned to the phone and sent the information from Ben on to Nick, adding that if he didn't have an appointment by the time she finished at the bakery on Tuesday, she would make one for him. Followed by: *You better hope that doesn't need to happen.*

CHAPTER 27

Gracie waited until ten but didn't see anything else. Not a vehicle. Not a person. Not even a shadow. She drove home, showered, and went straight to sleep.

A mockingbird woke her at five-seventeen on Tuesday morning. She dressed in a sky blue dress with cap sleeves and a gathered skirt. With it, she could wear a thigh holster. She didn't like wearing the same concealed holster two days in a row. No matter how well made, they tended to chafe.

She paired her dress with the cowboy boots Trinka had given her for her thirtieth birthday—the ones with the hand-worked bluebonnets on them. They looked really cute with the dress. A headband held her hair away from her face. Maybe she could find a flowered Fiesta comb or clip from a street vendor to replace the plain headband.

The sound of Donovan's voice echoed in her head. She looked forward to working next to him today. Even if she didn't qualify for the bimbo he was looking for. That was okay. She could still enjoy some eye candy.

Yesterday, her worries were about Webb and whether she should say anything about seeing him on the street. It didn't take her too long to figure out that it would be better to keep a secret or two.

No calls or texts had come in overnight or so far this morning. The day would begin with a clean slate. She put her phone on vibrate and placed it in the pocket in her boot before she got out of her Jeep.

At Jalapeno Cupcake, she knocked on the glass door and smiled when Donovan came out from the kitchen. He smiled, too, as he came toward her.

Gracie's mouth grew dry just watching him. *Stop ogling and smile.*

He unlocked the door and opened it for her. "Good morning!"

"Same to you. I can cross owning a bakery off my list. Getting up early isn't a problem. But every day and being happy along with it may be asking too much of my body clock."

He laughed as he relocked the door. "Not an early bird?"

"Not when it still takes an hour to see the sun."

"You hide it well." His voice quietened. He looked at her from head to toe and back again. "You look good to me."

She smiled. *He's interested!* "Thank you. Now I need my apron so I can get to work."

"Grab a fresh one from the back shelf." He returned to the kitchen while she tied the sash.

The morning went smoothly. Webb, Maricelia, and Natalie were friendly and chatty. Donovan was all business, but every once in a while their hands brushed. Or their arms. Each time, Gracie smiled, pretty sure the touches were intentional on Donovan's part.

She hated to leave at her break, but a walk in the fresh air would keep her fresh. This was a job, and she didn't need to let her mind keep wondering about Donovan's kisses. As soon as she moved out of his view, she ducked into a storefront and pulled out her phone. She hadn't noticed any vibrations and wasn't surprised that nothing showed.

It would be up to Gracie to jerk the strings today, lest someone felt like dropping the ball. She went to the same little shop as the day before, got a bottle of water, and headed to the back. Sitting on a stool at a window counter, she called Nick.

"I made an appointment. Two-thirty tomorrow afternoon. It's my day off." He sounded upbeat.

"Excellent."

"Thank you. I know I didn't say that before, but I know you're right. The referral come from your cousin?"

"Yes. She owed him a favor."

"Tell him thank you, too, for me."

"I will. Oh, I forgot to mention that she's not charging you a fee."

"What? I can pay for an attorney."

"Not this one. Ben says she's the best. You'll have to pay for filing fees, court costs, service fees, and the like, but she'll reimburse you. I gather she owed him a damn big favor."

"I'll talk the reimbursements over with her. But thanks again."

That was Nick. Proud. No charity. "My pleasure. I need to get back to the bakery."

After disconnecting, Gracie glanced at the time. *Yikes! I've got to hustle.* She tossed her empty water bottle into the trash as she left. She fast walked back, holding the door for a departing Jalapeno Cupcake customer before she went inside.

"Sorry I'm late. Call from my mother." *Sorry Mom.*

"If you're late, I didn't notice." Donovan wiped the top of the display case. "I know how mothers are. Believe me. Mine moved to Phoenix. Not sure if that's better or worse."

They both laughed.

Webb Truitt came out from the kitchen, wiping his hands. "The cupcake order for the eleven-thirty pickup will be ready to frost in about five minutes. You asked me to tell you."

"I want Gracie to watch so she can be excited when she talks to customers about them."

Webb turned to her. "Bet you didn't know anyone could get excited about cupcake frosting, did you?"

"I've never been excited about putting it on, but I've been plenty excited about eating it off. I'd love to watch."

"Okay. Five minutes."

Gracie put her bag back into the drawer and retied her apron.

Donovan stopped her. "Before you go to the kitchen, bring me some of the paper bags with handles that we use for larger orders. We're almost out up here."

"Sure. Where do you keep them?"

"I guess I didn't show you the supply closet. The door on the other side of the restroom."

"Got it. Be right back."

Now she wouldn't need to sneak in to see if there had been any deliveries. She opened the door. A large box sat in the center. She pulled out her camera and snapped a picture of the box and another one of the shipping label. Someplace in Fort Worth called Ave Amarillo, in all capital letters across the top of the shipping label. Gracie was surprised it was shipped from Fort Worth instead of Amarillo since Avenue Amarillo was the name.

She sent them to Jackson. As soon as she slipped the phone back into her boot she searched for the bags and grabbed a stack.

When she turned back toward the door, she screamed.

CHAPTER 28

Each time Slate came to Austin, the last stop he made before returning to the Lone Star Ranch was the condominium building overlooking the Colorado River. He parked in the space allotted to Unit 1101.

The elevator took him directly to the penthouse floor. He rang the bell. A woman he'd never seen opened the door, wearing a white silk robe and fuck-me pumps.

"Yes?"

"I'm Louie."

She stepped back. "Come in. I'm Rosemary."

Sure you are. Slate asked for a different woman for each visit. He wanted nothing familiar about her. But he was always Louie, and she, Rosemary.

Slate stepped into the upscale impersonal interior and untied the belt of Rosemary's robe, taking in her naked beauty. The service had his explicit requirements. Blondes only. Under twenty-five. Slender. Slate never wanted to look at a Rosemary and be reminded of his daughters. Nor did he want her to possess any of the features of his wife, Courtney. Rosemary was for his fantasies.

He led Rosemary to the bedroom. She continued on to the bathroom, where she knew to wait until he called.

Hot, moody jazz played softly, and in the corner, a small lamp glowed. He removed his clothing, taking his time, getting himself in the mood. Rosemary's perfume bottle sat on the dresser. Naked, he sprayed the air and inhaled. The scent brought back all the memories.

The sex with Rosemary would be hard and fast and rough. All the things he wouldn't do with Courtney. All the things that freed him. Slate's muscles were hard and strong. Cowboy muscles. He knew how to control them, and how to control himself. Otherwise, it would be too easy to really let go. He sprayed the air again.

"Rosemary! Get in here."

The bathroom door opened and the woman sauntered toward him. She'd retied the robe, and in the soft light, every movement she made showed through the silk.

Slate grew rock hard.

Rosemary stopped in front of him.

He again untied her robe. This time, he slicked it down her arms into a puddle on the floor. She handed him a condom.

As she stepped out of the ridiculous heels, Slate rolled on the condom. When she looked up, Slate brought his lips down hard on hers, thrusting his tongue to the back of her throat. He pulled back and pushed her down to the bed.

Rosemary used her arms and feet to propel herself toward the pillows. Slate followed her movements until his face was even with hers. He straddled her and grabbed both her wrists in one hand while spreading her legs with his knees. With no warning or foreplay, he plunged inside.

She cried out.

"Shut up, you cunt." He thrust again.

Rosemary fought him. The woman must work out. She had some muscle behind her. The fight made him thrust harder. One punch landed on his cheek.

He might need to think of how he would explain a bruise there. He pulled out and rolled Rosemary to her stomach.

"Raise your ass."

She followed his command. In the faint light, he made out a faded tan line. He caressed her smooth cheeks. She flexed her muscles, and he spanked her. She flexed again, and he applied more force. She flexed the third time. Rock hard and near the bursting point, he spanked her again. She moaned.

He slammed inside her. She was so tight. And she fucked him good. He lasted a minute, if that. Afterward, it was his turn in the bathroom.

When he returned, Rosemary lay under the bedcoverings. Her instructions were to remain there until he left the apartment.

Slate dressed quickly. He withdrew his wallet to leave her a tip. On a scale of one to ten, this Rosemary was an eight. A nine if she hadn't punched him on the face, accidently or not. He counted out eight one-hundred dollar bills and left them on the dresser.

CHAPTER 29

Gracie screamed again. She watched in fascination as a furry black spider as big around as a cherry landed on top of the box.

She held the bags with both hands and smacked them down atop the spider. "No! No! No!" With each word, she smacked the ebony... fuzzball... and all... eight... woolly... appendages... to arachnid... hell.

"What the—" Donovan appeared in the doorway.

"No!" Smack. "No!" Smack.

"Gracie, what is it?"

She looked at him and backed up until she bumped against the shelf. Her gaze strayed to the top of the box. No spider. Where was it? She turned the bags over.

And screamed again, tossing the bags toward Donovan.

He stepped back just as Webb Truitt walked up. They both stumbled.

Webb stepped around Donovan and into the doorway. "What's going on in here?"

Gracie had regained her composure. "Sorry." She shivered and rubbed her arms.

"Are you all right?"

She nodded. "I am now. A spider." She grimaced and rubbed her arms again.

Webb stared at her. "A spider?"

"A big, black, furry spider. Hanging in front of my

face." She shivered again.

"Did it bite you?"

Gracie backed up. "Oh, God, no."

"What's all the fuss? Where is it?"

"On one of these bags."

"On a bag."

"Yes. I hate spiders." She swallowed. "I'm afraid of them. I tried to kill it. But I may have just knocked it out."

"You tried to kill it with a bag?"

"All the bags. Someone else will need to pick them up. I'm sorry—I can't do that. It may still be alive." *Snakes, rats, felons, meth heads, a whole gang of thugs with guns. Arterial spurts, splattered brains, gutted intestines—no problem.* She tried to get her breathing under control. "I don't know why I'm so afraid of spiders. There's no reason."

Webb laughed. So did Donovan. Finally Webb said, "If it's dead, you probably scared it to death."

Donovan gave her a hug. He smelled really good. She was glad she didn't have on her hip hugger holster.

Webb held up a bag. "Found it." He turned it over. Dead. For sure.

The black blob made her shiver. "Thank you. I can get the rest of the bags." She scooped up the ones at her feet and handed them to Donovan.

"You go on in and watch Webb frost those cupcakes. I'll take care of this."

Webb passed them. "Now I have to wash my hands again."

Gracie took a step, but Donovan stopped her with his hand on her arm. "You scared me half to death. I'm glad you're all right."

She might have scared him all the way to death if she'd pulled her Glock and shot the furry little fucker.

#

The rest of her shift was busy but uneventful. Her phone had vibrated once. She'd taken only a few steps past the door when she was met by a reporter and camera person. *What the hell?* "Excuse me."

"Wait!" The duo blocked Gracie's progress. "We're Rita and Raul, and we're doing YouTube interviews for StreetSides. It'll only take a minute."

Jackson would have twin cows—her orders had been to keep a low profile. "Sorry. I'm late for a meeting."

They trailed her as far as the alley. She wondered if they were taping. Would she be the rude woman of the day? Probably.

She pulled out her phone before entering her Jeep. It was especially hot inside, and the A/C blew hot air. Gracie looked to see who called. She didn't recognize the number, but the caller had left a voicemail.

"Hello, my dear. Sorry I missed you. This is Father Tim at Holy Cross."

Father Tim. Well, well.

"We found something that belongs to you. If you can stop by this evening about seven, we'll be happy to return it to you. No need to confirm unless the timing is a problem. We'll see you at seven here at the rectory."

"I'll be damned."

Her phone rang. It was Jackson. "Stop someplace and bring lunch for two."

"Did you get the photos?"

"Yes—can't talk now. I passed on the information to be checked out." He disconnected without saying goodbye.

Gracie stopped at Taco Cabana and bought street tacos, chips, salsa, and queso. While she waited, she filled tiny containers with pico de gallo.

As she approached her car, two black SUVs sped to a stop behind it, preventing her from reaching the door. The front and back doors of the first vehicle opened, and out popped Rita and Raul from the street.

Only this time, they had badges clipped to their waists.

"Come with us, please." Raul took her elbow and ushered her into the backseat while Rita jogged to the driver's side and slid in beside her.

CHAPTER 30

What am I supposed to do? Beat them over their heads with plastic containers of food?

Besides, she was ninety-nine percent the badges she saw were Homeland Security. Why would DHS stage a sham takedown? Bastion worked with them all the time. Why didn't they introduce themselves on the street earlier? Who rode in the second vehicle?

The SUV was rolling.

"Where are we going? I have someone else's lunch here."

They stopped at the street to wait on a break in traffic. A moment later, a woman on the sidewalk opened the front passenger door and got in. As she buckled up, the traffic cleared and the SUV made a right turn onto San Pedro.

She turned to Gracie. Short white-blonde hair, blue eyes, straight nose, smiling lips, oval face. "Pardon me for the grand entrance, but sometimes it pays to be overly careful."

Gracie agreed with that statement.

"I'm Paulina Villanova." She took off the blonde wig, revealing dark brown hair in a pixie cut. "Now you see the real me. I was elsewhere on another job when we got the news, so in pulling things together, we decided it worked better for me to meet everyone here. I'm the leader of our particular unit, and the reason we snatched you off the street is to take you to

143

your lunch meeting with Roland Jackson."

"Okay. Why didn't all of you just go there yourselves?"

"We'll let Roland explain that to you. Rita and Raul will stick with you when we arrive. I'll follow after the three of you are on your way up. Sit back. Relax. Let us do the driving."

Gracie tried to put the pieces together. Possibly DHS had unearthed a problem. Or maybe they were tracking Victor. Probably it had nothing to do with the Cantus' killer or they would've phoned it in to SAPD. Homicide got touchy. Everybody knew that. Or maybe, since all of this was taking place after she sent Jackson the photo of the box, the Jalapeno Cupcake delivery had triggered this pick-up action.

They rolled up to the building. Instead of stopping to let her and the StreetSiders out, the driver pulled into the garage and up to the elevator. A few seconds passed before he said, "Go."

Rita and Raul both pulled their Glocks and exited the SUV. A second later, Rita ducked her head back inside. "Okay, Gracie. Come on."

She knows my name. For some reason, that made Gracie's palms sweat. Not a heart-stopping fear like that damned spider, but more like it made her uneasy. Her stomach sank, and her heartbeat sped up. She slid out. Two agents from the second vehicle also stood in the garage with their weapons drawn.

The neon light in Gracie's mind blinked on. *It's you, Gracie. They're guarding you.* But that was crazy thinking.

They entered the building through the Bastion door, Raul in the lead with his badge in hand.

Saul Gallego was on duty. "I was told you'd make an entrance and bring a party. Elevators are ready."

"The original party girl. Thanks."

Through their exchange, Raul kept them moving.

He entered the elevator first and motioned her to stand behind him. Rita entered last and pressed the button for Jackson's floor.

Several seconds later, the bell dinged, and both Raul and Rita raised their Glocks to firing position.

Gracie could've told them there would be no worries here, but she decided to let them have their fun. As soon as that thought entered her head, she tried to clear it. *Take it back, take it back.* She didn't want to jinx anything and run into someone with an automatic rifle standing outside the door. She pulled her own Glock.

The doors opened and Gracie blew out a stream of air before following Rita.

Jackson stood at the reception desk. "That better be my lunch in the bag, Hofner."

"Yours and mine." She raised the bag. She still held her Glock in her right hand.

Rita nodded. "They're on the way up."

Gracie stood beside Jackson beneath the Bastion logo. Rita and Raul faced the elevator, their weapons pointed at the floor.

The elevator dinged and the duo assumed a firing stance. The door opened. Two armed men stepped out followed by Paulina and another man Gracie didn't recognize. He looked about fifty, with dark hair that was graying at the temples. Laugh lines marked the outer corners of his brown eyes. His haircut, paired with a dark gray suit, pale golden yellow shirt, rusty red and black tie, and black shoes, wrote Washington all over him. He must've been the passenger in the second vehicle.

Jackson nodded to his guests. "Welcome. Follow me." He walked toward the main conference room.

Maybe he planned to assign her to a new case. Could be as early as now if the box was the delivery she had been watching for. If so, she wouldn't see

Donovan again. She would miss him. Then she remembered his number was on her phone. Maybe she'd make a date for drinks on Saturday night, if the new case allowed for that.

She entered the conference room and chose a chair at the rear. Before sitting, she holstered her Glock. Everyone, except for Gracie and Jackson, milled around at the far end of the large room.

Jackson said, "I told them we needed a few minutes to eat. Enjoy this meal. I only know the basics, so who knows what's going to break."

Gracie nodded as she set the food out. They devoured most of it in about ten minutes.

Jackson scooped a bite of queso. "You look like you want to say something."

"I do. Two somethings. The box. Is it what I was waiting for?"

"Unlikely. I asked for background on Avenue Amarillo. Low priority, though, unless something changes."

"I suppose I don't get details."

"Correct. Unless it does prove to be the delivery. Just because we have information available doesn't mean it's wise for everyone to have access to any of it unless it pertains directly to an assignment."

"I know I bitch about the need-to-know basis, but I'm glad it's that way."

"The only way to fly, Hofner. What's the second thing?"

"Paulina said you'd tell me why they brought me here instead of just meeting us."

He swallowed and looked at Paulina, who was talking to Rita at the other end of the room. "She lied."

Gracie understood. It was expedient. Wait and tell the story once. And if Jackson did know, he chose to let Paulina tell it for him. In Paulina's shoes, or Jackson's, Gracie would've done the same. She nodded and pulled out her lip gloss, smoothing some onto her lips.

While Jackson used the last few broken chips to shovel out the remaining queso, Gracie counted the people in the room. Jackson, herself, Paulina, Rita, Raul, the man in the suit, plus four agents she didn't recognize. Two stood at the door. Two guarded Suitman. Whoever he was, he was important.

Jackson put the last container into the bag and took it to the hall, confident someone would take care of it. He motioned to Gracie. "Let's join the others." She stood and followed him to the other side of the room.

CHAPTER 31

Slate had called Courtney to meet him in town for lunch. He pulled into the Bungalow Grill parking area and spotted her white Escalade at the far end of the lot. After parking next to her, he checked his cheek again in the mirror. A slight discoloration had appeared and was turning a deeper blue. It wasn't large, and the skin wasn't broken. He could easily work around that.

The times he and Courtney spent together after he visited Rosemary were extra special, and he looked forward to them as much as the times with Rosemary. He explained to his wife how being away from her for a short time made him miss her, and that missing her made him desire her more than he already did. She fell for it every time. He was already getting turned on again.

Courtney stood just inside the door and smiled when he entered. "I barely beat you here."

The hostess returned. "Two?"

Slate scanned the restaurant and inclined his head. "The booth in the back, please."

"Yes, sir." She grabbed two menus. "Follow me."

Slate ordered half a bottle of Courtney's favorite wine. "Anything exciting happen while I was away?"

She glanced at her wrist. "All twenty two hours? Not much. Two of the girls got in a fight over which one would use the purple towel at bath time, and

I planted the last of the rose bushes by the south pasture gate."

"I do love all my girls."

Courtney smiled, then frowned and cocked her head. She pushed her hair behind her ear in a gesture Slate loved. Her frown lifted as she leaned forward. "Aw, sweetie, what happened to your cheek?" She brushed the bruise with the tips of her fingers.

The thrill of Courtney's touch where Rosemary had struck his cheek aroused him even more. "I got shampoo in my eye this morning. When I reached for the washcloth, I hit the knob. Lucky my cheek took the hit instead of a few inches higher. I could've knocked myself out."

"It's not too bad. I'd kiss it and make it better, but I can't reach."

Slate took her hand. "You can kiss something else and make it better after we leave here."

"I can't wait."

Slate smiled and squeezed his wife's hand. He recognized good fortune when he saw it, and because of Courtney, his home-front world rocked. His life was exactly the way he wanted it.

CHAPTER 32

Paulina stood up and faced the assemblage. "Everyone knows who I am, so there's no need for introductions. I apologize for the speedy and unorthodox way we pulled this together, but it was the best we could come up with, under the circumstances.

"First, Gracie. We were hoping to relay a message to you via the StreetSides ruse, but you outsmarted us."

Gracie pumped her fist, and a few people chuckled.

"Someone has placed a tracking device on your Jeep. I'll get to how we know that in a few minutes."

Why would someone track her? Was it a current case or something from the past? Certainly nothing personal. She hadn't been involved with anyone for a few months, and none of her friends or relationships were controlling types.

"I spoke with Roland, and we agreed it's best to leave it untouched for now. Just know that someone has taken an interest in your activities and is keeping track of your location. Roland said you were last checked the first of the month and you were clear. So the interest has begun sometime between then and now. You two can get your heads together on your own time to figure it out."

Maybe someone got the wrong Jeep. "Thanks. Are you ready to get to why my tracker came to your attention?"

More chuckles. Jackson shook his head. "She's like that. Never a moment's peace."

Someone snorted. Gracie thought it was Rita.

Paulina smiled. "That's all right, Gracie. If you decide you want to come over to our side, just give me a call."

Gracie turned to Jackson and wrinkled her nose. She liked having options and open invites, even though she had no intention of leaving Bastion.

"Our unit has been charged with keeping track of a shipment of large, uncut diamonds." Paulina waited a beat for that to sink in. "They moved from South Africa in an unconventional manner to Dubai before continuing on to Brussels, where we expected them to be cut. But instead of being cut, they were couriered to Oslo."

"Oslo?" The word popped out of Gracie's mouth before she could stop it. "Sorry. I didn't mean to say that out loud."

"No problem. That's about how we felt. We were certain this particular shipment was inspected in Dubai, would be cut in Brussels, and sent back to Dubai. There were rumblings that the cut diamonds would be sold in a black auction and the profits funneled into the terror pipeline. But while they were in Oslo, they vanished."

Gracie didn't understand how the diamonds figured into the tracking device on her Jeep, so she wanted to hear more. "How do you know the diamonds vanished? Maybe they're still in Oslo." If they'd had that close of an eye on the diamonds, they would've noticed something suspicious.

"I can't tell you how we know they aren't there. It's classified. But I can tell you with one hundred percent certainty that they are no longer in Oslo at the original destination. We have eyes-on confirmation. We also know they are still uncut."

Gracie rubbed at the knot forming between her shoulders. "If you know where they aren't and know they are still uncut, can't you just check and track diamond cutters who would be attracted to this type of job? Someplace they're bound to show—" Gracie stopped mid-sentence. "Oh. I think I know how you tracked them. And why you can't find them now."

"We'll talk later. One thing we have been able to track, that's been constant, has been the code words they use in their chatter. It's the chatter that led us to you and to Bastion. That's how we found the tracker on your Jeep."

"How could stolen diamonds lead to me? I've never been to Norway and I'm not a thief."

"No, we checked. You haven't. Nor to any other location pertinent to this operation. But you are working on a case to find a missing woman and her daughter."

"Jessica and Maya Cantu. Obviously, you're aware of other elements of the case as well."

"We've recently been informed of the details, yes."

Gracie shook her head. "I'm following what you're saying, but I'm missing a connection or two. Terror diamonds wouldn't land in the hands of a woman who spends most of her days shopping. I don't see a common ground."

"It's our belief the killing of Hector and Therese Cantu occurred as collateral damage while in pursuit of a larger goal."

Collateral damage. Jackson's fingers circled her wrist in a warning for Gracie not to let loose on the messenger. She clenched her teeth and took a deep breath. "What would that larger goal be?"

"I'll let Mr. McAlister explain that. Ian McAlister is part of our Intelligence and Analysis unit." Paulina looked at Suitman. "Your turn, Ian."

Gracie thought Ian McAlister would be the fussy

sort with his clothing. Instead, he stood right up without checking cuffs, tie, or creases. "Sorry to crash in like this. Had I known I'd be in Texas for lunch, I'd have worn jeans and boots. I'm from Fort Worth, so I'll try to get over feeling overdressed and give you the facts as we currently know them."

Gracie bit her lips to hide her smile. Ian McAlister hadn't lost all of his Texas drawl. She wondered if it sometimes got him made fun of. Or if he used it as an icebreaker.

"Paulina told you about the diamonds. They've been missing for a week. At first we believed they were auctioned early or a buyer paid enough that the cutting and auction weren't needed to achieve their terror needs. We weren't having any luck at tracking the money when we heard squawking from Dubai about a theft. That's when we knew the diamonds had been stolen."

Gracie turned to Jackson and held her palm from her cheek to his. "They operate like we do."

He whispered back, "Only with about a hundred times more people and money. We probably use as many resources as they do, though."

"After that, we turned our attention to a different area, listened to different conversations. Yesterday, we picked up some interesting tidbits, but nothing definite. Overnight, those tidbits were fleshed out a little. About the time I got to work this morning, we got the breakthrough we'd been working toward."

Jackson cleared his throat. "It must've been some breakthrough for you to come all the way out here."

"I'm not a big somebody, but I'm good at what I do. Which may not be exactly what you're thinking my job is. I'm not allowed to tell you more. But I can tell you the reasons they sent me are because I'm from Texas and I was handy. They think I can relate better to you and sell you on our theory."

"Theory?"

"It's really more than that. It's developing rapidly and we have new information already since I left this morning."

"Let's hear it."

"The diamonds are in Chihuahua, Mexico."

Gracie touched Jackson's arm. "Lupe said..." She let her voice trail off on purpose.

Jackson shrugged one shoulder and nodded toward McAlister.

"You had suspicions about Chihuahua?" McAlister asked.

"Regarding a different case." Jackson shifted in his chair. "We didn't know anything about diamonds."

That was all Jackson shared. He said nothing about Victor. Gracie would do her best to follow his lead.

McAlister smiled. "I've heard Bastion is sharp. It's a pleasure to be here. Let's get to the nitty-gritty, shall we?"

Jackson jerked his head in a nod. "Do it."

CHAPTER 33

"Before we get started, I'm also here to help in any way we can. Your excellent reputation precedes you, Mr. Jackson." McAlister smiled again. "It's an honor to work with you, sir."

Jackson acknowledged the compliment with a bounce of his head.

"If needed, I can deploy a rapid response team. Agents here can connect to our computers and databases if you need computer or cyber assistance. We're not here to take charge—just to offer assistance and provide an overview of facts you may not know. If you hadn't demonstrated you're as good as I've heard, this would be a different story right now."

"I appreciate that."

"We got a blip from the diamonds this morning. It was short, less than two minutes' duration. But more than long enough for us to pinpoint them. Because we have the ability to do that, we believe they've changed hands."

Yes! Gracie did a mental fist pump. She'd thought it had to do with a new chemical coating she'd read about. Someone must have opened the diamond container, and the diamonds must have been sprayed with the new coating. Gracie tried to remember where she'd read the article. It had been several months before, and she'd remembered thinking at the time that if they were writing about it in a magazine, somebody was already using it—and it wasn't anything secret for those in the know.

"Since we've been in San Antonio, we have on-the-ground intelligence from Chihuahua."

"Quick action."

"We called in a favor."

Nick and her cousin's favor popped into Gracie's head. And just as quickly, she remembered where she'd read the article—one of her brother's *Popular Science* magazines. Kern had loved science since he was a boy, and now he taught it to high schoolers. The substance was a spray-on coating that dried invisible to the naked eye. Some of the particles could be detected under some microscopes, but detection usually involved a lab setting and specialized instruments. Or a receiver designed solely for the purpose. She tuned back into the conversation.

"Four agents arrived onsite within minutes." McAlister was totally engrossed in his story, but a glance at Jackson told Gracie he'd seen that she'd been off visiting her imagination, except in this case it had been her memory. "They shadowed the first four people to leave the location who appeared to be likely couriers. They're still tracking two of them."

"What about the other two?"

"Proven to be uninvolved. Of the two they're watching, one is still in Chihuahua proper. One is moving west. It's possible the diamonds left before we arrived. Or after our people left."

"Maybe they're still at the same location." Jackson wasn't fond of what-ifs.

"Possibly. The blip came from a large market with multiple exits. We worked on the theory that whoever possessed the diamonds would depart quickly. That may have been incorrect, but it was our best guess with limited manpower." McAlister's phone beeped. "Excuse me a moment."

Gracie couldn't leave the coating situation alone. She focused on trivia as much as she focused on every aspect of each assignment she worked. Jackson told her she often had no filter. Maybe so, but it didn't seem that way to her—more that she needed to learn for herself what was important and what wasn't.

Right now, the coating took center stage. It emitted a radio wave that sounded like a constant ping. It could be adjusted for one of a predetermined set of frequencies. It didn't deteriorate or corrode into anything else. Nor did the coating affect the physical properties it adhered to. The only way the ping couldn't be detected was to enclose the coated object in titanium—like inside a box or tube.

She needed to talk to Jackson, but he was typing a text.

Paulina walked toward her. "You know about the coating." Her words were a statement, not a question.

Jackson looked up from his phone.

"I read about it a while back. Whoever stole the diamonds in Norway put them in a titanium container. He had to know to do that."

"Yes, he did."

"I think the person who now has them took them from the container for a visual verification and put them right back in. This person may or may not know about the coating."

"Good theory. Possibly the correct one." Paulina spoke in a quiet voice. "How do you think the person who contracted the theft knew about the diamonds? Much less the coating?"

"I haven't figured it out yet, but I have a few ideas, all somewhat interconnected. Rough."

"Will you share?"

Gracie glanced at Jackson. He raised his chin in a go-ahead.

"The original purchaser had the diamonds coated

at the mine. Our government found out about them and started tracking. Or, the whole Dubai/Oslo thing is a sham and the diamonds were ours to begin with. Why our government would purchase them I don't know—and don't want to know. If they weren't ours, I don't have the slightest idea how some American citizen, with enough spare change in his pockets to buy half of China, learned about these particular diamonds on the other side of the world. I don't want to know the answer to that either. Add to all that, I think you already know all the details, but somewhere, something went sideways."

Gracie hoped she'd made herself clear enough. The Federal government was not her thing. Too big, and too many rules. Both of those concerns were her main reasons for leaving SAPD for Bastion. More than that, once you knew any of the Feds' secrets, they thought they had you under their control.

It wouldn't be so bad if she learned the answers for herself. But she didn't want anyone to tell her, even if they believed she needed to know.

Jackson leaned forward. "Paulina. What's really going down here?"

A corner of Paulina's mouth smiled. "You always could see right through me. Good to know one thing hasn't changed."

Jackson stared at her, waiting for her to speak.

"Don't turn loose of Agent Hofner. She's sharp. Takes after you."

Gracie stayed silent. She didn't want them to send her away.

"The diamonds are ours." She sent Gracie a quick grin. "We put them out there with every expectation of getting them back—either cut or uncut, it didn't matter. We didn't expect them to be stolen."

"Tracing a pipeline?" Jackson asked.

"You could say that. Close enough."

"Have you plugged the leak? Is it your op?"

Paulina shook her head. "No. Homeland, but not my team. South Africa, Oslo, the rest—that's all true. We only got word when the diamonds showed up in our backyard. Our job is to get them back, not worry about how or why they were stolen."

"Excuse me." Gracie felt like the baby sister at a family meeting again.

Both looked at her.

"Go ahead," Jackson said.

"It would be a big help in finding the diamonds if you knew who had them stolen or even why. So if you could share that with Jackson, we could provide a lot more assistance."

Jackson laughed.

"What's so funny?"

Paulina touched Gracie's arm. "He's laughing because he knows how we work. Ian and I have told you all we know, with the exception of what I just shared. I wouldn't have said what I did if you hadn't already figured it out. Other teams are working to find who and why answers. I'll tell you what I do know. Whoever stole them... the person who made the actual grab... that list is down to a few high-priced thieves. Finding them and having proof to arrest is likely impossible. The diamonds themselves are in the eight digits uncut. Maybe more. After they're cut, the value increases exponentially. We cannot allow them to reach the black market."

CHAPTER 34

"Understood." Jackson leaned toward Paulina. "I do want to clarify one thing."

"If I can."

"Did you or someone on your team contact the Rangers about a delivery being made in San Antonio this week? Or do you know or have any intel about such a delivery?"

"No. I've heard nothing about a delivery. It would've had to come from another team if it came from Homeland."

"Thanks."

"No problem. I need to go corral Ian before he gets caught up in another fire." Paulina waved and turned away.

Jackson led Gracie to the other end of the conference room. She caught the tiniest whiff of leftover chili powder at the table where they'd eaten lunch. "I'm glad you need to talk to me, because I need to talk to you, too."

"Go ahead." Jackson rubbed his forehead. "We're probably going to talk about the same things."

"This is blowing my mind a little bit. So quick. So big. I mean, why are they really here?"

Jackson smiled. "That's the least of our worries. Feds drop in from time to time. You've seen a few. It's just the first time for you with this particular bunch. Paulina can be intense."

A weight lifted, but then she remembered. "What about the tracker on my Jeep? Who would do that?"

"Don't know. I've made it a priority to find out, starting with anyone connected with the bakery delivery—set that in motion already. I also have a call in to SARIC to find out the latest with the Cantu case. We have a standing email, but I need to ask questions. When I get back to my office, I'll get someone to look into the last few cases you worked, and the ones that we believed were on hiatus. Could be something new perking on any of those."

"That sounds good. I'll be more alert. What about the box? The one I sent the photo of?"

"I forwarded your photo to my contact. They said, and I quote, 'Your agent will know when it happens and what to do about it.'"

"So now I'm supposed to be clairvoyant? That's Ariana's thing, but she's on a cruise. Wait... if I'll know, then it must not be something normal."

"What's that mean, Hofner?"

"Normal. Like mail or supplies or ingredients. Things that could come any day of the week and no one would look twice."

"Makes sense."

"So maybe it's like someone will drop off a lost dog or forget a baby. Or throw a pipe bomb through the window."

Jackson shook his head. "That gives you a wide range of possibilities. You're on the right track."

"Just so we're clear—so I'm clear—your anonymous tip for this delivery came from the Texas Rangers, right?" That's what he'd said to Paulina, but she wanted to confirm.

"Correct. But I still don't know where they received their information. Cord McCullough passed it on to me. I didn't question it then. Given the new circumstances, I'll see if I can learn more."

Cord McCullough was one of the three Bastion partners. Jackson, McCullough, and Dominic Russo—all former government employees. Jackson, CIA. McCullough, Texas Rangers. Russo, Army—Special Ops. They understood one another. If more details were out there, Jackson would find them.

CHAPTER 35

Even though the diamonds and their disposition were of utmost importance, Maya and Jessica still occupied the number one spot on Gracie's list.

Jackson inclined his head toward the front of the room. "Looks like we're about to find out for sure why they're telling us about the diamonds."

Gracie turned. McAlister pocketed his phone and stopped to talk to Paulina, who nodded as he spoke. They returned to that end of the room.

"I'm sure it's about Victor being the diamond courier." Gracie banged her knee on a chair and grabbed it to keep it from tipping over. "That explains the collateral damage, the bug, all of it. Whoever killed the Cantus saw me at the scene and at Lupe's. They want to know who I am."

Paulina claimed her seat, and the others in the room resumed their previous positions. Gracie sat next to Jackson and looked at her knee. A little reddish line surrounded by a dime-sized circle of blue meant she'd have a sore purple spot before tomorrow. She sighed.

Ian returned to the front. "Sorry for the interruption. To continue, while we've been monitoring the diamonds, one of our processes has been to also monitor those individuals on our radar screens who've been involved in or been suspected of such activities in the past."

No one should be surprised by that.

"Not only are we monitoring the individuals, we're also set up to listen for devices used during previous instances of suspect behavior."

Gracie shook her head. *Fed 101*. They liked to string out a large net and see who else they could snare. Other agencies, even Bastion, did it to some extent, but no one equaled the Feds in execution.

"This morning, a device that hasn't been active in more than three years pinged in San Antonio. Our technology has improved over the last three years. What we found was an older tracking device. It didn't take too long to pinpoint it. We learned who the Jeep belonged to and that the owner worked for Bastion. So here we are. Questions?"

"Yes." Gracie's hand shot in the air. Despite trying, she hadn't been successful at breaking that old habit. "So somebody that does something to attract your attention every once in a while is now interested in tracking my movements."

"I'm afraid so. You said your interest in Chihuahua didn't have anything to do with diamonds—I'm sure you believed that—but my guess is that it does."

"We think it may, too." Gracie looked at Jackson, who nodded his assent. "Just because we didn't know about them until today doesn't negate the circumstances."

"Unfortunately, I have more news. The call I received a few minutes ago also has implications on this operation. As everyone can see, this is very much a developing situation."

"Aren't they all?"

Everyone nodded at Jackson's comment.

"The information I received is that one of the two people we were tracking in Chihuahua was ambushed and killed. Not by us, I might add, in the event any of you think we were involved. We were unable to do anything except watch from a distance before departing in order not to become casualties as well."

Gracie quickly got that picture.

"As a result, an apprehension was made of the second subject by the Mexican police. Our people are questioning that individual now, but no diamonds were found on his person. The stones are still in the wild."

CHAPTER 36

Slate had just stepped from his second shower of the day when his phone rang. "Yes."

"One package is in his possession. Plans are in place to pick up the second."

The check-in had proceeded as ordered. A good sign. "Did he give an indication of which package?"

"No. I pressed, as instructed. He hung up."

Slate toweled his hair with one hand. A minor problem, but one to be dealt with quickly upon the man's return—so he knew who was in charge. "Keep me posted."

"Yes, sir."

Slate disconnected and dried off. He'd expected both packages to be in Texas and on their way to him by now, but a delay had always been a possibility. One package was good. Two would've been better, but the second should be forthcoming by the next check-in.

He tossed his used towel over the hamper. He'd hired amateurs. Professionals would have put Slate's puzzle together early on and wanted more cash to do the deal. Amateur problems couldn't be helped.

The view caught his eye, and he stopped to admire it. He never tired of looking at his land. His nearest neighbor's property abutted Slate's a good two miles away from his home. Good enough in normal times.

But these times were not normal. There was no

way in hell he would allow that bastard of a neighbor who now called himself a Texan and a rancher to sell his property to a big East Coast development firm that didn't give a damn about Texas or its people.

Especially not when he knew just what to do to prevent it from happening.

CHAPTER 37

Gracie sat across from Jackson in his office. "Did McAlister say he'll get back to you with names?"

"Yes."

"What's our position if either of them is Victor?"

"Bastion doesn't have a position."

"You know what I mean. Do we tell SAPD? The sisters?"

"No, DHS would inform SAPD. I don't know who would tell the sisters. One of them. Or someone from the Department of State if a takedown is made in Mexico. They would also notify the wife, if she can be found. Maybe just the wife. I've never been involved in the mechanics of that."

Gracie removed her headband, rubbed her head, and put the band back on. "All kinds of things are floating in my mind right now. I'm trying to herd my thoughts into separate pens so I can think. My phone's vibrated at least three times, maybe more. I've got to sort out what I have before I add what's in the phone to the mix."

"Take your time, but don't take too long. What's on your schedule?"

"When I leave here, I'm going back to Taco Cabana for my wheels. I'm hoping someone will take me."

"No problem. I'll drive you."

"Thanks. From there, I'm going to talk to the Cantu sisters, see if I can wring some more information out of them. I expect it will be about five when I'm finished there. Earlier, I hope. Then I'm going home. I want to find the tracker for myself so I can check every day to see when it goes away. Then I need to shower and grab a sandwich so I can be at Holy Cross before seven."

"What's happening?"

"They called. I'm hoping the meeting will lead to the location of Jessica Cantu and her daughter. My gut's no longer tied in a knot."

"Excellent. Get in touch with me after. Time doesn't matter."

"I need to be in bed by eleven to guarantee any kind of alertness tomorrow because I have to get up at five-thirty. So anything extra that's on my phone needs to get squeezed in between the priests and bedtime." She paused to run everything through her head again.

"Anything else?"

"I also have to check in with Nick—I expect he's the originator of at least one of my messages. And I have to call a friend of Jessica's to see if she has any news."

Jackson stood up. "What are you waiting for? We need to get a move on. Time's a-wasting, girl. You can check messages while I drive."

She followed Jackson to the elevator. "Oh, yeah. Somewhere I have to find time to get an ad in the paper for my aunt's garage apartment."

#

Buckled in Jackson's car, Gracie pulled her phone from her boot. One voicemail and five texts. She chose the voicemail. It was from her brother closest to her in age, Axel.

"Hey, baby sis. I'm out here at the old Rastetter place on Mason Road. Somebody's redoing the farmhouse. They were cleaning out the attic and

169

found some ancient high school yearbooks. Oma and Opa are in some. I'm wondering if you think Mom would like those for Mother's Day. Let me know."

She sent him a text. *Hell, yeah! I hate you. You win the perfect gift award this year.*

She'd no sooner sent the text when he replied. *Score!*

She sent him a smiley face and turned to Jackson. "My brother found some old yearbooks with our grandparents in them. He's giving them to Mom for Mother's Day. She'll love those until the day she dies—and remember Axel for giving them to her. I'll give her perfume that she'll probably give away at Christmas."

"She'll still love you. Trust me. That's one less gift she had to purchase. Where did your brother find the books?"

"Working on somebody's old house. He's a contractor. Carpenter. Handy Guy. He can do most anything but tries to sub it out so he doesn't have to work."

"My kind of job."

"I know." *Who was he kidding?* Jackson was a Type A's Type A. He couldn't be still for a second unless he was eating. "Now I need to get on my messages."

Nick: *Call me.*

Nick, ten minutes later: *Still need you.*

Rachel: *Call me. I heard from Jessica.* "Yes! Jessica checked in."

"Now you know she's safe. Probably their daughter, too."

"I'll follow up on that in a sec. I'm not done."

Trinka: *I got in a new order of flip flops. Do you want me to pick some out for you? How many?* "Oooh, cool."

"What?"

"My sister has a shop. She just got a new order of

flip flops and is going to hold some for me."

"I'll never understand the love affair between you women and your shoes."

Nick, an hour later: *Where the hell are you?*

Jackson pulled into the Taco Cabana lot. "Where's your Jeep?"

"On the side."

He pulled into the space next to it. "You want to finish your texts here?"

"Planned it that way. You don't need to wait unless you just want to hear me talk. I'll send a quick text to my sister, but I need to call Nick and my contact to Jessica." Gracie unbuckled her seatbelt.

"Nah. Go ahead. I'm going to drive through and get something to drink. You want anything?"

"I'm good. Stop back here before you leave, and I'll fill you in on any news."

CHAPTER 38

Gracie texted Trinka to save her five pairs if there were that many different styles. Otherwise, three colors. Trinka knew what she liked.

Then she called Rachel, who skipped the hello. "Gracie, Jessica texted me right before I texted you."

"What did she say?"

"She and Maya are safe and waiting for Victor. I shouldn't try to reach her again until she calls me from home. She hopes it's soon. That was it."

"Good news. She didn't indicate where they were?"

"No, just that they were waiting for Victor. So I guess he's one place and they're at another."

True. "Thank you for letting me know. That takes a load off my mind, and I'm sure yours, too."

"Yes! She's my friend."

"Will you let me know if she contacts you again?"

"Of course."

"Great, thank you."

Gracie ended the call and huffed out a ball of air. It was good that Rachel heard directly from Jessica. On the flip side, Gracie had hoped that Father Tim was going to deliver Jessica into her hands tonight. Now, it appeared that wouldn't be the case. But Jessica's and Maya's safety was all that mattered.

Jackson must've run into a crowd at the drive-thru. She called Nick.

"Well, if it isn't Queen Gracie."

"Shut up. You would not believe my day. For real."

"Try me."

"It all started when I had to watch the baker frost cupcakes."

"Enough! I believe you. Some of us have been working."

"Whatcha got?"

"When I first called you, the Homicide detectives returned to San Antonio Lighting. They were in Victor's office when a disturbance occurred in the front of the store."

"What kind of disturbance?"

"Some guy raising a stink because his fixture didn't fit the jacked-up opening in his ceiling. You know the type of guy. Mountains out of molehills until the volcano inside boils over like a science project."

"All too well." They made the news way too often.

"The detectives returned to the office, and a table had been moved."

"So?" O'Conner was good at spotting details. But not always good at putting patterns together.

"The table stood against the wall as—O'Connor's words—part of a vignette. I have no damn idea what a vignette is. But she said the table wouldn't have moved itself, and there was no reason for anyone to have moved it. She started searching, and found a hidden door."

"Like an old English mystery novel. O'Conner scored. A vignette is a small group of furniture and things like art and books and stuff that all looks good together. I think. Trinka talks about things like that."

"Sticking that in my trivia file."

"Never to be seen again." Nick was clutter-free in the useless information department. She had often wished she could free her brain of random data as efficiently as he could.

"Most likely. Anyway, inside the hidden space

were two cots, two pillows, some bedding. A toilet and sink. A microwave and bar fridge. There were no people."

"Son of a bitch." Jessica and Maya must have been hidden inside, but now they were missing. Except Jessica texted Rachel they were safe. "The disturbance in the showroom created a distraction for Jessica and Maya to leave unnoticed."

"That's what they think."

"I wonder if they left the table out on purpose so someone would find the space?"

"O'Connor said she didn't think so. That it was overlooked because they were in a hurry."

Jackson drove up.

"Hang on, Nick. Jackson had to bring me to my car and he just drove up. I want to tell him." She shared the news from Rachel and from Nick.

"Everything's moving from all directions now. It won't be long. Call me later."

Gracie rolled her window back up. "Jackson thinks the pot's boiling so it won't be long until dinner."

"I think he's right."

"Finish telling me the story."

"Right. So, of course, no one knew anything or saw anything."

"Of course."

"That was what the first two texts were about. Then I texted you again about something else."

"Oh, there's more?"

"I wouldn't have bothered you again for old news. Yes, there's more. This afternoon, I'm stopped for a light at 1604 and Culebra. Who pulls up to me but a priest in a white Acura. Then I see a little girl's head pop up in the backseat and go right back down again. I'd swear on that priest that the little girl was Maya."

Maybe there was hope for Father Tim after all. "I'm working on the lead I got from your CI—the sister is a goldmine. I'll update you when I can. If we don't talk before your appointment tomorrow, don't hold anything back from your attorney. Even if it's bad. As long as she knows what went on, she can use it to your advantage or protect you from anything that may come from Kim's side. Get over being embarrassed or ashamed. We're all human."

"I keep telling you Kim's not like that."

"Right. I keep forgetting. Listen to your attorney. She knows what she's talking about. If you don't, you and I'll get in the ring. You know I can kick your ass."

Nick laughed. Only because he knew it was true.

CHAPTER 39

"Daddy, I need some help with my photography project." Hannah, Slate's oldest daughter, stood in the doorway.

He clenched his teeth. As quickly as his anger flared, he brought it under control. This would be a good opportunity to bond with Hannah. Besides, he had no one to blame but himself for not locking his door. "Didn't your mother tell you I was working?"

"Yes, but I want to take a montage of El Rojo. He's in the pasture just outside, and the light's good. You said you don't want us around him without you. My project's due next Monday. Please?"

Slate sighed and locked his computer. "Okay, but make it quick."

Hannah hugged him, and his back stiffened.

"What's the matter, Daddy?"

"Nothing. Just a pulled muscle. Let's go."

Slate stopped at the barn to pick up a ladder. El Rojo stood in the middle of the pasture looking at them.

"Stay several feet away from the fence. If I tell you to move, do exactly as I say. Understood?"

"Of course. Jeez, I'm almost seventeen, Daddy."

Slate set the ladder about ten feet back from the steel pipe fence. Four horizontal steel bars with sturdy posts every six feet.

"What's the ladder for?"

"In case the fence is in your way. Or to give you a better angle."

"Thanks. I don't think this will take too long."

I don't, either. The more he watched Hannah move, the more he was certain.

Not too much ever upset Rojo, but one thing that did was constant motion. And that's what he'd known Hannah would give him. He'd seen her in photographer mode before. Left to right and back again. Up on the ladder every once in a while. Rojo showed her his profile, the first sign he wasn't happy.

"Look, Daddy! He's posing for me." She clicked away.

Hardly. El Rojo put his head down.

"Hannah!" Slate's voice sounded like a rifle shot. "Don't turn around. Back up. One step at a time."

Before she took the first step, Rojo charged.

Slate expected her to scream and run. That was okay—the fence was plenty strong.

Instead she kept shooting, moving her camera to one side and another to take multiple shots of the longhorn rushing toward her as she backed toward Slate.

Rojo stopped several feet from the fence. Longhorns were damn fast, but not for long.

"Keep backing, Hannah. Follow my voice."

He kept talking to her, and she kept clicking. At one point, she dropped to her knees for a few shots before continuing her progress toward him.

His oldest daughter looked like a carbon copy of her mother, but he'd just learned she was like him on the inside. Determined, and a risk taker who didn't scare easily and didn't take no for an answer. He didn't have any sons and had wondered what to do about keeping the ranch in the family. Now he knew.

Hannah had one more year of high school. Over the summer, he could introduce her to how he ran the

Lone Star. He would need to steer her toward Tech or A&M to study ranch management.

"Stop, Hannah."

She stopped and turned around.

Her face flushed with excitement, her eyes sparkled with confidence. "Did you see that! I've never seen him charge before—he's always been a gentle giant. I got some great shots—I know I did! This will be my best photo project yet."

"Go on. Go look at your pictures."

She ran off but turned after a few strides and ran back, giving him a huge hug. "Thank you, Daddy!"

Slate closed the ladder and carried it back to the barn. He'd set out to teach Hannah a lesson about interrupting him. Instead, she'd shown him something new and valuable about herself. Now he'd have to find a way to focus her attention on the ranch and figure out a way to make her want to stay here.

But he'd have to fight Courtney over that. There would be more than one battle, but he would prepare well. And he would win.

Where the ranch was concerned, Slate always won.

CHAPTER 40

Gracie parked in front of Lupe's house. A different officer sat outside. She approached the patrol car, and he exited before she'd taken half a dozen steps, his hand on his service weapon. He also had sergeant stripes on his sleeve. They'd bumped this up in priority. Gracie stopped and showed her Bastion ID. "If Erin's inside, tell her I'm here."

"Wait back at your car, please."

She did as he asked. Only when she'd returned did his hand move off his weapon. He pulled out his phone and made the call. A few seconds passed before he motioned her over.

"Detective Montgomery wants to talk to you."

Gracie took his phone. "It's me, Gracie. Are the ladies decent?"

Erin laughed. "We're all going stark-raving mad. Come on in and join us."

#

"I can't believe how different you look today."

Carmen smiled.

"I can tell you're feeling much better." Gracie was happy to see Carmen looking almost vibrant. She looked as young as her sister.

"Like normal. Do you have news?"

None she could share. "First I need to talk to Erin."

Erin left her spot by the door. "Let's go in the kitchen."

They stood in the far corner, between the sink and refrigerator. Erin leaned against the counter so she could see the opening into the living room.

Gracie faced Erin so her voice wouldn't carry. "If we don't find this guy, do you have your plans set for tomorrow and Thursday?"

Erin nodded. "They're chomping at the bit to get Mom and Dad in the ground. The M.E.'s holding the bodies until we give the okay."

"Good."

"Keeping them inside is next to impossible. Especially Carmen. She's accustomed to being outside all day. And Lupe's hyper."

"You need help."

"We don't have it."

"I understand."

"We go out back at random for a few minutes during the day and night. Best I can offer."

"Bastion offices are a fortress. Plus we have a few safe suites, fully stocked, inside the offices. There would need to be an explosion that levelled the building to destroy it—and my own feeling is that it would still survive. If you can get SARIC and Homicide to agree to move them, I can get my boss's okay. Willing to give it a go? Carmen will still be cooped up, but they will have wide views through the windows. Their safety will be guaranteed."

"Sure. When would you want to do this?"

"As soon as possible. Preferably just at dark tonight. The shooter won't be expecting anything then. He won't be looking for us to do anything until about four in the morning. If he's looking at all."

"That would put us moving out about eight-thirty tonight. Do we need vehicles?"

"No. Zero fanfare. Keep the patrol on the street. Change them out exactly as you've been doing. Have them use the phone to check in with you like the

180

uniform did today. It would be good if one could be in the alley starting tomorrow, to show we're beefing up for his Wednesday night deadline, but I know you don't have units to spare for decoys."

Everything she told Erin was true—to a point. Except she'd had no plan to suggest any of it until she'd stood in the kitchen. While Erin had been telling her about the sisters becoming restless, the same feeling had come over Gracie as the last time she was here. A smothering, dark, ominous cloud that made her want to flee. It took all her grit not to pull Erin outside.

As soon as she forced herself to stay, another thought came. *Get out of the house. Get the women out of the house.* She just knew. Plain and simple. And complicated as hell. She was Gracie Hofner. And Grace Elizabeth Hofner did not have premonitions.

"Maybe I can get one more, given the urgency. How do you want to move them?"

"I'm working that out in my head. I only had the thought when you said you go outside at odd times. They can't go outside in the bunker, but they can see out. Almost as good."

"Better for them."

"I can come in through the alley and haul everyone in my Jeep. If you get the okay, I'll get cover help and we'll get it done. Don't tell the sisters. Make sure the coffeemaker, stove, oven, and curling irons are off. No candles burning. Leave the lights on. Don't tell the patrol. I'll call or text when we're in position. Bring them out and we'll load up. Or it could work better if you're all outside between eight-thirty and nine. I'll leave that part up to you."

"Plan. I'll use my bag of tricks to disguise them." Erin held up her fist and they bumped.

"Call your peeps. I've got something to tell the ladies. You're welcome to listen in."

Gracie returned to the living room. "I have to send a quick text, then I'll fill you in on what we know so far."

Both sisters nodded.

Gracie typed the message to Jackson: *I'm booking a bunker for the duration. As of tonight. I'll need your help about 8 o'clock. Will call in 30 or less.*

Her phone beeped with Jackson's reply before she got started with the sisters—*10-4.*

Gracie sat between the two women on the sofa. "I really came by to talk with Erin, but I do have one tiny bit of news to share with you."

"Yes!" Carmen touched Gracie's hand.

"We received a short message from Jessica."

"Oh, thank God!" Lupe crossed herself.

"She and Maya are all right. We don't know anything more, but now we have hope."

Carmen reached across Gracie to grab Lupe's hands for a moment. When she released them she faced Gracie. "Thank you for telling us."

Gracie stood. "I enjoy sharing good news. Let me say bye to Erin, and I'll be on my way."

Erin gave Gracie a thumbs up as she entered the kitchen. "The suits were happy to ditch responsibility. We're a go."

"I have your number. You have mine?"

"Yep."

"It's okay on my end, too. I'll be in touch."

CHAPTER 41

In her Jeep, Gracie called Jackson before giving the area one last scan and pulling away from the curb. He answered right away. "Sorry to spring the news in a text."

"Not a breakup text, so that's okay. I still love you, Hofner."

Gracie smiled. She and Jackson had a casual working arrangement, but he was still her superior. "Same here. Just don't tell Sabrina."

"She's right here. You want to tell her?"

"That's all right."

"Fill me in."

No way was she telling him about the get-outta-there feeling. She shivered thinking about it. "The sisters are getting antsy. Erin is taking them out for a few minutes at a time. Random. Into the backyard."

"Not good."

"Agree. That's when I thought about the bunker. Erin agreed and got it cleared on her end."

"They were probably happy to oblige. Less responsibility. Less cost."

"That's what Erin said. I want to move them right after dark—I mean immediately as it gets dark. The shooter will think we'll try something before dawn in the morning. He won't be expecting anything to happen at that time tonight."

"I thought you had a seven o'clock appointment?"

"Right. I can't cancel, but I can push it along. If I leave there by seven-forty-five, I'll have enough time. Without a traffic backup, I'll be early. I hoped the meeting would be to pick up Jessica and Maya, but it doesn't look that way now. Have you heard any more from Paulina?"

"No. I'll call first thing in the morning and find out what they've learned. Tell me what you need tonight."

Gracie filled him in on what she wanted him to do and where to meet. Then she called Nick.

"It's officially my day off as of one minute ago, Gracie."

"I don't care. I need you."

"Women. You always need a man at the wrong time."

"God made it that way to keep you in line."

He laughed. "In your dreams. What's up?"

Gracie gave him the details and shared her repeat experience of needing to leave.

"Somebody somewhere is telling you. If you'd listened the first time, I wouldn't be working on my day off."

"You know I don't believe in that woo-woo crap. But the thing is, as soon as the thought came to move the women out, the feeling vanished. It had to just be cop instinct taking a new form. Seriously, though— thank you, Nicky. I'll call you when I'm on my way."

#

Gracie pulled into her driveway seconds after she hung up. She drove into the garage, jumped out, and slid underneath the Jeep, grateful that it wasn't a low-slung sports car. She might not have fit.

Using the flashlight on her phone, she checked the undercarriage with no results. Then the driver's front wheel well. *Gotcha, you sucker!* She yanked the tracker off.

The more she thought about the meeting with

DHS and the diamonds, the more she believed they were connected to the Cantu murders. The tracking device tied them together in her mind. Unless the tracking device had to do with the delivery she waited for at the bakery. In all, nothing fit directly together, but in her head, each part was a puzzle piece. She didn't know if they all belonged to the same puzzle, but the tracker had to belong to one of her current projects.

It hadn't been there a couple of weeks earlier. None of her assignments between then and now would rate someone wanting to know her whereabouts—she'd located a runaway teen and helped her get into a rehab program, presented awareness and confidence-building programs at several junior high schools, participated in some neighborhood watch programs, and assisted SAPD with some DWI checkpoints. She'd also been involved behind the scenes of a county-wide outstanding warrants roundup. None of that would've enticed someone to want to know her whereabouts.

The big question for her was if the delivery, the Cantu murders, and the diamonds were in any way connected. It didn't sound like it, but she'd learned early that sounding random didn't make it so. She could waste a lot of energy on what-ifs, but all she really needed to remember was that someone wanted to stay informed of her location. That was a concrete fact she could deal with.

Gracie closed the garage door and went inside. First a shower, then a sandwich, then up to Holy Cross. Her phone rang, and she smiled. "Hi, Mom."

"Have you found a renter for the apartment yet?"

"No. I haven't had a chance to run an ad."

"Good. Do you remember Katie Ullrich? Well, it's Miller now."

Katie had been in the same grade as Gracie. They hadn't been close friends, but they had a few friends in common. Nobody had ever talked smack about her. "Sure. Is she interested?"

"I saw her at the beauty shop and she asked about you. In the course of the conversation, I said you were always busy and now you had to find a new renter. You know how that goes."

With her mother, she certainly did know. Her mother would tell a stranger the life stories of herself, Dad, and all the kids. "Right."

"Katie said her cousin was moving to SA from Houston and wanted something that sounds just like Elissa's apartment. He doesn't want to live in a complex, and he's not ready to buy a house."

"He?"

"He."

"I don't want to rent to a man. I want to rent to a middle-aged woman with three cats and no husband, kids, dogs, or grandkids. I'm going to put an ad in the tearooms around here."

"Get over it, Grace Elizabeth. You'll never find another Ariana, and you'll get in all kinds of trouble if you refuse to rent to a qualified tenant. I shouldn't have to tell you that."

Gracie sighed. "I know." She pulled out the clothes she planned to wear.

"You're dragging your feet. I took matters into my own hands. Elissa and I FaceTimed this morning. She agreed."

Sometimes it was hell living in her mother's sister's home. Even with all the perks. "So tell me about Katie's cousin. He must be weird wanting to live here and not in a complex with babes of both sexes all around. Whichever he prefers."

"He's not right out of college. Katie said he's thirty-five or thirty-six, she couldn't remember, but a few years older than her. Single. No kids."

So far he didn't sound like too bad a renter. "Why's

he not buying a house?"

"That's being nosy, Gracie."

"It's part of my job. Speaking of jobs, I assume that's why he's moving here. What's he do?" She grabbed a towel and washcloth.

"I don't know. Katie said he's transferring with his company."

"Good. Renters need a steady paycheck."

"Anyway, he's going to be in San Antonio on Friday. I gave Katie your phone number, and she's going to give it to him to call you."

Gracie removed her holster. "Okay. I don't suppose you got Katie's number or her cousin's. What's his name, so I'll know who he is when he calls?"

"No. I can find out her number if you want it."

"I'll let you know." She turned on the shower. "What's the cousin's name?"

"Milo. Milo Porter."

CHAPTER 42

Gracie dressed and put her hair into a ponytail. It stuck out everywhere and was too short to hang down, but it would have to do. Given what was going to take place in a few hours, she opted for black tactical pants and running shoes along with a close-fitting black Henley. Father Tim would have to deal.

She ate a grilled cheese sandwich and a big spoonful of jalapeno-stuffed olives while standing at the counter looking outside at the garage apartment. It didn't look like Ariana anymore. Gone were the colored pots on the stairs that held a mix of herbs and flowers. Her wind chimes no longer tinkled in the breeze.

Now the apartment was a clean slate, ready for a new occupant—it was more prepared and willing than Gracie. She hated the thought of getting to know someone new. Someone who would probably come and go and never say hi. Never pop down for a beer. Certainly no one who would bring down a massage chair and work out Gracie's tension for free.

She finished her sandwich and olives. It was just after six. She had a few minutes, so she called Donovan. When he answered, she said, "I just want to thank you again for saving me from the spider monster."

He chuckled. "I couldn't imagine what was happening. Then I couldn't believe how scared you were of one little spider."

"Not little. It was huge!"

"I'm glad you're all right. Would you like to meet for a drink later? I'm making dinner for all of us, including my lazy sister who's sitting here giving me the evil eye, but I could meet you in a couple of hours."

Wouldn't you know? "I can't tonight, but thanks for the invite. Another time?"

"Tomorrow. Earlier."

She had no idea what tomorrow would bring. It was deadline day for Lupe. "I have three brothers and a sister plus a friend going through a divorce. My time is rarely my own. I may have a spare hour tomorrow to squeeze in a drink, but I'd rather not have to drink and run. How about Friday?" She hoped everything would be over by then.

"Friday it is. If you have time, we'll include dinner. We'll play it by ear."

"Wonderful! It's a date."

"I like the sound of that."

"Me, too." Maybe. She'd been fooled by good looks before.

#

Gracie arrived at the Holy Cross rectory a few minutes early and parked next to a white Acura that had been parked in the same place the previous night. Father Tim must be home.

Tonight she looked the part of law enforcement—black tactical pants, black running shoes and socks, her Bastion ID clipped to her belt, and her Glock clipped under her Henley at her back.

She didn't think Father Tim would mind her being early. He may object to her choice of dress, but too bad. She pressed the doorbell.

He answered the door himself. "Look at you." He didn't smile.

"I had a hot date and no time to change."

"Well, I can say that I'm pleased not to have been your date. You look like you mean business."

"I do, Father. And I have another engagement after I leave here. I knew you'd understand the importance of saving a life over looking pretty."

"Maybe I should take lessons from you, child, about getting to the point. Please step inside for a moment. Since you indicated you are pressed for time, I'll get straight to the point myself." He led her into a small office off the entry. "Have a seat."

He rounded the desk, opened the center drawer, and withdrew the envelope she'd handed him yesterday. "There is something inside for you, placed there by our mutual friend. I'll withdraw for a few minutes to let you read without thinking I'm looking over your shoulder."

More than she'd hoped for.

Father Tim passed the envelope across the desk. He also placed a yellow notepad and pencil in front of her. "Feel free to tell her anything you wish. I'll return in five minutes."

"Thank you." Gracie waited until the door closed behind him before she opened the envelope.

The items she'd sent were all there, still clipped together. No notes or comments. At the back was a sheet of notebook paper with neat handwriting.

Thank you for getting in touch with me. You're thorough. It's clear you know more than Victor believed anyone knew or would be able to find out.

I appreciate your offer of sanctuary, but we must follow Victor's instructions. We have been safe, and we will continue to remain safe until his return. He is the best at hiding people.

Please do not try to find us—I beg you. If there is anything urgent, you may relay it through Father Tim. Both Victor and I trust him implicitly. He is a good man. You can trust him, too.

Maya sent a drawing. She said it's for Aunt Lupe.

Thank you for understanding. Victor will return soon, and this nightmare will be over.

Peace,

Jessica Cantu

Gracie pulled another sheet from the back. Maya had drawn a yellow bird with a big blue eye, a red beak and legs, and long black eyelashes. Beneath the bird she'd written *I love you, Aunt Lupe* in blue crayon.

The girl's picture made Gracie smile. She picked up the pencil. Her message needed to be clear and honest while relaying as little real information as possible.

Jessica,

I'll see that Lupe gets the drawing.

Since I'm not the decision maker, I can make no guarantee as to whether we will continue to seek you out. I can only share my opinion with those in charge, but I'm happy to learn you and Maya are both safe.

Father Tim is an excellent intermediary, and I will continue to use him as needed. I promised to make a donation. He won't refuse.

Stay safe.

Gracie

She clipped her note to the front of the papers and returned them to the envelope.

Father Tim opened the door as she folded the note and drawing and put them in her pocket. "Did I give you enough time?"

"Yes. Thank you. There's a message for Jessica in there. I appreciate your confidentiality."

"Comes with the collar. Respect and honor. Treat others the way you'd want to be treated." He clapped his hands and threw them apart. "Enough sermon for tonight."

"Thank you for being one of the good guys, Father Tim. By the way, I haven't forgotten the donation, but things have been hectic."

"I have faith in you, child." He made the sign of the cross. "Go in peace."

CHAPTER 43

Gracie had time to spare, but she needed to go ahead and call Erin, Jackson, and Nick so they could get into position. She left the church property and drove to a nearby shopping center to refresh the map in her memory.

Her first call went to Erin.

"The sisters are doing the dishes. I'm getting their things ready for our evening excursion."

"Do you do them up every day, or will they think something's going on?"

"Every time we go out. We're cool."

"Good. Things are running on schedule. Don't come out until eight-thirty. I will be standing where you can see at least my face, if I have to poke my head through the bushes. What's it like back there? I don't remember."

"There's a gate with a lock on our side. I have the key. Stand near there in view. I'll direct the ladies away from there while I keep watch for you. As soon as I see you, I'll be the best herding dog you ever saw."

"If I'm not there by eight-forty-five, abort. I mean abort totally. Get them out of that house because something will be drastically wrong."

"Got it. But nothing will go wrong. Have faith."

They disconnected. Erin had more faith than Gracie did.

She called Jackson next since he lived the farthest.

"I want you to go to the house just the way I'm telling you, so write it down."

"You sound like Sabrina. Okay, shoot."

"Get on 410 West. At the interchange take I-10 East. Exit at West Woodlawn. Turn right."

"Onto Woodlawn?"

"Yes. Exit 567. Woodlawn is a little ways down on the feeder."

"Okay."

"After about a mile on Woodlawn, you'll see Woodlawn Lake. Keep going straight for about another mile. You're going to turn left onto Camino Santa Maria. It's the street that runs in front of St. Mary's University." She gave him specific instructions how to reach the alley behind Lupe's house.

"Is the alley paved?"

"No. It's dirt and a little overgrown. You'll have to watch for it—it's narrow. Back in and keep the engine running. I'll be coming out your way, and Nick will be behind me. Text Nick and me when you're in place."

"Will do. Give me his number."

She did. "I'll make sure he has yours, too. Time your arrival for sometime between eight-twenty and eight-twenty-five. Nick's arriving earlier and blocking the other end. He's going to run the alley to make sure it's clear, and he'll make sure it stays clear."

"Sounds good."

"There are three streets in there that run east and west before you get to the university. Try not to go on any of those."

"You got it."

"I'll come into the alley from Nick's end, and he'll close it behind me. As soon as I'm in the alley, I'll switch to parking lights and stop about halfway to you. When I turn my headlights back on, I'll be headed your way, so be ready to go. I don't want to have to stop."

"Yes, ma'am."

"We'll go back the way you came in. Woodlawn to I-10, to 410, to San Pedro. Unless you have a better idea."

"No, good for me."

"Questions?"

"No, I'm good."

"Text me if you need to."

She ended the call and pressed the button for Nick. "I want you to come in via Culebra. Go to the back side of Saint Mary's, and turn north." Then she gave him the same type of directions she had given to Jackson.

"Okay."

"Block it off. Park parallel until I get there because you'll have to let me in. Then pull in behind me but stay put until I turn my headlights back on."

Gracie made herself stop talking and take a deep breath. Her heart pounded. *I hope we're not too late.* She took another deep breath and forced the air out through her mouth. "After you park, I want you to run east down the alley to the next cross street. Get there between eight-ten and eight-fifteen. Jackson should be there by the time you get back to your truck."

"I just left the gym, so I'll look and smell the part."

"You always smell the part, Nicky."

"Yeah, yeah."

She gave him Jackson's phone number. "Let me know if you need anything."

Gracie was nearing the Loop when Jackson called. She pressed the answer button on the steering wheel. "Are you lost?"

"Someone's tailing me."

"Are you sure you don't have a tracking device on your car?"

"After you left, I had it swept and secured. I'm clean. Speaking of tracking devices, what about yours?"

"No worries. Where did the tail pick you up?"

"Just before I reached West Ave. Instead of heading toward you, I'm on my way to North Star Mall. If I can shake him, I'll call. If I'm a no-show, you'll know why."

"What's he driving?"

"A silver Chevrolet Malibu."

"Do you think you can lose him there?"

"Best shot I have this time of day. Do you want me to call someone else in the group?"

"No. Keeping it close."

"If I can't lose him, I have another idea. I'll be in touch."

That was the way, unfortunately. It only took one little something to make the best plan go belly up.

She called Nicky to relay the information.

CHAPTER 44

"**D**o you want me to call somebody else, Gracie?" Nick asked.

Traffic thickened a little as Gracie neared the airport, but nothing out of the ordinary. The timing was still good.

"No. Jackson asked the same thing. We need to keep this close. You watching my back is good. Like old times. I'm coming up on North Star Mall."

"I just parked. Will run it now and walk back. Call me when you cross Bandera Road. When you do, I'll get in and start her up, and we'll keep the line open."

"Plan."

As she drove past the giant boots at the mall entrance, she frowned, wondering if Jackson was already there. Nicky would be able to watch the alley, but there was little he could do if someone entered from the other end. Ahead, only the very top of the sun cleared the horizon.

A few miles later, she exited at Babcock, took it to Hillcrest, and turned south.

Pre-op jitters settled in. Gracie drove the speed limit through a residential area and wiped each sweaty palm down the top of her pants. The light at Bandera turned yellow as she approached, and she stopped. Her phone beeped. A text from Jackson. She checked the time. She had about two extra minutes.

The light changed. She crossed Bandera and

pulled into a parking lot next to a fried chicken place to read Jackson's text.

In restroom to send this quick. Can't shake. Have half a description. Will try to get tag number on way out. I texted an order and a code to Bastion for them to go down as soon as they receive confirmation from you, and you will be there prior to 9 pm. They know why you're coming. Call in and repeat my code. It's CUPCAKE REVENGE. I had to think fast.

Gracie laughed out loud and texted back. *Yessir, Capt. Cupcake.* She called Bastion, identified herself, and said, "Cupcake Revenge. As per Jackson." They were good to go.

Then she called Nick. "I'm at the light at Bandera."

"Okay. I'll get started. Still clear."

"Jackson texted. He won't be here, but we're clear for Bastion. You just stay on my tail. No matter what."

"I hear you."

"Just passed the St. Mary law school."

"You'll be at Woodlawn in seconds."

"Turning now."

"As soon as I see you, I'll back up. I see you now."

Gracie let up on the accelerator as she approached, put on her brakes, and turned in front of Nick into the alley.

Her wide Jeep barely fit. She hoped there was room to open her doors. A few branches brushed her sides and roof, but all was okay. She counted houses and hoped she had accounted for each one.

Gracie stopped. There was a gate. After she put the Jeep in park and turned the headlights down to parking, she opened the door. Yes! There was room to move. Behind her, Nick cut his lights down.

She got out and walked to the gate. It was still light enough she could make out the sisters checking what Gracie remembered were rose bushes. Erin was looking directly at the gate. Gracie raised both thumbs. Erin did the same before turning to the sisters and shooing them in Gracie's direction.

In three minutes, everyone was inside Gracie's Jeep and she grabbed her seatbelt. The sisters sat in the back and Erin rode shotgun. "Ladies, one of you on the floor, the other flat on the seat. I want you out of sight of any curious eyes for the full trip. It will be short and bumpy."

Erin checked that both women were in place. "It's important people believe you're still inside your home. I'll explain later." She turned back to the front.

Gracie turned on her headlights. "Okay, Nicky, let's roll."

They bumped out of the alley onto the street without incident. That was the part she'd been most afraid of. Nick stayed right on her bumper through the neighborhood and down Woodlawn until they reached the freeway. He allowed as small a space as possible for safety and once blocked a car from cutting in between. At the San Pedro exit, he again closed the gap, staying right with her as if his truck were a trailer.

Erin and the sisters remained quiet while she drove. She could hear murmurs from the sisters from time to time, but Erin's focus was squarely on the surrounding traffic. "Thanks for the extra set of eyes, Erin. We were supposed to have a lead car, but he picked up some company along the way and couldn't send them home."

"I get that. I'm in this, too, so just looking out for *numero uno*."

"Mmm-hmm." They always had to look out for themselves because no one else looked out for them. If they wanted to serve and protect others, they had to be around to do so.

The building housing the Bastion offices was in the block ahead on the right. She put on her blinker a few yards before turning in. Nick rode her bumper through the parking garage until she pulled to a stop in front of the doors to the elevator lobby. He stopped inches away.

She counted eight Bastion agents. Knowing how Jackson operated, she knew at least four others were scattered nearby, one a sniper.

Saul Gallego, stepped forward and opened her door. "You do like to make an entrance."

"Any time I get the chance. In the front passenger seat, Detective Erin Montgomery, SAPD/SARIC. In the back, sitting up now, are our guests for the next few days, Lupe and Carmen." She'd debated whether to give them assumed names for their time here, but decided against upping their stress levels.

Gallego leaned down. "Detective Montgomery, exit and stand by the back door on your side, please."

Erin did as requested, her hand on her service weapon.

"Who's back there making love to your bumper?"

"My former partner, Nick Rivera. SARIC detective."

Gallego motioned for Nick to lower his window. Nick stuck his head out. "Yo."

"Stay behind the wheel at the moment. Remain alert."

"You got it."

"Okay, let's get these ladies inside the lobby." Gallego motioned to the men, who moved to create a protected path for Carmen and Lupe to move to the lobby door. "Detective Montgomery, follow us inside. Hofner, you and your partner park right over there in Bastion parking and come inside." He stepped through the men and opened the Jeep's back door. "After you, ladies."

When Erin entered the lobby, the agent closest to Gracie's door pounded the Jeep's roof. "Move out." In her mirror, she watched him motion to Nick to follow her to her parking space.

She got out and waited for Nick by her back bumper. That's when she noticed the agents stationed at both the entrance and the exit. When Bastion participated in a project, they owned it. No one was getting inside without a firefight.

Maybe that's why she still felt the tightly wound spring in her gut.

CHAPTER 45

For the second time that day, three of the four elevators stood open and waiting. Erin wanted the sisters split. She took the elevator with Lupe, and Gracie rode with Carmen. Bastion agents rode in each. Nick rode with Gracie, Gallego with Erin.

They rode up in silence and were greeted by more armed agents. The Bastion agents made themselves at home walking on through to their spaces, chatting as they moved. Nothing out of the ordinary.

Erin and Lupe were ahead, but beside her, Carmen's eyes were wide. "Are you all right?"

Carmen nodded. "All of this for us?"

Gracie smiled. She was relaxing more with each step. "Yes, ma'am. The Bastion touch. People first. You and Lupe are safe here."

Gallego motioned to Gracie to catch up. He used his handprint to open a door to the security area. "We have your information, Hofner. Who's going to be here with the ladies?"

"Me." Erin stepped forward.

"Here's what we're going to do." He looked to see how many people were working. Looked like a full crew to Gracie. The processing wouldn't take too long. "I'll take the three of you back and wait for them to take the information they need from each of you. Then we'll come back here. We'll all go to the security suite together. Except for him. No offense." He pointed to

Nick.

Nick gave him an affirming nod. "None taken. Good to me."

"Then I'll wait until Gracie sees that all her chicks are in good hands before bringing her back, explaining what she needs to do to visit. Questions?"

No one raised a hand or uttered a word.

"Okay, ladies, follow me." He turned back to Gracie. "Give us twenty or thirty minutes. Probably less, but that will allow for any screw-up."

The door closed behind him, and Gracie turned to Nick. "I totally owe you. I had no idea what would happen during any of this. I need to text Jackson that everyone's safe."

"Go ahead."

A minute later, she stuck her phone back in her pocket. "Okay. As I said, thank you for having my back."

"Anything for you, Gracie. And those women. They must be basket cases by now."

"Erin says they're holding up quite well, considering everything."

"This is the first time I've been inside Bastion. Quite an operation."

"Told you."

"Right. You did. I still think my spot is in SAPD."

"We're all different. So, are you all set for your appointment tomorrow afternoon?"

"Almost. Rayann asked me to pull some things together, and I'll finish up with that in the morning."

"Good. Call me after so I know how you feel after meeting with her."

"How about you? How's the bakery gig?"

"Easy enough except for getting up so early and having to be perky at the same time."

"Not your strong suit. I remember those early shifts."

"Exactly."

The door opened and Jackson marched in. "I thought I'd find you here."

Gracie stood up, and Nick followed. "Nick, this is my boss, Roland Jackson."

"Pleasure to meet you. Gracie's always telling me 'Nick this' and 'Nick that.' It's good to put a face to the name."

"She likes you, too. I hear the same."

"Guys, I'm right here."

"So you are." Jackson moved a chair so he could face them. "Sit."

"What happened? Tell me everything." Gracie didn't doubt for a minute that he would. Jackson was a firm believer in open communication.

"He had to have been watching from around the curve of my street to see if I'd leave. At first, he followed at a distance, but I assumed it was a neighbor. He followed me onto West. I still wouldn't have known anything was amiss if he hadn't had to jockey to get into my lane when I stopped to check the air in my right front tire."

"The little things. Maybe Bastion should offer a course in rolling surveillance so we don't give ourselves away if we're doing it."

"I've been thinking that, too. In the morning, I'll mention it at the partners' meeting. So he kept going when I pulled in the station, but was back behind me when I stopped at the light at 410. That's when I decided to head to the mall. He changed lanes a few seconds after I did and remained with me all the way."

"You actually had to go inside?"

"I did, and I bought a tie. Spotted him pretty quick, so I led him around for about ten minutes before turning the tables. I went into the Cheesecake Factory."

"Dark in there. Well, dim, I guess. And cavernous.

Plus the entrance is always crowded."

"I made my way to the back. Along the way, I found one of those big trays leaning against the wall. I picked it up and held it over my head. He knew I wasn't a server, so I automatically became invisible."

"Quick thinking." Nick was hooked. He looked like a kid listening to a campfire story.

Working with him again had been fun. She still wished he would consider moving over to Bastion. Maybe tonight had given him the push he needed to put the possibility on the table. She hoped so.

"I made it to the men's room. There's a little alcove where I could watch his movement. He searched for me for a good ten minutes before the manager ushered him out to the mall area. Using the tray again, I found a back door that opened on a utility hall, then the parking lot. Of course I came out on the other side of the mall from the garage, so I got my run done in spite of myself."

Nick's eyes glowed. "Did you wait for him?"

"I did. It didn't take long. He walked past, saw my car, and kept going. I followed him and got his tag number. As soon as I get to my computer, I'm going to run it. I waited until he left, gave him three minutes lead time, and took the back roads to get over here. No one followed."

"What did he look like?"

"Ball cap, so I don't know about hair. Maybe five-ten. Stocky. Like a wrestler."

"Webb Truitt."

CHAPTER 46

"You can't be certain it was Truitt, Hofner. I'll go run it right now."

"Wait. Before you go, did anyone report seeing Jessica today?"

Jackson shook his head. "Afraid not. The second shift is on duty. I'm keeping a twenty-four seven lookout until six o'clock Saturday morning. Or until Victor Cantu reappears. Whichever comes first. I'll see you before you leave."

As soon as Jackson left, she turned to Nick. "Truitt is the link."

"What link?"

Gracie had to be careful what she shared. "This afternoon, I learned someone put a tracker on my Jeep. Since then, I haven't been able to shake the feeling that the bakery job and the Cantu murders are connected." *The diamonds, too, but I can't mention those.*

Nick frowned. "Why would you even think that?"

"Because my Jeep was clean the first of the month, and nothing I've worked on between then and now comes remotely close to meriting a tracking device."

"Maybe."

"Then again, why did I think we needed to move Lupe and Carmen? Maybe I'm going crazy."

Nick looked at her hard. "No. You wouldn't think you were if that were the case." He winked.

She sank to a chair and rubbed her temples, slumping forward until her elbows rested on her knees.

Nick sat beside her. "What's the matter?" His thumb and fingers massaged the sides of her neck.

"Nothing. Everything. That." She sat up. "I really miss working with you. We're in tune. It's like you're in my head and I'm in yours. Tonight was good. I felt alive again. Not that I didn't before, but tonight was different."

"I felt that, too. There's nobody like you for a partner. "

"I didn't realize how much I missed what we have."

"Same. It's like we never stopped working together."

"There's also something I shouldn't share with you yet, but nothing else will make sense if you don't know it."

Nick put his fingers over her mouth. "Don't tell me anything until you know it's all right. You know and I know we're tight."

Gracie nodded as he moved his hand. "Vegas."

"Stays right here."

They smiled at each other. Their old code.

She leaned back. "No one else knows how we work and relate, but I think Jackson suspects."

"Exactly. I don't want you to get in trouble for oversharing. I trust you, Gracie. That won't ever change."

She gave him a quick hug. "Same for me with you. Always." *Partners.*

"I think you're right about Jackson, and I can see why you like working with him."

"Good. He likes you. I could tell. Oh!" She snapped her fingers. "Will you do me another favor? It will be easier and quicker than this one. I promise."

Nick grinned. "You're such a con."

"I know. Will you?"

"Of course. What?"

"Go to the Marriott Rivercenter. Not the Riverwalk one, the Rivercenter one. That's the northernmost one."

"Did you forget we worked central as rookies? I know which one's which."

"No. I relied on you. I still get them confused."

"You're a girl, so..."

Gracie punched him on the arm for the girl crack.

"Ouch. With a wicked right jab. I forgot."

"Talk to someone at the desk. A bellman, concierge, bartender, server, maid, whoever's around. See what you can find out about a guest—male, last name Bernal."

"I'm on it."

"Learn what you can, and let me know. All I know is he's an optometrist from El Paso. Here for the convention. He's also Jessica's cousin."

"You think she's there."

"Possibly. You don't need to do anything, just a fact-finding mission. Do your chummy guy thing and keep an eye out for the stocky wrestler-type man with or without a ball cap. Don't let him overhear anything."

"Got it."

"Oops! I forgot you have to get papers together for tomorrow. Never mind. I'll do it after I get off at the bakery."

"It's not a problem. I have more than enough time for both."

"You sure?"

"I'm positive."

"You win the best partner award again."

The inner door opened. Erin entered first, followed by Carmen, then Lupe and Gallego.

Gallego moved between the women and the outer

door. "Everyone's now in the system, so I'll take you on back and show you around. Hofner, if you come back in to visit, place your palm on the reader in the hall like you saw me do. Just because we're Bastion, not everyone is allowed in here. It's on an as-needed basis. You're part of that as long as these guests are here. Ladies, I can't foresee you venturing out of your new home away from home without a Bastion agent. Everything you need will be in your new area. But should that happen, your palm print will also allow you entry. Everyone follow so far?"

A chorus of *yeses* followed. Gallego grinned, and Gracie thought he must be enjoying the feminine attention.

"You all saw what happened when we entered— not much. They knew we were coming. However, when someone is allowed entry, an alert sounds back there and one or more people will appear behind that black glass. They'll make sure you're the real thing and not some thug holding an automatic rifle."

Lupe's eyes grew huge.

"The chances of that occurring are slim to none, but Bastion protects against those as well as more likely scenarios."

Lupe visibly relaxed. "I'm glad about that."

"Someone back there will talk to you and make sure you're not under duress. When they're satisfied, they'll release the lock on the door at the end of this space and you can enter. You'll be met by another Bastion agent who will take you to your own space. Ready?"

This time, the only yes came from Erin, who would probably be happy to get some sleep.

Before Gallego could open the door, Jackson came in from the hall. "Take them on back. I need to talk to Hofner."

Gracie gave each of the women a quick hug. "I'll

try to get by here tomorrow, but I'm not going to promise. It's hopping right now. I will promise to keep you updated the best I can. With any luck at all, you won't be here but a night or two before you're back in your own beds."

When the door closed, she went back to Jackson and Nick. "Well?"

"The car is a rental."

"Are you shitting me?"

"Language, Hofner."

"My ass." Then she remembered Webb's angry march away from the car dealer. "It's him. I saw him at a dealer's body shop yesterday and walking afterward."

"The rental is registered to Thomas Shoemaker."

"What?"

"You heard me. It's not him."

"It has to be him. He used a false ID."

"I have no way to confirm that. After I got the name, I did run Thomas Shoemaker. Here's his DMV photo."

Gracie all but yanked it from his fingers. The guy did look like Webb a little bit. She could tell he was stocky from what she could see of his neck and shoulders. "Where does he live? In your neighborhood?"

"He could've been visiting someone."

"No. He tailed you. Why?"

"I don't know yet."

"Know what I think?"

"Tell me."

"I think Webb Truitt found someone who resembled him, took a photo, and had his own fake TDL printed. Probably more ID than that. If you find the real Thomas Shoemaker, you'll learn he wasn't anywhere near North Star Mall last night. But I'll bet he's been to the Jalapeno Cupcake within the last couple of months. Or to a bar where Webb Truitt saw him, and maybe they even talked about how they looked like one another."

Jackson just stared at her. She didn't back down.

"I've known her a little longer than you have," Nick said. "She gets like this."

Jackson shook his head. "I know. This isn't the first time I've seen it. Thing is, she's probably right."

Nick nodded. "That's usually the case."

Jackson looked back at Gracie. "I'll find Mr. Shoemaker in the morning. Do not approach Truitt with anything. You're still the temp. Keep it that way."

"Yes, sir. I'll check in tomorrow."

In the parking garage, Gracie and Nick stood between her Jeep and his truck. Agents were still posted at the entrance and exit as well as in the elevator lobby. Neither had said anything since they left Jackson at the elevator.

Gracie touched his arm. "Sorry you had to witness the Gracie Bitch. I know you thought you'd never have to see her again."

Nick gave her a hug. "I kind of missed that chick. She's not bad when she's chatting with someone besides me."

Gracie snorted and pushed away. "We're all crazy, you know that."

"A little crazy is what keeps us sane."

CHAPTER 47

Courtney snuggled into the crook of Slate's arm, her chestnut waves dark against the pillow. "I missed you."

He kissed the top of her head. "I missed you, too. And the girls. Did you see Hannah taking photos of Rojo this afternoon?"

"No. You two went out while I was working on dinner."

"I learned she loves this ranch and the cattle." *Okay, maybe I stretched that truth a little. More like slanting it to make my point.* "And that there's not much she's afraid of. She wants to jump into life with both feet."

Courtney sat up and faced him. "You got all that from a few minutes outside with her?"

Something in her voice told him he needed to tread carefully. "Of course not. Those are all separate things I've noticed about her as she's grown up. Today, they seemed to all come together and make her really shine."

"I see where you're going, Slate. The answer is no."

Damn her. "There's no question, hon. Just a comment."

"There's always the same question from you. 'Who's going to run my ranch?' Do you have any idea what Hannah wants to do?"

"She wants to go to UT, and last I heard, major in

art history. What the hell kind of a degree is that?"

Courtney slowly moved her head from side to side. "Hannah wants to go to design school in New York. Have you seen her room lately? You don't need to answer that. She's redone it. And Amanda's. She's working on Callie's and Greer's now."

Better to cut his losses and build a better argument later. And he would. No way was he allowing his daughter to go to school in New York. She needed to stay here in Texas where she was born and raised. Where she belonged. He arranged his face so he appeared properly chastised. "I didn't know. Of course she needs to do what she's good at." Like running this ranch. Her ranch.

"Not only what she does well, Slate. All our daughters need to do the things they love. Letting them follow their passions and dreams is the only way any of them will ever agree to return here to live."

What fucking bullshit. "I never thought of it in that way."

"Well, you better start. I'm not letting you bulldoze your will on our daughters."

We'll see about that.

CHAPTER 48

As soon as Gracie got home, she placed the tracker back where she'd found it on her fender well. On her way to the patio, Ariana called. "Hello, sailor."

"Hello, yourself. I hope I caught you before you went to bed. Time is weird out here. They serve food all hours. I haven't known what time it is since we left, but I don't care. This is so much fun!"

"I'm glad. Why aren't you out having more fun instead of being a party pooper and calling me?"

"Because I have a message for you."

Gracie laughed. "A message? Who's on there with you that I know?"

"Zoe, of course."

Ariana's spirit friend. "So does Zoe want me to tell you to lay off the tequila so you don't fall overboard?"

"No, silly." Ariana giggled. "She says she's happy you finally got the hint to move the women. Whatever that means."

Gracie stopped walking. "Say again."

"Zoe said she's happy you finally got the hint to move the women. I don't know what that means. I just knew I needed to convey the message. What does it mean to you?"

"That's crazy, Ariana."

"Ahh, it does have meaning. One day, Gracie, you'll listen."

"I paid attention this time, obviously, but I

certainly didn't hear Zoe telling me."

Ariana asked what happened, and Gracie told her about the dark, oppressive feelings telling her to leave the house.

"There was a time when you would've totally ignored those feelings, Gracie. You're learning to listen—to heed what you feel. You've come a long way."

None of this was logical. "I don't know about that."

"Trust me. I need to hang up so I can afford this call when I get the bill. We'll talk more when I get home. I'll tell you about this great couple I met yesterday."

#

The closer Gracie got to the bakery, the more she anticipated seeing Donovan again. It had been a while since she'd allowed a man into her life, and she wasn't sure she was ready. Ariana had told her that she would never be ready—that she just needed to jump in. Gracie wasn't as sure.

She'd been the one to end most of the relationships she'd been involved in, and there hadn't been that many. Her being a cop hadn't helped any of them. But Donovan was safer. He didn't need to know she'd been a cop. He would be returning to Austin in a few weeks anyway. A few months at most.

But now there was the problem that if she was right and the bakery was linked to the diamonds or the murders or both, Donovan could be involved. Even if in only a peripheral way, it was still involvement. If he was the informant, how could he have known about the gems without knowing of the murders?

She shook her head. Untangling these thoughts was worse than fighting herself out of a cornfield maze. One wrong turn crashed everything.

On the other hand, it could be a really fun fling and give her a little more experience at being a man's lover instead of his sister or friend or work partner. She'd never thought of herself as being the type for a fling. Maybe it was because she'd never met the right man. Donovan was perfect fling material.

She hoped their Friday date would go off without a hitch and she wouldn't need to cancel. "I won't cancel. No matter what." When she said something out loud and heard her voice with her own ears, it made her decisions more permanent.

After a Friday date, they would be able to share a secret on Saturday morning. Except there may not even be a Saturday morning at the bakery for her. Her assignment would end as soon as the delivery arrived.

Why was she so indecisive? Usually she had no trouble making decisions and sticking with them. Because Donovan Beck was one hunky man, that's why, and she was realizing she needed a man in her life. Someone to share the day-to-day with. It must be her body clock. She'd just have to knuckle down and get through it.

She turned the corner. Donovan waited at the door. She waved before seeing he was on the phone. He nodded and turned away.

Why would he step outside to make or take a call? At six-thirty in the morning?

CHAPTER 49

As Gracie worked to load the display case, she carried on a running banter with Natalie and Maricelia. The shop was small, and there was no way for Donovan and Webb to ignore their teasing and gossip. Each one joined in from time to time, but she failed to learn anything new about Webb.

Donovan never told her who his phone conversation was with. Maybe he really was an informant. Or talking to a wife or girlfriend. *Stop it right now, Gracie!*

A parade was taking shape on Broadway, and the Jalapeno Cupcake was the busiest she'd seen it. There had been a line since a little after eight, once even extending beyond the door. She and Donovan didn't have time to fill orders and keep the case loaded. The activity kept her mind busy, too, and all but free of Donovan's presence inches away from her.

Natalie brought out a tray of assorted cookies, and Gracie stepped back against the rear counter to allow her room. She closed her eyes and rotated her neck in a circle, scrunched up her shoulders and pushed them down.

"Okay, you're all set."

Gracie opened her eyes to the *whish* of the case closing and Natalie's back entering the kitchen. A man was bent down looking at the goodies. "Welcome to Jalapeno Cupcake. How may I help you?"

He stood up. Gracie's eyes widened. It was Nick.

"Hi. I want one of those chocolate cupcakes." Nick looked at her the same as he would a Starbucks barista, indicating she wasn't supposed to know him.

She paid attention. "Excellent choice. Those are my favorite. To die for." She licked her lips.

Donovan worked with another customer, and Nicky gave her the *spare me the diva act* look.

She grinned. He was here for a reason, she knew that much. She didn't know what the reason was, though. With so many people around, it wasn't as if they could have a quiet conversation.

"You know what? I better get something for my wife and little girl, too. They said they didn't want anything, but I know if I come back with this cupcake and nothing for them, they'll be all over my case."

Wife and daughter. Nicky knew where they were. Or at least where Jessica's cousin was. "You're right about that. What would you like?"

"Tres leches. A cupcake and a cookie bar."

"Perfect."

As Gracie bagged the items for him, he said, "Are you from San Antonio?"

"Not originally, but I've lived here a long time."

"You wouldn't happen to know where West Woodlawn Street is would you? I'm looking for eleven thirty-seven."

Eleven thirty-seven. That would be Jessica's room number. *Thank you, Nicky!* "Take any of the downtown east-west streets going west until you get to North Flores. It's about six blocks west of Broadway—that's the street out here with the parade. Turn right and stay on North Flores until you reach Fredericksburg Road. Turn left. That will take you to Woodlawn. You'll have to look for the number."

"North Flores to Fredericksburg to Woodlawn."

"Correct. It's about three miles out there from town. Good luck with finding eleven thirty-seven. And thanks for coming to Jalapeno Cupcake. Donovan will ring you up. Enjoy your goodies."

CHAPTER 50

For half an hour, Slate had ridden across the rocky land that was his Lone Star Ranch. He alternated Arabella between a walk and a trot until they reached the gate from the trail into a large, hundred-acre pasture. Plato had romped ahead, barking off and on, a smile plastered across his face.

Slate moved his cattle from range to range to give the vegetation time to grow, seed, and mature again. This particular plot hadn't been grazed in over a year, except by marauding white-tails. It was looking good. He planned to move a small herd here in the fall.

It looked wild and native, but Slate and his ranch manager, Art Cochran, planned and decided on every plant for every pasture and saw that each got off to a good start before turning the reins over to Mother Nature.

Slate dropped the reins and let Arabella find her own way. Because he visited this particular pasture more than the others, she knew where they were heading: to the top of a craggy bluff fronted by mesquite and scrub. Arabella had made her own trail.

Plato scampered ahead, making sure it was safe. He barked when he reached the top. Slate and Arabella joined him a few minutes later. He dismounted to give her a short break and looped the reins around a low branch.

The tree line marked where his property joined

that of his neighbor, Joshua Brackett. Slate raised his binoculars. In the distance, the metal roof of Brackett's show barn gleamed in the sun.

"You stubborn old son of a bitch. It didn't have to be this way. I warned you, and you gave me no choice. When it goes down, you just remember that."

He left Arabella to graze and whistled for Plato. They walked the length of the bluff and back. Along the way, Plato picked up a stick. They played fetch a few times until Plato took an interest in a small herd of rabbits.

"Come on, boy. Time to go home."

He'd just mounted Arabella when his phone beeped. "Yes."

"Both packages are secure and at the meeting point. I just talked to him."

Slate glanced at the time. "He's early. Tell him the pickup will be made at two o'clock, as scheduled, and to return then. He's to confirm with you as soon as the handoff is made."

"Yes, sir, boss. Consider it done."

"No need to confirm—only if you don't hear and can't reach him." Slate punched off. The stock auction would be finished by one, if not sooner. That would give Cochran time to grab a bite before picking up his extra cargo. Everything was going according to plan.

As he walked toward Arabella, Slate thought about the man on the phone. Soon his time as a free man would end. Slate had already set his plan in motion. Webb Truitt had served him well, but he knew too much. Not only would he hit up Slate for more money in the future, but he now knew enough to cause a problem if Slate didn't pay.

He looked out again toward Brackett's land. "Adios, amigo. This is the last problem you'll ever cause me. Enjoy your dinner tonight. It will be your final one on God's green earth."

CHAPTER 51

Webb passed by the counter at his usual quitting time without a word to anyone.

Gracie turned to Donovan. "What's wrong with him?"

"I guess he's tired. Like me."

"Same here."

Donovan smacked his forehead. "I just realized no one took a break this morning."

Gracie blinked. "Didn't cross my mind. I didn't know what time it was until I saw Webb leave."

"Take your break now."

"You sure?"

He grinned. "Go."

On the street, Gracie tried not to hurry. She pulled out her phone as soon as she rounded the corner and called Jackson.

"You have two minutes. I have a conference call coming in."

"Room eleven thirty-seven at the Marriott Rivercenter."

"Do I want to know how you know that?"

"Nick. That's all I know. You need to confirm that it's registered to a Bernal from El Paso."

"Sending the request now."

"If it's confirmed, do we pick them up? Do I do it? Or do we keep them there?"

"Let me think on that during the conference call.

Give me a ring when you leave the bakery for the day. I'll have more answers."

Gracie finished talking right before she reached her favorite stop. She paid for a bottle of water but instead of taking her usual path around the block, she turned to retrace her steps. As soon as she turned the corner, she unscrewed the cap and took a big gulp.

"Hi, there." The voice came from her side, and she jumped.

Part of the water went down the wrong pipe, and she coughed. It took her a minute to realize it was Webb Truitt standing at her side.

"You okay? I didn't mean to startle you."

"Fine." She coughed again. "Or I will be in a sec."

"I left my windbreaker in the kitchen. The old brain doesn't work like it used to. I just wanted out of there."

"Today was crazy. Donovan said you came in early to bake extra."

"Yeah. Two hours."

"I may have just been going to sleep around then."

He laughed. "You're still young. You can pull those kind of hours. I need every minute of sleep I can get."

"You have a long way to go to be that old. I sometimes catch up on the weekend. Party Friday and catch up all day Saturday kind of thing." *Okay, your turn.*

"I can't sleep in. Too many years of waking up before three o'clock. Messes you up. Other people don't realize I'm ready to go to bed just about the time they're sitting down for supper."

Thud. Webb, old buddy, are you cranky because you were chasing Jackson around the mall at eight o'clock last night instead of getting your beauty sleep? And then you had to get up two hours early? I'll bet you a jalapeno cupcake you are.

CHAPTER 52

Gracie tried to engage Webb in conversation on the short walk back to the bakery, but he was quiet, except to tell her his car was in the shop and he had to go pick it up. At least he was upfront about that. When he walked into the bakery, he waved at Donovan and went straight to the kitchen. She was still tying her apron when he came back through, waving his windbreaker in farewell.

The rest of her shift was uneventful. Before she left, Donovan came to stand next to her.

He squeezed her shoulder. "I'll miss you."

Gracie turned her head toward him and smiled. "I'll miss you, too. But we're both going to be busy after we leave here."

"You know what I'll be doing. What about you?"

Was he asking because he was interested in her romantically or was he questioning her to learn where she planned to be? *But look at that face.* His eyes were intent on her in the way a man looks at a woman he wants. She had to stop reading the worst into men's motives. It was the reason most of her relationships had failed.

But she couldn't be exactly truthful either. If she told him she might be going to kidnap a woman and her child and take them to a secret hideout, he would bolt faster than grass through a goose. "I'm starving. As soon as I leave, I'm grabbing lunch. Then I'm calling an old friend to see where we're going to meet. It's usually something fun when we get together. Then I'm supposed to meet another friend—in the process of a divorce—for drinks. That's probably going to work into dinner and another drink or two." The truth, more or less, minus a few important details.

Gracie made sure Webb wasn't any place in sight before she approached the parking lot and her Jeep. Nothing stirred her subconscious and no hairs stood up on her arms, neck, or anyplace else on her body. She got in and drove to a nearby fast food drive thru. As she'd hoped, the line was long.

She called Jackson. "What's the decision?"

"More than one. The room is confirmed to belonging to one Kevin Bernal, an optometrist from El Paso. I sent a team with a listening device into the room next door. They picked up sounds of a television plus a child's voice and a voice belonging to a woman. It's the best confirmation we can make without a visual. The drapes have remained drawn and no housekeeping service was requested."

"It's them. Are you picking them up?"

"Bernal's on a panel at one-thirty. We have a team onsite ready to extract them at one-forty."

"She's going to fight you. She's adamant about following her husband's instructions. He's a control freak, so she's probably thinking of the hell she'll have to face afterward if she doesn't."

"The team has a short video from Lupe and Carmen assuring they are safe. Carmen says if Victor was aware of all the circumstances, he would insist on her joining them. Then Lupe appeals directly to Maya."

"Playing the kid card. Smart."

"In this instance, yes. The hotel situation puts too many people in danger. Also, I want you to be aware that SAPD is sending a K-9 unit to Lupe's later this afternoon to check for explosives and accelerants."

"Excellent." Not that she believed they'd find anything. No matter what Zoe said to Ariana.

"Everyone agreed it was the smart thing since the caller's Wednesday evening threat is approaching with no sign of Cantu. I need you to come in and talk with Jessica after she's here and has had a few minutes to reconnect with Carmen and Lupe, but before she has time to get comfortable. Can you be here at two-thirty?"

"Yes. I'm in a drive thru line now and need to make one quick stop. If I get there early, I'll hang out with the white hats and learn some new tricks."

"One more thing. I talked to Cord McCullough this morning about the source of the delivery information you're watching for. He said the source is anonymous."

"No such thing. There are ways."

"I pushed. Told him some background so he could see why I was asking. He said this same individual has provided tips in the past, and all have been fruitful. Each time, Bastion or the Rangers have tracked and located an abandoned burner phone in various locations around the country. McCullough believes he may be a trucker or an airline employee."

"That's probably what the source wants us to believe."

"I agree. I told Cord that this level of intel usually meant a higher level source. We agreed to keep each other and Dominic apprised of anything remotely related at future partner meetings. It may take a while, but we'll figure out who it is."

When they disconnected, she called Nick. "Thank you for the room number. I owe you a beer."

"Consider it payback for hooking me up with the lawyer. Can you believe I'm actually a little nervous?"

"She won't bite you. Unless you ask nicely, that is."

"Ha, ha. I haven't been nervous about anything in a long time. Maybe it's a good thing."

"It could be. Is her office downtown?"

"Near the courthouse."

"Where are you now?"

"At home."

"Meet me someplace in fifteen minutes."

"What's up?"

"I need to give you the tracker on my car. I'll explain later."

"The Walmart parking lot on 410 by NSA. Up near the bank."

By the time Gracie got her food, she had to hustle to make the meet with Nicky on time. As she turned into the lot, he approached from the opposite direction, stopping in the center of a row of empty parking spaces. Seconds later, she parked so her left front wheel was across from Nick's window.

She got out, yanked off the tracker, and handed it to Nicky. "Just stick it on the floor someplace. Call me after you finish with the attorney. I'll buy you a beer and pick it up. I'm going to Bastion, and I don't want this son of a bitch to know where I am or believe I'm at home."

CHAPTER 53

Gracie hadn't been in the Bastion office for even five minutes when Jackson found her.

"Come on in here with me."

She followed him into his office.

"They're bringing Jessica and Maya up now."

Her head fell back. "Yes!" She took a deep breath and blew out the air. A smile spread across her face.

"They'll rush Jessica through the process. We'll print Maya, but won't input hers into the access pad software. Don't want her sneaking out and getting lost."

Gracie nodded. So many things could've gone wrong. Only now did Gracie realize how knotted up she'd been. "By the way, I ditched the tracker last night and today. I'll pick it up again after I leave."

"Figured as much."

Gracie's phone rang. She didn't recognize the number. "Mind if I take this?"

"Go ahead. I'm going to welcome the new ladies to the family. Maybe reassure that little girl. I have cookies."

"A dirty old man with cookies for a little girl." Gracie shook her head. "Get out of here."

Jackson wiggled his eyebrows at her as he went out the door.

She answered the call. "Gracie Hofner."

"Hi. This is Milo Porter. My cousin gave me your

number. Katie Ullrich. Miller. She said your mother told her you have a garage apartment for rent in San Antonio."

His voice was warm and deep, the kind of voice she liked. She moved to the window to watch the traffic. "I do. Actually, though, it's my aunt's apartment."

"Sounds like your mother is looking out for her sister and her daughter."

"That's Mom."

"I have the same situation. Family is great, but they can sometimes be—"

"Insistent. I know. My mother called me last night and gave me your name."

He gave a short laugh. "I told Katie I'm looking for something specific, but she prides herself on being able to locate the perfect thing people are looking for, no matter what it is."

Gracie smiled. "I didn't know that about her. We lost touch after high school."

"She gives great Christmas gifts."

"I'll bet. That's a fantastic perk."

"Right. Anyway, I'm not sure I can find what I need in an apartment. I'll probably end up renting a small house."

"Tell me what you want. Maybe I can help you find it. Or point you in the right direction. I'm not hung up on that, though, like Katie. Just so you know. I may need a prod or two—my life is hectic."

"Nobody's hung up on it like Katie. It's just me, so I only need one bedroom and one bath, but I need one or two separate spaces apart from the living area."

"For..."

"I do freelance illustration—in addition to my real job. I do get a regular paycheck."

"That's always good. What kind of illustrations do you do?"

"I figured you'd think so. Mostly ads. I've done a

couple of kiddie books."

"Cool."

"I need a separate space with a little elbow room. Not cramped like an armoire desk that folds up."

"Son of a bitch!"

"Excuse me?"

"Oh, not you. I didn't mean you. A small car just got creamed by a van. Can you hang on a second?"

"Sure."

Gracie laid her phone on Jackson's desk and picked up his line, punching in the outside code plus 911.

"Emergency. How may I help you?"

"Reporting an accident on San Pedro just north of 410."

"We have previous reports. Units and paramedics are dispatched. ETA three minutes."

"Occupants are exiting the van."

"One moment."

Gracie hoped those in the other vehicle were all right.

"Thank you for holding. You're calling from Bastion?"

"Yes."

"Units are a block away. You may hang up now."

Gracie did and picked up her phone. "Sorry about that."

"You sounded like a cop—calm and in control."

He was a quick study. "Former. Now I'm a law enforcement consultant." He didn't need to know all the ins and outs of that right now. Maybe never.

"I've never known a cop before."

"We don't bite. Just don't piss us off. Maybe I'm kidding about that."

"I could tell. Maybe."

He was a little dorky. But she was, too. "What do you do?"

"Marketing and Communications. You ask a lot of questions."

"I do?"

"You just did."

Oh. He's right. I do. "I guess it's part of who I am. You were saying you needed one or two extra spaces. One I get—an office. What about the other one?"

"Music."

"Amps and all that?"

He laughed. "No. I have *all that*, but it's in storage. I used to play in a band, but I won't wake you at three in the morning."

"Good. The lots aren't that large here." Sirens wailed below.

"It doesn't have to be a big space, just large enough for a keyboard, a chair and table, and a little room for me to move around. Or one larger space for both pursuits. Plus space for a washer and dryer. That's a must."

"The apartment has a washer and dryer. If you have your own, I can have someone move these out."

"I planned to purchase new ones, but I can use the ones that are there."

"You'll like them. The previous tenant kept them spotless."

"Can you tell me about your apartment? Do you have what I need or do I need to look for a house?"

"I'm not in the real estate business, so it's just a guess on my part. How much do you want to pay?"

He told her.

"My aunt can work with that." Ariana had paid less, but her aunt wanted more from a new and unknown renter. "The apartment is about twelve hundred square feet plus a covered balcony across the back that's twelve by thirty."

"Sold!"

"Right. I haven't told you about the apartment

yet." Gracie was beginning to like this guy. He made quick decisions.

"I suppose I should hear about that."

"It was built around about twelve years ago and was my aunt's studio until her husband was transferred. So it's been an apartment for about seven years. One tenant. It's been cleaned and repainted. It has clerestory windows on the side that faces the backyard—for my privacy and yours. French doors, more windows facing the other side and a neighboring garage roof. Two skylights—my aunt's a natural light freak."

"So am I."

"It has a large living space, one bedroom, one bath with a walk-in shower, an office or extra room without a closet, and a half-bath with toilet and sink. Wood flooring, granite counters, high-end appliances and finishes. The balcony is covered and has three big, lazy ceiling fans. That's about it. My aunt designed it for what she would want if she lived there."

"Sounds perfect, but I'm worried about location. I'm only somewhat familiar with San Antonio, and I don't want to spend too much time commuting. What general area is it in?"

"Southtown. In the King William area. Do you know where that is?"

"I think so. If I'm at Hemisfair Park, I turn on one of those streets in that area and go south?"

"Pretty much."

"That's one of the areas I was looking for. I need to be centrally located."

"Do you want to come look at it?" *Because it's all going to hinge on what kind of vibe I get off you in person.*

"I'd like to see it this weekend—sometime between late Friday afternoon and early Sunday afternoon. Whatever works with your schedule. I can come almost anytime, but that's the time that works best for me."

Jackson poked his head in the door. "Come on. Jessica's going back to Carmen and Lupe now. I want you in there early."

She nodded and talked as she followed. "I'm working and have to go. As soon as I can, I'll call you back to set up a time. Call me if you haven't heard from me by tomorrow afternoon. Leave a message if I don't answer, so I have a reminder. Sometimes things get a little hairy."

After they hung up, she remembered she'd forgotten to tell him about the garage space and the storage. At least she'd have something to talk about when she called him back. She wondered what he looked like.

"Hurry up, Hofner."

CHAPTER 54

On the way down the hall, Jackson's phone rang. "You go on. I'll meet you inside."

Gracie entered the bunker and hurried the short distance to the suite the sisters were sharing. She faced the camera and knocked rather than just use her palm print and enter.

Lupe greeted her with a hug. "You found Maya! Thank you!"

"Others were involved, not just me."

"If it hadn't been for you, others wouldn't have cared. I know. You were the only one who fought for her. For that, I thank you. And I thank you for my brother." She raised clenched fists into the air only to lower them half a second later and pull on her hair. "I hope he'll remain alive to learn his lesson."

Gracie patted her on the back. Now that Lupe didn't need to worry about Maya, her thoughts were trained on her brother. After he returned, she wouldn't have anyone to distract her from grieving over her parents. Lupe didn't realize that yet. "Why don't you introduce me."

"Sure. Everyone's in the kitchen." The miniature kitchen was maybe five steps from where they stood.

"Aunt Lupe! You kept my picture!" Maya sped around the corner. Her eyes appeared huge in her heart-shaped face.

"Of course I did." Lupe scooped her up. "I almost

can't lift you anymore, you're getting so big."

Maya giggled and snuggled her head into Lupe's neck. Gracie's relief at seeing the little girl in the flesh, happy, smiling, and as carefree as possible, lifted her spirits and gave her an instant energy boost. *Better than a double shot of espresso.* She smiled and caught Lupe's gaze, angling her chin to indicate for her to go ahead into the kitchen.

"Hop down, *mija,* and let's go find your mama."

Maya skipped the few feet ahead.

"Jessica, someone to see you."

A tall, slender woman turned her head, her brows raised over bright brown eyes. Her dark hair hung in a single braid, and she wore no makeup. She had the most beautiful skin Gracie had ever seen. Victor was crazy for wanting her to hide it under makeup.

"This is Gracie Hofner. She's part of Bastion. Gracie's the person who was determined to make sure Maya was safe. This man's a monster."

Jessica held out her hand. "I believe we met through Father Tim."

"What?" Lupe's eyes grew as huge as Maya's had.

"I'll tell you all about it later," Jessica said.

Gracie took Jessica's hand. "Good to meet you in person. Father Tim is a good man. You didn't have any worries."

"He's been our friend for a while. Victor was certain I could trust him."

"He's a good man. I'm glad you and Maya are here and with your family. I need to ask you some questions." Gracie turned to Lupe. "Is Erin here?"

Jessica stiffened. "Who's Erin?"

Carmen touched her arm. "Jessica, chill. You only know your part of the story. After Gracie leaves we'll all sit down and talk. Then all of us will be aware of everything that's happened."

"Victor won't be happy."

"Victor is never happy. These people are professionals. They've earned our trust. Let them do their jobs."

Lupe nodded toward the other side of the open space. "Erin's back there. First door on the left."

#

Jessica had settled Maya in a soft armchair with her favorite game and headphones. Gracie introduced Erin and waited until she was seated at the table with everyone else. Erin opened her notebook.

Gracie tried to make herself look relaxed and non-threatening by leaning back against the wall. She felt silly, so she stood straight. "I'm going to update everyone with what I know and elaborate when possible with what I think. So pay attention. If I get something wrong, wait until I finish and we'll sort it out. It won't take long. Everyone cool with that?"

All the women nodded.

"First, Jessica. The reason Lupe and Carmen are here is because the man who killed their parents has threatened to do the same to Lupe if he hasn't received positive word from your husband by tonight."

Gracie had chosen her words with care to shock Jessica and bring her into the folds of sisterhood. She wasn't sure if she'd succeeded. Jessica had flinched a couple of times, but her facial expression hadn't changed. "It's my belief the only reason he chose Lupe instead of you or Maya is because he wasn't sure where you were."

The sisters showed more reaction to that than Jessica did.

"It took us a few days, but we figured it out. We showed up at the lighting store yesterday not long after you and Maya left. You were spotted in Father Tim's Acura on the way to the hotel. It's fortunate the person who identified you was a police officer working on this case and not the shooter."

236

Jessica began to shake.

Gracie went on. "If I hadn't found Rachel, I wouldn't have known about your cousin as quickly as I did. You can bet the person who murdered your in-laws has been researching the entire family. Sooner or later, he'll either find Rachel or tumble onto your optometrist cousin and the convention in town. My bet is sooner. He's smart, and he's ruthless."

Jessica's head had drooped, her braid falling forward against her cheek. She raised her head. Her face had paled, and the pulse at her temple beat visibly. "Victor will be furious."

Gracie glanced at Erin's notebook. She'd just written *domestic abuse victim* and *counseling recommended*. "You let us worry about Victor."

CHAPTER 55

Slate brought Arabella back to the stable. After brushing her and making sure she had water, he handed her over to one of the hands.

Waiting for the call from his ranch manager made Slate's nerves stand on edge. The pickup should've been made a few minutes ago. Little things could mount up to a delay, but he knew the call would come as soon as possible.

If he returned to the house, Courtney would pick up on his mood. He needed to calm the hell down and finish this business first. Another horse snickered at him, so he made the rounds, rubbed their heads, talked to them. He left the barn from the door that didn't face the house.

Several rusty troughs leaned against the back of the barn. Courtney had been after him to bring one of them up to the house so she could use it for a planter. This was as good a time as any. The activity would dispel some of his nervous energy.

He'd just rounded the corner with the trough when his phone rang. About damn time.

"We're rolling toward home." That meant he'd picked up his passenger.

"Good. Did all the bulls sell for a good price?"

"Yes. I have the paperwork. The money's been sent."

"I need to talk to him."

"One second."

The rustle of the phone being passed was clear. Cochran would be taking the exit for San Angelo about now. The assassin had requested he be dropped off at a location near Sunset Mall, saying he would arrange his own transportation from that point.

"Hello?" It was the same accented voice Slate had spoken to before. He didn't know if the accent was real or fake. Slate knew him only as Verdugo, Spanish for executioner.

"Welcome to Texas. Your plans are still the same?"

"By this time tomorrow you will hear the news. If you fail to hold up your end, as you Texans say, I will find you."

"I won't fail. But the same holds true for you."

"It is good we understand one another."

Yes, they did. Slate didn't know how it would happen, but it was past the point of no return. Before this time tomorrow, Joshua Brackett would leave this earth and meet his maker.

And Slate's plan to purchase his neighbor's property would be set in motion.

CHAPTER 56

The door to the bunker opened, and Jackson entered. "Don't get up, ladies."

Gracie smiled. He carried a tray loaded with ice cream sundaes and placed it in the center of the table. One of them had extra cherries on top.

He picked it up. "Where's my girl?"

Lupe pointed to the living area, and Jackson delivered Maya's personally.

Gracie picked up the last sundae. She hadn't eaten ice cream since last summer back at her mom and dad's. Her mouth watered.

Jackson returned. "A Homeland Security chopper has spotted Victor."

Jessica's spoon stopped halfway to her mouth. "Is he safe?"

"Right now. He's heading east on I-10 toward San Antonio. He's still several hours out—in the middle of that long stretch between Fort Stockton and Ozona. He's alone. Odds are he will make a pit stop in Ozona or Sonora."

"No." Engaged now, Jessica returned her spoon to the parfait glass. "He never stops in those places. He stops in Fort Stockton and not again until Junction. It's his routine."

Jackson pulled a barstool to the table and straddled it. "Mrs. Cantu, we need him to stop before then."

Her back straightened as if a pulley stretched it into place. "What are you going to do?" She laced her fingers and squeezed until her knuckles turned white.

Jackson patted her hands. "We're hoping you'll help us."

She gasped. "Me? How? I'm here."

"We'd like for you to call him. Convince him to stop at a particular location."

Jessica shook her head. "No. I can't do that."

Carmen launched herself at Jessica. Lightning fast, Jackson stopped her mid-lunge. "Settle. I'll get to the bottom of this." Jackson's words were gentle.

Carmen returned to her chair. Her face was flushed and her eyes flashed with anger. "Victor may be her husband, but he was my brother first. Still is my brother. I'll always love him and his family, but this attitude of his—this wanting all the marbles—it has to stop before our entire family is murdered, just like Mom and Dad were."

Gracie kept her face quiet and still, but inside she was cheering Carmen on. She doubted Jessica realized she was enabling Victor's control issues, and in turn, his desire to have the biggest and best of everything, no matter the cost. A domestic cluster fuck if ever there was one.

Jackson nodded to Carmen and looked from her to Jessica, who stared at the table. He touched her hand. "Tell me why you won't call your husband."

"He doesn't like it. He's afraid someone can track him if I call. He usually keeps his phone turned off until he gets back to San Antonio."

Erin and Gracie looked at each other. They both knew what could've been easy now would be difficult. This was an opportunity for Carmen to turn things around in her marriage, but Gracie didn't imagine she saw it as such.

"Does he have a burner?" Jackson's voice

maintained its gentle tone, but a little muscle in his neck hopped around like a drop of water in a pan of hot grease.

"A burner? I don't know what you mean."

"A burner phone. A prepaid phone like you can buy at a convenience store. Do you know if he has one of those? Or a satellite phone?"

Jessica didn't answer. Which meant he did.

Jackson touched her arm. "Do you know the number?"

She remained silent.

Jackson closed his eyes. Bad sign. His patience was used up. When he opened them, they were filled with fire. "We hoped you'd help us, Mrs. Cantu. Get him to pull into a rest area where someone from Bastion would drive his vehicle and he would be driven back to SA in an unmarked vehicle and brought straight here to join all of you."

Or brought by helicopter, if Gracie's suspicions were correct, but she didn't say anything. This was Jackson's show.

"Now we'll have to pull him over in a traffic stop. It's dangerous on a good day, arouses suspicion on a bad one. And on days when nothing goes right, it can bring death and destruction. The choice is yours."

Jessica stared at the melting ice cream on the table and stood up. Her arms flopped around, her hands touching her face, smoothing her skirt, pushing back her hair, scratching her neck. Clearly she didn't like making difficult decisions.

"Oh, for God's sake, Jessica." Carmen bounced up again. "Grow up. This isn't just a regular trip to Caballo Canyon. Mom and Dad are dead. I don't know why this bastard chose Victor, but he did. Obviously Victor refused until the screws were turned. Now we're all in the boiling pot. Each of us has to make our own difficult decisions. It's time for you to forget my brother's precious feelings. He needs to know it's time for him to let go of that machismo thing he's got going on, and time for you to stand up to him and tell him what's what. Because that's exactly what I plan to do when he gets back."

"And it's time he buries La Luz." It was the first time Lupe had spoken. "His time is over. He's no longer needed."

You go, girls!

Jackson stood up and put his arm around Jessica's shoulders. "Think about your daughter, Mrs. Cantu. Let her keep her daddy. More importantly, let her be proud of a mommy who's a strong and positive role model."

CHAPTER 57

Jackson was damn good at playing the kid card, and not bad at laying on a guilt trip. Jessica was misery on a stick, her face drawn, her eyes downcast, her fingers constantly touching her hair, twisting and pulling at her braid. She couldn't hide her inner fight between fear, anger, and love.

Gracie had stayed out of it so far, but time was running short. "Jessica, listen. I don't know you or Victor. And I surely don't know what your life with him is like. From all I hear, it's a bit manic and his demands have increased."

Jessica's head jerked up. She didn't voice the words, but everything about her said *back off*.

The sisters snapped to attention.

"I know what we're asking you to do goes against everything you've done to cater to and coddle your husband over the last few years."

Jessica hadn't moved.

"I want to share something with you that my grandma told me when I started dating." Gracie paused for a couple of beats, totally for effect. It worked—Jessica's shoulders slumped half an inch. "I can still see her. She was a stern-looking woman with a big, soft heart. She said, 'Gracie, you've been a scrappy little thing ever since you were born. The way you keep up with your brothers and big sister beats all I've ever seen. I swear, child, you're not afraid of anything.'"

Gracie stopped for a bite of ice cream. Also to make Jessica wonder where the hell she was headed with this story. "So then Grandma said, 'Your mama tells me you're going on your first date tomorrow night.'

"I went on to tell her how cute he was, and how excited I was. And something like I felt as if I was finally a woman. Grandma gave me one of her fear-of-God looks. After all, I was only fifteen."

Jessica's lips curled up for half a second.

"Then she said, 'Remember this. You won't be a real woman until you have a battle of wits with your man. And despite his pigheadedness, you win. Until then, you're just a girl—like all the others out there. Real men want real women. And that has nothing to do with putting out in the backseat."

Jackson burst out laughing. "Your grandmother really told you that?"

"Swear to God." Gracie guessed she'd never be a real woman. She'd never loved any man enough to armor up over anything that really mattered. If he didn't agree with her, she just walked away. *Sayonara, sucker.*

Jessica cocked her head and looked at Maya with a sweet smile softening her face. She faced Gracie. "Thank you. And your grandmother. Victor has always been in charge. If I stood up to him each time we disagree, we would spend all our time fighting. But I don't want my daughter to have a marriage like mine. This is a story I will tell her the night before her quinceanera."

"That's fine, but what about now?" Gracie asked. "What are you going to do?"

"I'm not quite ready to meet your grandmother and have the Man Versus Woman conversation, but I will make the call to Victor. After all, I should have at least one good story of my own to tell Maya when she's fifteen."

"Wonderful."

Jessica looked at Jackson. "I'll need my phone back to call him. He won't answer any other number."

Jackson left to retrieve Jessica's phone. While he was gone, Jessica went over and talked to Maya in a hushed voice. Maya giggled and went back to her ice cream.

Gracie was surprised her grandma's words had made such a difference. They'd made a difference to Gracie, but she'd been a teenager. It was the only story she could think of on the fly, except for the shotgun one—and that one wouldn't have worked, for sure. Oma had a lot of hidden fire for a little German farmer's wife.

Jackson returned. "I need you to write Victor's number down. While you do that, I'm going to jot down the points you need to cover with him. We'll want to talk to him direct to set up the meet." He pushed across an index card and a pen.

"You want the prepaid number or his regular number? Or his satellite number?"

Well, well. Victor was prepared for anything.

"Put them all down. Indicate which is which."

Jackson pulled a phone out of his shirt pocket and placed it on the table. He and Jessica started writing.

Gracie read over Jackson's shoulder:

Speaker
Not alone
You and Maya are OK
Carmen and Lupe here
Department of Homeland Security tracking him
Meet at Sonora rest stop

His pencil paused before he wrote *I will talk to him as well.*

He assumed by giving her guidelines that Jessica

would lead the conversation. Gracie didn't think there was much chance of that, even after hearing Oma's words. Standing up to Victor would take perseverance and much practice.

Jackson traded notes with Jessica. "Ready?"

Jessica nodded and picked up her phone. She licked her lips before placing the call.

"Put it on speaker before he answers." Jackson pointed at her phone.

"Now?"

"Yes."

A little tension returned to her face, but she followed Jackson's instructions, putting the phone back on the table.

Gracie counted four rings before Victor picked up. "Jess?"

"It's me, baby."

"Are you all right? Maya?"

Jessica nodded. "Yes, we're fine."

"Why are you calling?" His voice took on an edge.

"Because something else has happened."

"Did you follow my plan?"

"Yes." She took a deep breath. "Victor, Maya and I are not alone."

"Your cousin is there. I know."

Jessica pushed at her slicked-back her hair. She was growing frustrated. "The phone is on speaker. Maya and I are in a safe place with Carmen and Lupe."

"What? My plan didn't include my sisters. You fucked up."

Jackson pulled the phone closer to him. "Watch your language, Mr. Cantu. And your attitude."

"Who are you? What are you doing with my wife?"

"Look in your mirror, Mr. Cantu. See that car back there a couple hundred yards? He's about to flash his lights at you."

"Son of a—who the hell are you?"

"I'm the man you fucking don't want to mess with. Now listen up."

For half a second, Gracie wondered how Jackson had pulled off the light trick. Then she realized he'd called the Bastian agent in the car and left the line open. So when the agent heard Jackson talking to Victor, he just flashed his lights on cue.

Gracie glanced at Carmen and Lupe. Both were smiling. She'd never worried about Carmen, but she hoped Lupe was growing into her shoes.

"My name is Roland Jackson. I'm a director of a group you've never heard of. Bottom line, we are law enforcement consultants, working with different agencies and organizations to make their jobs a little easier. That's all you need to know. Right now, we're working with the San Antonio Police Department to identify and locate the person who killed your parents. At this moment, we're coordinating efforts with Homeland Security to bring you safely back to San Antonio to rejoin your family. Questions?"

CHAPTER 58

Slate was pulling the trough to the spot Courtney had marked off when his phone rang again. He recognized the number. "Yes."

"I understand the handoff has been made."

"That's right." Slate wiped his forehead on his sleeve.

"There's been no change to my account."

Greedy motherfucker. "It's a long drive. As soon as I have what I've paid for, you'll get your money. Sometime within the next twenty-four hours."

"That wasn't our agreement."

"It is now. That's all you need to know." Slate uttered the words through gritted teeth.

"Twenty-four hours. If the money's not there—"

"You'll what? Don't threaten to do something you can't back up. Lowlifes like you are cheaper than Saturday night hookers. Remember that. I said the money will be there, and it will. Stop wasting my time." Slate ended the call. *Stupid fuck!* He'd definitely chosen the right time to end their relationship.

"Oh, good, you're bringing it up." Courtney crossed the patio and stood by the place she wanted the trough. "I love watching you work."

Slate pushed his anger down. He raised his head and smiled at her from under the brim of his straw hat. "Yes, ma'am!"

"You're crazy." She ran to him and wrapped her

arms around his neck.

"Crazy and sweaty."

"Watching your muscles work makes me hot. Now we're both sweaty. We need a shower." She kissed him full on.

He was hard in an instant. "Let me get this in place, then we'll go inside." Sometimes Slate thought Courtney was as crazy as he was. He didn't care. He liked it.

They barely made it to the bedroom before Slate pulled Courtney to him. "How long before the girls get home?"

"At least an hour."

He kissed her hard. She responded in her own way by digging her nails into his back.

Then she pulled away. "I want you to strip."

"My pleasure." He wore a western shirt with snap buttons. It came off in a second.

Courtney kicked off her sandals.

He sat to pull off his boots and socks. When he stood, he unbuckled his belt. As much as he desired to use it lovingly on Courtney, he wouldn't. She'd put a stop to that long ago. He didn't like her decision, but he respected it. Next came his jeans. He unbuttoned them and pushed them and his underwear to the floor, stepping out of them toward Courtney. "As directed."

Courtney kissed him again, and her hands and nails seemed to be everywhere—his back, his chest. Her lips followed down his neck, across his chest. Her hands found the muscles on his arms, and the next thing he knew, they cupped his ass. He was throbbing. Courtney liked to prolong the high, and this was one of the days it would take all his willpower to do so.

Her lips continued across his belly until she took him in her mouth. Holy mother of God. No one could give a blow job like Courtney, but he knew this was just a tease. After half a minute she stood up.

It took Slate a few moments to focus. When he did, he saw she'd stripped and was smiling at him.

"Come on, old man. Let's get in bed."

He followed her like a puppy. But once they were under the covers, he took charge. Her breasts were exquisite, and all natural. That's what having four baby girls had done for her. Watching those babies go after her had been its own turn-on, but those days were past.

His fingers entered her. She was wet for him. He replaced his fingers with the part of him that could never get enough of her. "I think this is what you wanted."

"Always."

He rode her hard, then rolled to his back, taking her with him. "Your turn."

Her hands worked through his chest hair until they found his nipples. He let her have her pleasure until he could no longer hold back, rolling again until he braced himself over her and buried his ache deep. "Let's rock and roll."

A few minutes later, Courtney's arms tightened around his back, and he plunged hard until he came inside her.

After a few minutes of stillness, Slate rolled to his side, gathering Courtney close. "Wake me in time for a shower before the girls get home."

CHAPTER 59

Jackson told Victor to stop at the rest area between Ozona and Sonora. Victor was adamant about not stopping until Jackson told him he would stop one way or another and he thought Victor would much prefer the easy way of doing it of his own accord. Jackson also told him Homeland would contact him directly concerning the meet, and that he would be wise to turn on all his phones and answer whichever one rang.

After the important items had been covered, Jackson continued. "I'll give the phone back to Jessica in a minute. Do you have any questions?"

"Yeah. How did you find them—Jessica and Maya?"

"We missed them at the lighting store by less than an hour, but we were watching the hotel as well. When the timing was right, we made the extraction."

Victor thought about it for a few seconds. "I was more worried about the lighting store than the hotel. How did you know to look there?"

"This is the information age. Very little is secret or hidden if you know where and how to look for it, Mr. Cantu. Our organization excels in that area." Jackson made eye contact with Gracie.

What the hell? Was he telling her he knew about her attraction to Donovan? Giving her a warning to keep her personal life out of her job?

"Any other questions?"

"No. I'd like to talk to Jess."

"Make it short. The call will stay on speaker." Jackson slid it back to Jessica.

"Victor—"

"I'm glad you and Maya are safe."

Had Victor's cutting his wife off been deliberate? If so, why? To keep her from saying something he didn't want them to know? Or to let her know that as far as she was concerned, he was still in charge? Gracie liked him less with each passing minute.

"I was so worried about you." Tears welled in Jessica's eyes.

"Wear your hair down tonight. And to the side. Does Maya have her pink dress?"

Jackson pulled the phone back toward him. "I don't think you understand the seriousness of the situation, Mr. Cantu. All of you are fortunate to be alive. It's no time to issue orders to your wife. This call is over." He disconnected and dropped the phone into his pocket.

Jessica sucked her lips inward and wiped her eyes. "Victor will be furious."

"You have no need to worry about your safety or Maya's. It's time your husband learned how to properly treat his wife. I will not tolerate behavior of that sort."

"And you shouldn't either, Jessica," Lupe said. "I don't know where Victor got that. Dad never treated Mom the way Victor treats you. He cherished her."

Go, Lupe!

Jessica looked at everyone in turn. "Victor has never struck me or hurt me in any way. Nor has he ever hurt Maya. He just needs everything to be like he wants it. Rachel, one of my friends, tells me how he treats me is still abuse. It's hard. I don't think I can be strong like all of you. I love him too much."

253

Gracie touched her arm. "It's fine to love him. We have little control over what the heart wants. But you should probably takes steps to have him respect you, as well. When this is over, I can give you a list of people who can help. Find one you like and get started." Gracie didn't tell her Victor was likely going to prison for a while unless somebody lobbied for a deal.

Jessica nodded, but she didn't look at Gracie. After several seconds, she looked at Jackson. "Thank you for letting me talk to him."

"Not a problem." Jackson stood. "He's not quite an hour from Sonora. We're patched into their conversations, and we have our own people out there. He'll be here by dinner, at which time we'll all talk again. After Maya's had a chance to visit with her daddy for a bit, one of our people will come in and take her to our break room for a burger and fries and some play time. I'll have food brought in here and all of us will talk again. We'll leave you alone now to reconnect and freshen up."

Jessica nodded her agreement.

In the hall, Jackson said, "Come to my office for a minute."

After Gracie entered, he closed the door. She chose her usual spot and composed her face so she wouldn't show any anxiety about Donovan. Not that there was anything wrong—she just didn't want Jackson being a voyeur in her personal life.

"I hope you got my meaning back there about not talking about your source. Want a cookie?" He reached back to his credenza and brought a white cafeteria bag to his desk.

"Sounds good. Thanks." Not revealing her source. Gracie released a pent-up breath. This chat had nothing to do with Donovan. She chose a fat, old-fashioned peanut butter cookie, complete with fork indentations. "I thought that may have been the reason for the look. You gave Victor a good dressing down."

"You know me. I have no use for arrogant, controlling people. Especially one who both curses at and uses a condescending tone with his wife. Mr. Cantu and I are going to have a long, friendly chat after we debrief him."

"Do you need me to stay here or can I come back later?" She took a bite of cookie. *Mmmm.*

"Later's fine. Cantu's close to Ozona about now, so the pickup point is thirty minutes or so away. A DHS helicopter will pick him and two of our people up at the Sonora airport. I look for him here under our roof in about two and a half hours, maybe three." He checked the time. "Plan to be here about six-fifteen. If it's sooner, I'll text you."

CHAPTER 60

Nick hadn't called, so Gracie decided to call Milo Porter back to finish firming up a time for him to see the apartment. If she didn't get it rented soon, her mother would come to SA and find a new tenant herself, and Gracie would have to deal with her mother's choice. She loved her mom, but she needed to make her own choices about who lived upstairs in her backyard.

Gracie was walking to her car when Nick called. She answered. "How'd it go?"

"Your cousin picked a winner."

"Are you being real or sarcastic? I can't see your face."

"Real. Rayann Dailey is amazing. I could be in love."

"I take it things went well."

"Meet me for a beer and we'll talk."

"Where?"

"How about the Friendly Spot?"

"I'd say yes, but I have to be back up here at Bastion at six-fifteen. The timing's iffy, though, so it could be earlier or later. What about up this way so I'm close?"

"Pappadeaux. They have a patio."

"Perfect. I'll go get a table."

#

It was still early, even for the happy hour crowd.

Only a few other people shared the large, shady patio. Gracie chose a table at the back corner against the wall. She asked the server to return when her friend arrived and pulled out her phone. If she didn't call Milo now, it could be too late after she finished at Bastion.

"This is Milo."

"Hi, it's Gracie Hofner—with the apartment in San Antonio."

"I remember. Let's see, it's been a whole hour or two, right?"

They both laughed.

"Right. I can do Friday afternoon if it isn't too late. I have dinner plans."

"I'm leaving Houston right after lunch, so I should be there about three or four. Is that okay?"

"Perfect. I'll show you around, we can talk, and I'll give you the paperwork. I *will* check you out."

"I don't doubt it. That's fine."

"After we hang up, I'll text you the address and directions—unless you just plug in the address."

"I do. I'm one of those."

She smiled at his quirky sense of humor. "Okay, I'll text the address. You have my number, so if you have any questions, just ask. Give me a call around the time you get to Seguin. We can set a more definite time. I'm on permanent call, so—"

"It's not a problem. I can work around your schedule."

Nick entered the patio, saw her. "Great. I'm meeting someone, and he just showed up. See you Friday."

While she disconnected, Nick dropped into the chair against the other wall. "Still working?"

"I have to text this guy my address."

"Oh?"

"Showing Ariana's apartment. I know, don't say

it—I have to stop calling it hers. My mother's involved. A friend's cousin. He's moving here and wants to look at it over the weekend." She sent the text and put her phone in her pocket. "Tell me what happened."

"Rayann already had a file on Kim. It seems a lot's been going on with her for a while. And I had no clue."

"Such as?"

"She had a part-time job—more than one, actually—and a separate bank account and credit card."

"Told you."

"You wouldn't believe some of the things she charged."

"I probably would. Easier than you, my sometimes-naïve friend."

The server came up.

Nick took both menus. "Leave them. Bring us two Shiner Bocks."

The server left, and Nick held a menu toward her. "I didn't know if you wanted to eat or snack or what."

"Maybe a salad or appetizer." Gracie took the menu and laid it across her lap. "We found the Cantus exactly where you said. Wife and daughter are with us. Thank you. They're bringing Victor in this afternoon, and we're going to have a gabfest. Jackson will have food available, but I'll be too busy to eat much, if anything. The session will last a few hours, I expect. I may need to leave before they're finished."

"Excellent. Maybe we'll get a solid lead on the shooter."

"Fingers crossed." Gracie hoped so. "I have this feeling it's going to lead back to Jalapeno Cupcake."

"Like the feeling you had about moving the Cantu sisters?"

"Not as scary, but it never wavers. It's stronger than a cop hunch. What's going on with me, Nicky? I may have a brain tumor."

"No. You've always had these hunches and feelings. You usually just ignored them or reasoned them out. I have hunches—most pan out in some way. Those that don't usually make everything worse. You operate more on instinct. Like those baby turtles on the beach. They know to crawl to the surf. You pick up on something unseen that most of us can't sense unless it stares us in the face. You've exercised that instinct muscle, and it's grown stronger."

"Strong enough to make me think I'm crazy. That's how it feels."

"Go with it Gracie. See where it leads. Keep talking to me about it. I'll let you know if you're making a mistake."

"Promise?"

"I do."

"Good. I'm going to hold you to it. What's the plan of attack for you?"

"We're filing against Kim. Guess where her part-time jobs were?"

"Not a clue. Didn't she used to work in retail? I'd guess that."

"Good try. Different men's clubs."

Gracie had been inside almost every gentlemen's club in the city, mostly undercover. She couldn't imagine a worse job. "Was she a dancer?"

"Cocktail waitress. You can rest assured she made more than her pay deposits. Rayann said the real money was in tips, and untraceable for the most part. She's still digging—all the way back to the beginning of the marriage."

The server brought their beers.

Nick raised his.

Gracie clinked.

"Here's to us."

They drank.

"So when are they going to serve the papers?"

Gracie took another sip. She needed to nurse this one beer along.

"They'll be ready Friday, and they'll serve her Monday or Tuesday. She refused to give her attorney permission to accept them, so there's probably going to be a problem. Rayann said the servers she uses are good, so I shouldn't worry."

"Kim thought she would cash out squeaky clean with all her chips and half of yours."

"Not happening. Oh, and another thing."

"What?"

"Three years ago, she had another affair."

Gracie grabbed his hand. "Oh, Nicky, I'm so sorry."

"Yeah, well, that's old news now. I was more surprised that I wasn't surprised. After everything else."

"You sure you're all right?

"Yeah."

"How did Rayann learn that? Who was it? I hope no one you knew."

"Kim had a second Facebook page under a different name and her other *edgier* look."

"Holy shit. I don't think I really knew her at all."

"Neither did I, as I'm learning. I didn't know the woman she had the affair with, either. But I got the impression she was well off. After they broke up is when Kim went to work at the men's club."

Gracie took a minute to process that not-knowing part. The Kim he loved had never actually existed. She'd been someone different all along. Then to be cheated on with another woman... that had to hurt Nick's man pride. It certainly would've busted her own self-esteem down to zero.

All in all, Nick was dealing with it better than she would have. "How do people even know if they're ever really in love?" She shook her head.

"You take a leap of faith, Gracie. In some ways,

I'm a better man for having been with Kim."
   "And in others?"
   "I'll let you know when I'm not still mad as fuck."

CHAPTER 61

Gracie ended up eating a cup of shrimp gumbo. Nick ordered half an order of oysters. Then they shared a slice of key lime pie. People filtered in. Nick ordered a second beer but Gracie went with water.

"Are you off tomorrow, too?" She moved her shoulders like Ariana had showed her, trying to relax the muscles.

"I am. Seniority is finally paying off. I get two back-to-back every once in a while."

"Meet me after work and I'll catch you up."

"Will do. Any place in particular?"

"I'll let you know."

They parted a little after five-thirty. Rather than fight heavy rush-hour traffic, Gracie took the back streets to Bastion headquarters. She walked in at six. Jackson wasn't in his office, so she sat in a guest chair and closed her eyes.

"If it's not Sleeping Beauty!" Jackson's words were filled with laughter.

Gracie raised her lids. "Not asleep, but I would've been shortly. Are we on schedule?"

"The helicopter touched down a minute ago."

"Just so we're clear... I'd like to leave no later than nine, since I have to be back at the bakery at six-thirty in the morning."

"That's fine. I don't expect this to take long. Our man says Cantu is exhausted."

"Good. All the way around on that."

They chatted until Jackson's phone beeped. "He's here. I'm going to take him back to get a handprint. Give me five minutes, and then go let yourself into the bunker. I want you in there before we come in."

"Okay."

"We're going to give him five minutes before Maya goes to eat. As soon as she leaves, we'll hit him hard for five. That's when they'll bring in food. After that, I figure we have an hour at most before he flakes out. Detective Montgomery will be in attendance, too."

"Plan."

Gracie checked the clock before getting up and moving around. She did some squats and lunges to get the blood flowing. When five minutes were up, she walked down the hall to the bunker.

Maya ran up to her, wearing yellow shorts and a white tee that said *Girls Rule* in large red letters. "I remember you!"

"I remember you, too." Gracie patted the top of Maya's head. "That makes us a team. What should we call ourselves?"

"Girls, silly." Maya giggled.

Gracie giggled. She was silly thinking she could outwit a first grader. "That's right. Is your mommy here? Your aunts?"

"They're in their rooms. This is a fun place. Mommy says she's making herself pretty for Daddy. Do you know my daddy?"

"I've never met him before, but I know who he is."

Erin came down the hall. "There you are. I thought we were playing hide and seek?"

Maya giggled again. "We were. But Gracie came in and found me."

"So we're going to play that way. Then I get to tickle you!" Erin grabbed Maya and tickled her ribs until Maya finally squealed for her to stop. Erin gave her a hug. "Go see your mommy, squirt. I need to talk to Gracie."

"Okay." Maya ran off.

"You're really good with her. What's up?"

"I was on the phone earlier with my sergeant."

"Something Bastion needs to know?"

"The detectives have been talking to members of groups the Cantus belonged to. Asked them about newcomers, new people they've worked with, helped, whatever. Anyone outside the normal loop. And if any of those had bonded especially with Hector or Therese. They hadn't expected any results."

"That's usually the way."

"Isn't it? A few names came up, but one came up more than anyone else. At the American Legion. When they checked him out, they couldn't find him."

"What did the guy do? Or why was he involved?"

"He joined the post last fall. Involved. Helped with functions. He and Hector hit it off. Some thought he'd been to the Cantu house a few times."

"What name did he use? Bastion can run it to see if it's a known alias for anyone."

"Thomas Shoemaker."

Gracie tried not to show her surprise.

"You know him?"

Evidently, the cover-up didn't succeed. "That name has come up in a matter on our end." Gracie didn't have a problem letting Erin know that. But she was less sure about sharing more.

"Anything SAPD needs to be aware of?"

"We'll let Jackson make that decision. I don't believe there's a problem sharing, but since he was involved, it needs to be his call."

"Got it. I already asked for a full check on our end, but we don't move as fast as Bastion."

Carmen and Lupe came in with Maya, who was bouncing around with excitement. Lupe stayed close to her. Carmen's lips were pursed and the skin around her eyes was tight. She was still pissed. Gracie was glad she wasn't Victor. Big Sister wasn't going to be his ally tonight.

"Is Daddy here yet?"

Lupe took her hand. Her lips smiled at her niece, but the smile didn't reach her eyes. "It won't be long. Come sit in the big chair with me until he gets here. You can tell me a story."

"No, Aunt Lupe." Maya giggled. "You're supposed to tell *me* a story."

CHAPTER 62

A few minutes passed before Jessica came in wearing a white sundress with a blue outline of a flower on the right front of the skirt. Her face was bare except for lip gloss and mascara. Gracie sniffed a hint of vanilla. Her dark hair was slicked back into a swirled double bun. Large silver hoops hung from her ears. Gracie wanted to give her a fist bump for not complying with Victor's demands. Small steps were the start of great journeys. There was hope.

"You look pretty, Mommy." Maya bounced over and gave Jessica a hug.

"Thank you, *mija.*"

The door opened.

"Daddy!" Maya ran to Victor.

He scooped her up, wrapped her in a hug, and didn't let go—until she started squirming. He shifted her to one side.

Jessica walked toward him, and she quickly closed the gap. Maya hugged both of her parents.

While their reunion occurred, Erin approached Jackson. Gracie couldn't hear, but she knew when Erin told him about Shoemaker. He sought Gracie out, giving her a little nod and a thumbs up.

The door opened again and another Bastion agent entered—a woman Gracie didn't know. But Maya did. "Ashley! Look, my Daddy's home!"

"I see that, little one. Give him another kiss. You

and I are going to find your favorite dinner while Mr. Jackson talks to your mommy and daddy."

Maya kissed Victor's cheek and patted the other one. "I love you, Daddy. I'm glad you're here."

"I love you, too, Maya. Go eat dinner. I'll see you in a little bit." He stood Maya on the floor and immediately grabbed Jessica's hand, as if he believed he would sink if he didn't hold onto something. Or someone.

As soon as the door closed, Jackson spoke. "Let's all move to the table. We can squeeze in."

Gracie grabbed a barstool and positioned herself next to Jackson and directly across from Victor and Jessica. She didn't know if he needed a shave or if he normally wore the stubbled look. The part of his face she could see was drawn and pale, with heavy creases around his eyes. He still held onto Jessica's hand.

"Everyone knows the plan. I want all of us on the same page—that's why we're all here. The two people you don't know are Detective Montgomery with SAPD and Agent Hofner with Bastion."

Victor released Jessica's hand. She pulled it back and rested it on his forearm near his elbow.

Erin smiled and nodded. Gracie followed suit. "I want to hear your story, but not just yet. First I want to know if anyone knows a man by the name of Thomas Shoemaker."

Head shakes all the way around. Not one of them showed any distress at the mention of the name.

"Okay. Now I have one more thing to relay. On Sunday evening, Lupe received a death threat."

"What?" Victor pushed Jessica's hand away as his head snapped to his younger sister. "Is that why she's here?"

"It's why both your sisters are here. We believe the caller is the same man who murdered your parents."

Victor's face turned dark and twisted.

Jessica touched his arm, and again he pushed it away. "I'll kill that—"

"There's no need for profanity." Jackson ended Victor's outburst before it began. "We had them well-protected at Lupe's house. Out of an abundance of caution, we moved them where we were one-hundred percent certain they were safe."

Victor clenched and unclenched his jaw. Popped his knuckles.

"Mi amor—"

Victor glanced at her without smiling. "I'm all right."

Jackson waited a beat before continuing. "This afternoon, a couple of K-9 teams went out. Again, an abundance of caution. We like to cover all the bases when we can. Lupe, what they found were two explosive devices."

Victor ground his forehead with his fists. Lupe's eyes were huge and she stared straight at Carmen, who put a shaky arm around her shoulders.

Gracie couldn't think beyond that. Her stomach sank, and she felt lightheaded. That feeling—no, it had been more than a feeling. She had known just as she knew her name. Without thinking or reasoning, just knowing—she'd had to move the sisters out. While she hadn't known what would happen, never had she expected explosives.

Still... she had known. She wondered if Ariana knew, too. This couldn't be real, but it was. She had no explanation.

"One device was buried under a bush next to the gas meter—barely under the surface."

Gracie shivered. A bomb like that could've had the potential to take out the block.

Victor pushed back from the table and stood. "This man has torn my family apart. When I find him—"

"Sit down, Mr. Cantu." Jackson radiated calm. "We are going to find him. And he will pay."

He waited for Victor to sit before he went on. "The second device was found in a big bush that grows at the corner. That's how the K-9 officer described it. It was wrapped in a section of newspaper dated the same date your parents were killed. They believe it was meant to be found in a search. The other one was intended to go unnoticed."

Lupe walked to her brother and gave him a hug. "The important thing is we're all safe. This is a terrible experience, but we have to go beyond it to live again. We have to stay strong as a family. That's what Mom and Dad would want. I believe that's what God wants. Don't waste your energy on destructive thoughts. Use it to build lives up. Yours, Maya's, and Jessica's."

Gracie hadn't expected such a speech from Lupe. She rocked it. Gracie wouldn't have been able to do that.

Lupe still held tight to Victor. His shoulders shook. Several seconds later, he wiped his cheek with the back of his hand. "Thanks, runt. I needed that."

Jackson pressed a button on his phone and went to the door. He came back pushing a cart. "Chow time. Put these on the counter, Gracie. Everyone can help themselves. Drinks are in the fridge." He handed Gracie two trays filled with sandwiches, a third with cookies, and the last with individual plates of pickles, raw veggies, and ranch dip. Next came a basket with individual chip packages. The sisters were moving plates and a variety of drinks to the counter as fast as Gracie set the trays down.

Victor held out his hand to Jackson. "Thank you. For everything."

Jackson shook it. "Don't thank me yet. We haven't even scratched the surface. You may want to change your mind."

CHAPTER 63

Victor ate like Gracie's brothers. They attacked every meal as if they hadn't seen food in a week and would go another seven days before eating again.

Since she'd eaten gumbo only a couple of hours earlier, she grabbed a portion of veggies and a cookie. She munched on a carrot and wondered again about how she'd known to move Lupe and Carmen out of the house. Nothing like that had ever happened to her before. Or since. She hoped it never occurred again. Yet it had saved at least three lives, probably more, so it wasn't all bad. Even if it had caused her a mini freak-out.

She swiped the last of the ranch out of the container with a broccoli floret and popped it in her mouth. Victor no longer shoveled food, and Carmen was clearing the table. Gracie joined her.

Carmen shook her head. "Go sit down. I got this. Too much nervous energy. I'll be sitting down as soon as Victor finishes."

"He eats like my brothers."

"And my kids."

Gracie bagged the trash and put a clean bag in the container. Carmen put the few leftovers in the small refrigerator and picked up the cookies. "I'll have to hide these from Maya. She has a sweet tooth like my dad."

Gracie found a plastic container for the cookies.

"This will all be over soon."

"I know." Carmen wiped at an eye. "Victor, are you done yet?"

He nodded, and Gracie left Carmen to finish.

Jackson leaned over when she sat down. He used his hand to mask their mouths from view. "I told Erin already that the only Thomas Shoemaker we located in the area is an elderly male. We're widening our search and will find him, even if he isn't our man."

Carmen returned to the table, so Gracie just nodded that she understood.

Jackson leaned forward. "Okay, everyone, let's get back to our little chat. Victor, I know you're tired, so I'll keep this as brief as possible. We need to know what you know about your parents' murders."

Victor gave Jackson a deep nod. "I figured that was coming. Appreciate you letting us eat first. You're probably going to be disappointed because I don't know much."

"Every piece of the puzzle helps. Just tell your story. I'm going to record beginning now." He tapped some buttons on his phone, and Gracie knew that although he'd left his phone on the table as if it were doing all the work, he'd actually activated the cameras and microphones in the space.

Victor wiped his mouth with his fingers. "It started about six months ago, only I didn't realize it then. People sometimes call the store, or come in, and ask for La Luz—I suppose you know about all that."

"We do."

"Everyone knows to refer them to me—they think the people have me mixed up with someone else, and I'll deal with them. I do the same if they come in. Polite and out the door. I would never work with someone I don't know."

Jessica nodded.

"This particular man called. And called. I couldn't

shake him. After about three months, he quoted a price for the job. I knew for sure then he was bad news. Ten grand for helping one person cross? That's got trouble written all over it."

Even Jackson was taken aback at the figure. He cleared his throat. "I take it that was the opening bid."

"Yes. Over the course of about six or seven weeks, the payment increased to twenty. I figured him for a cartel bigwig or a terrorist. Perhaps I should've contacted the Border Patrol or the FBI, but then I would've had to explain about La Luz. No one would've believed me."

Carmen touched his arm. "These people believe you. You may still be in trouble about that, but they believe you."

"She's right," Jackson said. "What happened after the twenty thousand?"

"Threats. Torch the business. Torch my house. Turn me in. Violence against my wife. Sisters. Even Maya." His head drooped briefly. "None of the threats ever materialized. I banked on the threat against Mom and Dad being empty, too. That's all on me. I'll figure out how to make my peace with it. Somehow."

Jackson cleared his throat. "Get back to the thread, Mr. Cantu. The man was making threats."

Victor nodded. "After he made what turned out to be his last threat, he was quiet for almost a week. On Thursday, he called about the time we were closing. He said this was my last opportunity. Thirty thousand dollars. I told him to go do you-know-what with himself, hung up, and put the phone on the night pickup and recording." He clutched Jessica's hand.

"Late Friday night my cell rang. We were already in bed. There was no Caller ID. I answered. He said he told me this was my last chance and to go check on my parents. I got scared. He said he knew it would take me a while to get there because I thought I was too good to live in the old neighborhood anymore, and he would call me back in forty-five minutes."

"What then?"

"I tried calling them. No answer."

Gracie's gut churned. Victor must've been in a panic all the way across town—especially when they didn't answer the phone.

"Seemed as if I'd never get there. Rang the bell. Beat on the door. No answer. I couldn't hear the television, so I thought they must've gone to bed. That this was a wild goose chase. I let myself in. All the lights were off, and I used the mini-light on my key ring. I expected to see them snoozing in bed, and I didn't want to wake them up. But the bed was still made. They weren't there."

Sweat popped out on Gracie's palms, her face felt flushed, and she shivered.

"I thought he'd taken them, and I panicked. As I headed to the kitchen to get a bottle of water or soda or whatever they had to calm me down before he called, I flipped on the kitchen light."

CHAPTER 64

Gracie vaulted out of her chair. Pain cut through her body like a million strands of barbed wire being pulled by an invisible hand. She hobbled to the other side of the room, gritting her teeth to keep from screaming. Darkness surrounded her, pushed at her, tried to get inside. She turned in a circle, trying to find a peek of light. Nothing.

Then Victor's face loomed in front of hers—huge, and almost touching. She knew, in the same way she'd known about Lupe's house, that she was experiencing his pain. Then his face vanished, along with the darkness. The room returned. Everyone stared at her.

This can't be happening. I must have a brain tumor.

Erin appeared in front of her. Gracie hadn't seen her approach. "Are you all right?"

Her words drifted in, disjointed and muffled. They didn't make sense. *Maybe I'm having a stroke.*

"Gracie?" Erin touched her shoulder.

Her touch was electric. Gracie blinked. "What? Did you say something?"

"What happened? Are you okay?"

Am I? What do I tell her? Think, Gracie. "Yeah, I just needed to move. A cramp. I haven't had a charley horse like that in a long time." *I'm going to Hell for lying.* She rubbed her leg.

"Probably from too much standing." Jackson

patted the table top. "Walk around a minute, then come on back."

She nodded and circled the living room's perimeter. Ever logical, Jackson had found a reason for her fabricated ailment. After the second circle, she approached the table on the lookout for a sensory attack. Nothing. She sat.

Jackson looked at Victor. "Go ahead."

"So... I saw them. My parents. I didn't touch them. There was no way they could've been alive. I backed out of the room and turned off the light as I passed the switch. That's when he called me. He asked me if I liked what I saw—said it hadn't been much fun, it was too easy. Like shooting fish in a barrel, he said. I wanted to punch him."

It would be a long time before Gracie forgot the scene. She wanted to punch the shooter, too—whoever he was.

"He said if I didn't do the deed, Jessica and Maya were next. This time, I couldn't risk a bluff. I caved. I should've gone to the police, but by then I was too afraid." Victor's head dropped into his hands.

Gracie could relate to that. If he hadn't been raised to be La Luz, he would've gone to the police at the beginning. But if he hadn't been La Luz, there wouldn't have been a beginning. Like so many things in life, Victor's situation wasn't black or white. But the murder of his parents appeared to be.

Jessica rubbed the back of her husband's neck. "I knew the instant he came through the door something was wrong. He told me what he found before he broke down. It took several minutes before he got to the backstory. Then it was as if telling me all of that gave him a jumpstart. He told me his plan for keeping Maya and me safe. We started packing and were on the road thirty minutes later.

"He drove us to the lighting store and made sure

we were safe. Before he left, he said there would be no more La Luz. Not with him, not with any of his children—Maya or any that may come. And not with Carmen's or Lupe's or any of his cousins, either. He promised me that."

Victor nodded. "I'd been thinking about stopping for a while, what with all the surveillance these days. Drones, planes, choppers. Each time was more difficult. That night, I made the decision. Too late. I meant it then, and I still mean it now. No more."

"Thank you, Jessica." Jackson patted her hand. "Let's keep moving. Victor, how did this man refer to himself? What did he tell you to do?"

A lopsided smile appeared on Victor's face for half a second. "Tommy. He said I should just call him Tommy."

"Anything distinctive about his voice?"

"No. I recognized it after hearing it enough, so I never called him by name after. Unless it was absolutely necessary."

"What did he want you to do? Did it ever change?"

"Never. Until the end."

"What do you mean?"

"Each time we spoke, he told me all I had to do was meet a man at an old church in Chihuahua, bring him across the river, and deliver him to a pickup point. I told him it was too dangerous going all the way down to Chihuahua, but he said it had to be done that way."

"He didn't say which church?"

"Not until Friday night. It was a poor church near the airport—Capilla Santa Maria. Small, very old, and in disrepair. He gave me rough directions from downtown. And told me I had to pick up a package from a drugstore before I picked up the man. It was a small metal box. Flat. Rectangular. I was to open it and count the number of pieces inside—there should be twenty-three. If there weren't twenty-three, I was to abort. Return the way I came, and wait for instructions. They were all there, inside a black leather bag. I don't know what they were. Rocks of some kind. Cocaine, heroin maybe. Or some kind of stones. I don't know what they have in Mexico besides amethyst and turquoise."

Gracie and Jackson exchanged a glance. Victor wasn't lying about looking inside the box.

"This was the scariest part. I picked up the box in a *farmacia*. When I came out onto the street, there was shooting. Two men were running toward us. Someone was shooting at them. I jumped in the car and we were out of there."

"You say we. Who was with you? Your contact?"

"Contact? There's no contact. He's my cousin. Trained the same as me. I told him he didn't have to go, that this wasn't about family but something I was being forced to do. He wouldn't hear of it. The Cantus are a proud family. We stick together and stick by one another, no matter what. He reminded me of that."

Gracie had witnessed their *la familia*.

"Who's your cousin, Mr. Cantu? We need that information."

"He's a man of God. A priest. I won't give you his name, even if it means I go to prison."

CHAPTER 65

A *priest. Of course. Why didn't I think of that?* One of the few ways he could have relatively safe passage through cartel badlands. It didn't mean much else. He could still be on one or more payrolls. Or piss someone off and be killed without warning.

Gracie tuned back in. Jackson was asking Victor another question.

"... cousin have cartel contacts? Do you? It's perilous to travel in northern Mexico these days without protection." Jackson was persistent.

"I have no idea about him. None for me."

"You do this year after year. How can you not have contacts?"

"I don't do this often. You still don't understand. We've brought family and occasional friends across the border one way or another. Relatives on this side travel with us because they don't have or want a passport. It's easier for them. But now they're on their own. I'm finished."

"How do you do that if you don't travel over there?"

"We contact each other to set up trips and meet at the border. Whoever has people crosses the river and is met on the other side. If we both have someone or a group, we meet in the river. It's shallow there except during monsoon—usually so shallow we can walk across on large flat rocks and never get our feet wet. The only other time I've ever been to Chihuahua,

I was about eight. Remember, Carmen?"

She smiled. "I do. Family vacation, Cantu style. Lupe, you were too little to remember, but you were there, too."

How many times had Gracie heard she was too little to remember? At least a million.

Victor yawned. "Sorry. Long day."

"One more question, and I'll let you crash," Jackson said. "Tell us about the man and the handoff. I want his description, your thoughts about him, his personality, what he carried with him, things like that. I want to know the same thing about the person you handed him off to. And where that was done."

Victor grinned. "You sure know how to pack a lot into one question."

Jackson laughed and shrugged. "It's my job."

"He was about my height—I'm five-eleven. Dark hair, cut short—like half an inch on top—receding hairline on the sides." He used his hands to indicate the pattern. "Dark, hooded eyes. Straight nose. Muscular. Fit. He had no trouble with the climb. He had clean hands and nails. Early forties. He had a backpack. A large backpack, like a hiking one."

"Nationality?"

"Dunno. He barely spoke—when he did, he spoke English. No accent. He didn't move like any Latino I know. Beyond that?" Victor shrugged. "One-word answers to my questions if possible. Nothing volunteered on his own. He was self-contained. Had his own food, water."

Water weighed a little more than eight pounds a gallon. That would add up in a hurry.

"Former military?"

A lot of military lived in San Antonio. Victor would be accustomed to seeing them.

"Possibly. I didn't ask many questions, and he didn't volunteer any information. He had the right posture. I can usually pick them out when they come in the store."

"Could he have been Middle Eastern?"

"I don't think so, but I wouldn't swear to it."

DHS would consider that a non-answer. They'd question him an hour on this point alone.

"It was dark when we crossed back into Texas. We spent the night in the car to sleep. I slept a little. I don't know about him. We didn't talk. After sunrise, we stopped in Marfa for breakfast, and then I zigzagged over back roads to get to the meeting point. We were still early."

Gracie was pretty sure he was telling the truth to this point. Maybe not all of it, but nothing fabricated.

"I'd been asked what vehicle I'd be driving and then instructed to park in a certain area of a truck stop in Fort Stockton. And wait. I was told a man wearing a straw hat would come up and ask my passenger if he was Jose. When he did, the man I picked up said, 'Si, para el jefe'—for the boss."

"A code, you think?"

"For identification. Yeah. I knew to wait until the man returned to get the package. He was parked out of sight. It took a good five minutes. He took the box without opening it. I was told to leave immediately. I did. Couldn't tell you what happened after that."

"Describe the man in the straw hat."

"Looked like a West Texas rancher. Or plumber, or carpenter. Someone who worked with his hands. They were rough and weathered. Little scars scattered around. Western shirt, jeans, boots. Sunglasses. That's all I got."

#

Fifteen minutes later, Gracie and Erin sat in Jackson's office, waiting for him to come in. Gracie took another drink of water.

Erin was quiet.

Jackson entered. "Evening, ladies. What do you think?"

Gracie dove in. "I believe the sisters were honest with us. And possibly an eye-opening, character-building experience for Victor. I don't know how well his follow-through will be."

"Erin?"

"I agree with Gracie. How committed is he to stopping?"

Gracie wasn't sure if this was the right time to bring it up, but she was going for it. "One thing niggles at me a little. Can Bastion get financial background on him? From what I learned, he's all about building his business. And they have that new house. His cash needs are certainly elevated above mine."

"Your point?" Jackson tapped a pencil eraser against his desk.

"They live day-to-day quite frugally. Did he really have enough cash and credit for that house from his businesses and investment? Or could the money for it have been laundered through the businesses? Bottom line, I don't know if we know enough yet about Victor Cantu to know how trustworthy he is."

Erin nodded. "Good point. I hadn't made it to that road yet. I do wonder how truthful he was. When he started talking about Tommy, his left leg started bouncing. I could feel it under the table. I also want to know about the crimes he's committed."

Jackson twirled the pencil between his fingers. "Interesting. We'll also see what more we can learn from and about Mr. Cantu while he's available here. The Feds will deal with him."

"Are you going to hand him off tonight?"

"No. What happens is everyone gets a copy of our recording. Every possible agency—city, county, state, federal." Jackson put down the pencil. "They also receive a report from the lead Bastion agent—me, in this case. It's up to them to decide the outcome. They may choose to take him to trial or not. It's clear Cantu understood he was breaking the law. He expects to be charged. And yes, there's a financial package included in the report."

CHAPTER 66

It was just getting dark when Gracie pulled out of the parking garage. She called Nick, and he picked up on the third ring. Lots of noise was in the background. "Where are you?"

"On your patio. With a six-pack that's warming up."

"What?"

"And my tablet. I'm watching a Spurs game."

"Why?"

"Because they're going to the playoffs."

Men. "Why are you on my patio?"

"Because I still have your tracker. I figured it would be good if someone believed you were home early for a change. Besides, you may want it for going to work tomorrow. Yes! Three pointer."

Gracie shook her head. "I'll be there in ten."

She walked onto her patio in record time, and Nick handed her a beer from a full six pack. "Cheers." He held a half-full bottle of water.

"Yeah." She took a long swallow. "Best thing I've had all day."

She picked up the tracker from the table. "Be right back."

When she returned, she gave Nick a playful noogie—just enough to make him squirm. "Thanks for being a great partner."

"No worries. Want to talk?"

It took a beer and a half, but as she told him the full story, she finally got a little perspective on it. "So somebody with some serious cash—"

"And a serious in with somebody to know about those diamonds." Nick downed the last swallow of his beer.

"Exactly. Whoever it is wanted both the diamonds and the man brought in. I wonder which is more important to him. Or her."

"Her? The voice on the phone was male. Lupe said that." Nick leaned back and propped his feet on another chair.

Gracie got up and walked. "That man's a flunky— hired, I'm sure, to find and convince La Luz to take the smuggling job."

"And when he balked, the guy with the cash turned the screws."

"So the flunky was running out of options. It's possible the money man doesn't even know about the murders. Or if he knows, he didn't connect them to his deal. Or doesn't care."

"He needed the man before the diamonds." Nick stood up.

"Why do you say that?" Gracie sipped her beer. She'd been thinking the opposite.

"He started working in that direction first. The diamonds came later."

"Huh. You're right."

"I'm always right. Except when you are. I gotta go. Put the beer in the fridge and go to bed. Get some sleep. I'll see you tomorrow. If nothing else, we'll do lunch."

"Date." She was too tired to move. They smacked palms. "Drive safe."

Nick waved back while walking to his truck. It felt normal talking over a case. She'd told him everything, except for the incident about Victor's pain. Ariana would be back Saturday. She'd tell her about that one.

CHAPTER 67

Slate and Courtney were getting ready for bed. Sticking to his routine helped to keep his anxiety down. He brushed and flossed. Courtney rubbed moisturizer on her face. It could be any other night of the year instead of the night that would change his life.

"Courtney, did I tell you I have to go to San Antonio on Friday?"

"No. What for?"

"Our investment company bought into an office building last year."

"I remember you telling me that. Near the Alamo, right?"

"That's the one. We've been talking about some capital improvements. The architect is making a presentation, and then we'll talk numbers before going forward. It's Fiesta—you want to tag along?"

"No way. I'm a no-crowd shopper and sightseer. You know that. Plus, the girls get out early on Friday and we've planned a spa day. We'll all be pretty when you get home."

He gathered Courtney close. "You're beautiful every day. I'm a lucky man." He rubbed her back. Inside, he released a sigh. San Antonio held no secrets, but it would allow him time to relax after the tug of war his emotions had played with him this week. "The meeting's at ten, so I'll be leaving here at seven. Gives me extra time for traffic and to review some points I want to discuss. I'll probably be back here before you beautiful ladies get home."

"Maybe tomorrow you can help me get the patio ready for my book club on Saturday."

"Sure. Whatever you need. Do you have enough wine?"

"You can never have enough wine, but yeah. And goodies."

"Do you ever talk about books?"

"Sometimes."

"Let me go put it on my calendar so I don't forget." He wouldn't, but it provided an opportunity to check for messages and missed calls. Nothing.

He prayed for a happy surprise in the morning.

CHAPTER 68

Gracie wanted to wear her hip hugger holster, but she couldn't chance that Donovan wouldn't hug her. She checked her wardrobe and chose a multicolor flowered dress with a square neck and a dropped waist. What shoes? Her white canvas Mary Janes. After she dressed, she pulled her hair into the world's shortest-ever ponytail and adorned it with a couple of combs with glued-on silk flowers to keep some of the flyaways in place.

Donovan waited at the door for her, smiling. She smiled back.

"Good morning!"

"Same to you."

"I like your dress."

"Thanks. What's new?"

"Not much. Except I've been waiting for you like a teenager on prom night."

Gracie drew back her arm to punch him before she remembered Donovan was a real man—not Nick or one of her brothers. She relaxed her muscles and smiled. "You're sweet."

"FYI—Webb is a growling bear this morning. Give him a wide berth."

"Thanks for the heads up."

"Any time. Tessa says he gets like this every once in a while. She gives him some space and he's over it in a day or two."

Gracie hadn't given up on Truitt being the voice on the phone and the perpetrator of the Cantu murders. On her break, she'd check with Jackson to see if anything new had turned up on Shoemaker. Back at the counter, she turned away from Donovan as she tied her apron.

"I said Margarita *cookies*." Truitt's raised voice. "What are we going to do with more cupcakes? You do remember how to make cookies, right?" Loud, angry, and condescending.

"Yes, sir." Poor Maricelia.

Gracie wanted nothing more than to march in there and dare Truitt to speak that way to her. She busied herself with loading the display case to keep her mind off him. The customer parade began within minutes of Donovan unlocking the door.

The third customer, a regular, was leaving when Truitt exploded again. Donovan whipped off his apron and pounded into the kitchen.

"Truitt! My sister worked long and hard to make this bakery happen. I won't have you tear it down in one morning because you're in a bad mood. Raise your voice one more time and you're out of here for the day. Understand me?"

The kitchen was silent.

A customer entered, a woman wearing a flowered Fiesta hat.

Crap. Gracie wanted to eavesdrop. "Welcome to Jalapeno Cupcake. What can I get for you?"

"A jalapeno cupcake, of course."

"Of course."

The woman continued to babble.

Donovan returned and put on his apron while Gracie bagged the woman's order. She hadn't heard Webb's response, but he hadn't stormed out, so he must've apologized. The woman continued to rattle, and Donovan responded. Gracie placed the bag at

289

the register for him to ring up. A minute later, the customer was gone.

"I guess you heard that." Donovan's voice was soft as he angled his head toward the kitchen.

"Actually, no. I heard what you said about Tessa, but then the customer came in. She talked the whole time, so I didn't hear his response."

"He apologized to Maricelia and Natalie. And to me. He said he'd received some upsetting news this morning and would take care not to let it happen again."

"Did he say what? His family?"

"He didn't say. I don't believe his apology. He said the words, but he didn't look apologetic—his eyes remained hard and he didn't smile."

A line of customers came in, and they didn't get a chance to talk further.

CHAPTER 69

Slate woke up every two hours through the night and wasn't ready to get out of bed when his alarm went off. As he had during the night, he checked his phone. Still no message.

His phone beeped while he was shaving, and he nicked his jaw. "Dammit!"

As soon as he grabbed the styptic pencil, he checked the message.

Confirmation arriving soon.

That should mean the deed was done.

He went to the kitchen. A note was propped against the coffeemaker.

Slate—

I have a dental appointment. Forgot to tell you. Will be home by nine.

Luv U!

He poured his coffee, took it with him into his office, and turned on the television. While the voices of the inane morning show hosts droned in the background, he checked the status of his portfolio.

The alert signal beeped, and the scene switched to the newsroom. Slate increased the volume.

"Good morning, ladies and gentlemen. This is Bob McMullen in the newsroom. We've just received word that longtime Llano County rancher Joshua Henly Brackett was found dead this morning in his home on the Rocky River Ranch. No word yet as to the cause

of Mr. Brackett's death. Tune in to News at Noon for updates on this breaking story."

Slate turned off the television.

It was done.

The triumph he'd expected to feel didn't tip its hat in his direction. He felt nothing. No happiness. Or sadness. His mood was no different than if he'd checked off an item on his to do list.

He needed to make the payments. He went to his personal safe and put in the combination, happy Courtney was out. If she ever found it, she would throw a world class bitch fit. He wouldn't just be sleeping in the guestroom, he'd need to find a hotel room. Maybe a new wife. That's why he'd been extra careful to conceal its location when he'd had it installed early in their marriage.

After retrieving his satellite phone, he placed a call to the Cayman Islands. Everything was done automatically, so he pressed in the account number, his PIN, and the safe word. Last came the amount. It was large, but worth every cent.

A second call went to a different bank, this one in the Bahamas. He made two transfers, the first to a bank in Sweetwater and the second to an account in Uruguay.

With the third call, he ordered a special delivery of a case of Dos Equis before returning the phone to his safe and relocking it. *Never hurts to cover all the bases.* He then used his regular phone to message the recipients. The first message was *Regards.* The second was *Confirmation received.*

CHAPTER 70

On her break, Gracie called Jackson. "What's news at your end?"

"DHS is watching the Victor Cantu interview now. I'm sure they'll want to conduct their own, but they'll do it here. He won't leave with them. They want to rattle his cage and see what happens after we turn him loose."

"Good."

"Cantu's agreed to cooperate fully. I'd like to eavesdrop, but while it's possible, it's not ethical in this instance."

"I get it." Gracie sipped her water.

"Earlier I made a call to my own DHS contact—and not Paulina."

Gracie had learned early that Jackson had friends in high and low places. His extensive network allowed for back channel negotiations and workarounds that would've been otherwise unavailable.

"They're requesting he be put on a long leash to see where he goes, who he sees, what he does. He won't be charged with anything at this point. They're telling him the case is still under investigation, but at this time, he's free to go."

"What if the shooter's still at large?"

"If SAPD nabs the shooter, the Cantus will be out of here immediately. Our deadline is Saturday morning. If there's no news of the shooter by then, our psychologists will begin transitioning them for release on Sunday afternoon. The current consensus is the shooter himself won't be a problem. His job is done and Victor Cantu has delivered the payload."

"You think there's someone else behind it." Her words were a statement, not a question. She was glad to hear Jackson hint at her own conclusion.

"Yes, and so does Homeland. I wasn't leaning in that direction until Victor confirmed the diamonds. When he leaves Bastion, he will have eyes on him twenty-four/seven."

"I agree. Regardless of what DHS said." Gracie started back to the bakery.

"Erin has been in touch with her supervisors. Everyone involved knows the same things we know."

"Give them a day and somebody won't be happy."

"I never expect anything different. Hang on a sec."

Gracie heard him shuffling papers. Then a voice. Someone must have walked in.

"Okay, I'm back. I take it nothing noteworthy has arrived yet at the bakery."

"Not when I left. Only thing different was Webb Truitt was in a foul mood."

"Two more days after today. Tough it out."

"What's happening with the Shoemaker search?"

"No news forthcoming yet. I'll keep you posted."

When Gracie approached the bakery, a delivery truck stood out front. The driver jumped out with another box from Avenue Amarillo. She held the door for him. Inside, there were no customers. Donovan was checking his phone.

He looked up. "Back already?"

"It's nice outside. I wanted to run away and play hooky."

Gracie donned her apron while Donovan signed for the box.

"How often do you order supplies?"

"At least once a week. We don't have a lot of storage space, so it seems as if we're always running out of one thing or another."

"Ordering so often would make me crazy." She was fishing, since the boxes were the only deliveries she'd seen all week, but she wasn't even getting a nibble.

"Webb does most of it. I tell him if I need anything, but Tessa stocked us up out here for the most part before she left."

"How's Emily?"

Donovan put his phone away. "Sweetest baby ever. Still. At least for the next thirteen years. Once she hits puberty, all bets are off. If she'd just sleep longer at a time, she'd be perfect."

CHAPTER 71

Courtney came in the back door just as Slate put the mayonnaise in the fridge. She kissed his cheek. "Egg sandwich?"

"My specialty. Want one? I'll make another."

She shook her head. "I want to enjoy my clean teeth until lunch."

He took a bite of his sandwich.

"Did you hear the news about Joshua Brackett?"

Slate almost choked.

"You okay?"

He nodded.

Courtney got him a glass of water. "He died last night. Everybody at the dentist's office was talking about it. His housekeeper found him this morning."

"What happened?"

"Nobody knows. He died in his sleep. At least that's what people say. Tina found him in bed with his pajamas on." Courtney started emptying the dishwasher.

"Tina Loomis still works for him?"

"Yeah. Put her kids through college. Joshua was good to her."

"Huh." Slate shook his head. "How old was he?"

"He must be close to eighty." Courtney stopped and looked out the window. "I remember Tina talking about his seventy-fifth birthday a few years ago. You know, we never did know him too well, and his ranch is right next to ours. When did he buy that property?"

"I was just a kid. He didn't move in right away. Dad complained a lot—called him a Yankee that didn't know a bull from a heifer, much less how to run a ranch. It may have been true, but he hired good people to operate it for him."

"Where was he from?" She continued putting glasses in the cabinet above the dishwasher.

"Colorado, I'm almost sure. Grew up on a farm. He hated cold weather." Slate finished his sandwich.

"Somebody said they heard he fell down the stairs, but someone else had heard he killed himself."

Slate was the only neighbor who knew neither of those was true. He didn't know how Joshua Brackett died, but he knew the death wasn't an accident or a suicide. Far from it.

CHAPTER 72

Gracie was loading up the cookie displays when Truitt left at the end of his shift. He didn't say anything to anyone, but whistled when he walked through. She didn't know if that was good or if she should be worried. It didn't matter if she should be or not—she was.

The rest of her shift went without a hitch. She took off her apron and found Donovan in the supply closet, emptying the box. "See you tomorrow."

His hands were filled with clear bags of Jalapeno Cupcake tees—black, white, pink, yellow, blue, sage, teal, and coral. "Okay."

"Those are cute."

"Take one. My treat. We're all going to start wearing them when Tessa comes back. Then they'll go on sale."

"You may sell as many those as you do the real thing. I'm going to buy a couple tomorrow if you'll let me be your first customer."

"Sure."

"I just need to decide what colors I want."

On her way to meet Nick at The Cove, she called Jackson to tell him about the delivery. She got his voicemail and left a message. When she arrived, she found Nick at a shaded patio table. He'd already ordered—fish tacos for him and a lamb burger for her. With two iced teas. They used to eat here when they worked homicide, and they ate the same food every time.

She hadn't been seated for even a minute before their food arrived. "Great timing, Nick."

"Don't get used to it." He picked up a taco.

It was like old times. She smiled. "I hope this burger is as good as it used to be."

Between bites, Nick said, "You still have an affair with food."

She nodded as she swallowed. "Still yummy. And spicy." She reached for her tea. Definitely old times. Work, food, friends. She was in her comfort zone. Even a mockingbird sang in a nearby tree—one of her favorite sounds. The afternoon was perfect.

She finished most of her burger and about half the fries before leaning back and closing her eyes. "It's so nice just to sit here and relax in the sun."

"Don't sit like that too long. You're too fair."

"I hate that. I've always wanted a tan."

"What are you doing this afternoon?"

"Ab-so-lute-ly nothing. I can't wait. Maybe a nap." She closed her eyes.

Nick laughed. "Now I know you're tired. *Siesta* isn't part of your vocabulary."

"I know. By the time I get home, I'll be wide awake. It's the cat syndrome—a full stomach, a little breeze, and a spot of sunshine. I want to purr." She opened her eyes and stretched. "What about you?"

"Going to start packing. I have to get the house ready to put on the market. The Realtor came over and looked at it."

"Did you list it already?"

"No. Rayann is working on tying up loose ends. The paperwork is already done. I read it and signed it. Much of what she found about Kim, I didn't know— didn't even suspect until recently... " He shook his head.

"Maybe Rayann used Bastion."

"Good possibility. She's filed everything and arranged for the papers to be served tonight. Tomorrow, if necessary—however long it takes for her process server to find her. She won't be expecting anything, so she shouldn't be hiding or using any evasive tactics."

"If the process server can't find her, have them call me. I'll have Bastion see if they can. They can come close just with her number. If I call and she answers, they can get closer."

"I'll pass that along to Rayann and give her your number. Teamwork. I like it. Anyway, as soon as she learns Kim has been served, she's going to talk to Kim's attorney. She knows him and thinks that with all the material we have, we'll be able to agree out of court and present a done deal to the judge."

"Hope she's right. Where are you going to move when it sells? I haven't rented the apartment yet, but I'm getting pressure. Aunt Elise and Mom have been talking, and someone's coming to look tomorrow."

Nick laid his hand on top of hers. "No offense, Gracie, and you know I love you... but I don't want to live right behind you."

Gracie laughed and patted his cheek. "None taken. I get it. You're my family as much as my blood siblings. You notice I don't live close to them either. Just remember I offered."

Her phone rang. "It's Jackson."

Nick got up.

"Stay." She grabbed his wrist and pulled him back to his chair. "I'm going to share with you anyway, so this way it's quicker."

She answered the call. "News?"

"Webb Truitt."

"I knew it!"

"Find Donovan Beck. Tell him who you are. Tell him

Truitt's a person of interest in an ongoing investigation and he, his sister, and her family may be in danger. I sent agents to round up the other two employees. They'll bring them in here for the afternoon to be on the safe side. Also the bakery owner's husband. He happens to work in this building."

"Good. Truitt's the type to lash out at whoever's handy when his world breaks apart."

"I talked with Sergeant Salazar, sent her what we have. She's getting a warrant—may have it already."

"Okay. What do you want me to do with Donovan and his family?"

"Bring them here. I think SAPD will have Truitt in custody before nightfall, but the sister and her family will have a bunker reserved. Just in case."

"What about Natalie and Maricelia and Donovan—in case Truitt's not apprehended?"

"We have options."

Options probably meant somebody's office. Or the conference room. That was another reason she liked Bastion. They worked projects from the people end and had the ability to protect potential victims before the perpetrator could act. In some cases, they also intervened with the potential perpetrator. Not all interventions were successful, but some were better than none.

Gracie filled Nick in and once again put him in charge of her tracking device. Instead of going home for the relaxing afternoon she'd planned, she drove back to Jalapeno Cupcake. She parked in her usual spot and hurried to the bakery. The door was locked.

She rapped on the glass, hoping Donovan was still inside. "Be here, be here." She rapped again.

301

CHAPTER 73

A few seconds later, Donovan came from the direction of the closet. When he saw her, he smiled and unlocked the door. "This is a happy surprise. I didn't expect to see you until tomorrow. Did you miss me?"

"Of course." She gave him a quick smile. "But I need to talk to you. Is there someplace we can sit?"

He locked the door. "The kitchen."

She followed him. A case of Dos Equis beer sat on the long center table. *This must be the delivery.* An envelope taped to the cardboard box was addressed to Webb Truitt. Under his name were the words *You Da Man!* Had someone identified him as the shooter? The person who had the diamonds brought across the border?

Donovan pulled two rolling stools from under a set of wall shelves and rolled them to the long center table. "Your wish is my command, m'lady."

"Thanks. First, tell me about the beer." Gracie sat and inclined her head toward the box.

"Someone brought it a few minutes before I closed up."

"A delivery service?"

"No. They weren't carrying any paperwork and I didn't have to sign anything."

"Man or woman?"

"A woman. Attractive. She rolled it in on one of

those little carts like sales reps use."

Gracie needed to talk to Jackson. "Remember the other day I told you that I was going to work for an international consulting firm?"

"I remember. Change your mind?"

"No. But what I told you wasn't the exact truth."

"Okay."

She took a deep breath. "I'm actually already employed by the organization, and while we do work in a global capacity, most of our work is done within the U.S. borders."

Donovan stared at her, so she went on. "I'm here this week because I'm on assignment."

"At the bakery?" Small frown lines appeared between his brows.

She nodded. "The firm is a law enforcement consultancy. We were retained by an agency to be here as an extra pair of eyes in response to intel they received." She kept her gaze on Donovan as she pulled out her Bastion ID, turning it so he could see.

He looked at it for several seconds. "You're good at the job. I never suspected you were anyone other than who you said. Is Gracie your real name?"

"Everything I've told you about myself, personally, is true. I'm Gracie Hofner, I have a whole passel of siblings, I'm not in a relationship, and I find myself attracted to you."

He smiled. "Okay. Why are you telling me this? Are you leaving?"

"Saturday will be my last day. Consider that bit of news an off-the-record heads up. You don't need to do anything. Monday morning, a real temp will show up. She won't know anything about me."

He nodded.

"The reason I'm telling you now is because there's a possibility you, your sister, and her family may be in danger."

"What? Why?"

"Webb Truitt is a person of interest in an ongoing investigation. He's at large. We're acting out of an abundance of caution. I'm authorized to take you to our offices, where you'll be kept safe until Truitt is in SAPD custody. Other agents are rounding up everyone from your family and the bakery."

Donovan blinked several times in a row, then paced a couple of steps in each direction before stopping in front of her. "Truitt?"

"Yes. I don't want to frighten you, and I'm not authorized to divulge information, but please believe me when I say it's possible he's armed and extremely dangerous."

"I'm still having a hard time about Truitt. But sure, I believe you."

"Good. I need to make a phone call before we go." She called Jackson. When he answered, she said, "I think it's here."

"Back up. Start at the beginning."

"I'm at the bakery. I'm certain the delivery is here."

"What is it?"

"A case of Dos Equis."

"X marks the spot? The person?"

"Don't know. But he is the most interesting man for us right now." She paused, but not long enough to give Jackson time to say anything. "There's an envelope attached with Webb Truitt's name on it. Under his name, it says *You Da Man!*"

"Open it."

"A beer?"

"Hofner."

Gracie smiled. "Oh, the envelope. I knew that. Hold on. I'll read it to you. It's not sealed. I'm pulling the contents out and leaving the envelope taped to the beer box. A thick card, writing on one side only. Not really writing. Printing. Like block printing."

"Okay. Read it."

"'Thank you for your faithful assistance. This will be our last communication.'"

"Sounds like Truitt just got thrown under the bus."

"That's what I think, too."

"Leave the beer in place. If we don't find him today, we'll watch the bakery overnight, along with the PD. They'll pick him up if he shows. Or wherever they find him. He'd be a fool to show up there, but you never know. Get on back here with Beck."

She hung up. "We need to leave now. Where are you parked?"

"In the alley."

"Do you go out the back?"

"Yes."

"Okay. Do whatever you do in the front to lock up, and I'll put this card back in the envelope. The beer stays here. Bastion or the police will pick it up at some point. You can move it to bake, of course."

"Good."

"You can take me to my Jeep and leave your car in that lot. I'll take you to our offices. Bastion will send someone to retrieve your car."

"I'll be just a minute. Lock-up is quick."

CHAPTER 74

Donovan drove a dark gray 4Runner. She climbed in and buckled up. "I'm in the next block in a parking lot."

Gracie directed him to the lot and her Cherokee, backed into the first space to the right of the entrance. The pay box stood to the left. The lot took up half of the block, with the other half occupied by a building. A mural of the Riverwalk area faced the lot. Vehicles filled most spaces.

"I see some spaces over there near the corner." She pointed with her right hand. "Let me out, and I'll drive over and pick you up."

Donovan's fingers tapped the steering wheel.

She touched his arm. "I know you're worried about your sister. She'll be all right. We're good at what we do."

Donovan nodded, but he didn't look convinced.

Gracie got out and walked to her Jeep as Donovan drove off. She got in, buckled up, and started the engine. As she put the transmission in drive, something cold and hard touched the back of her neck. She froze.

"Hello, Gracie."

Her stomach muscles tightened and sweat popped out on her palms. The voice belonged to Webb Truitt.

"Hey, Truitt. What's up?" She'd trained for this—she took a deep breath. *Don't panic.*

"Cut the crap. You didn't know I knew what you drove. I've been following you all over town with a tracking device. You didn't even know."

And you don't even know I knew. "So what do you want?"

"I need you to be a road dog and drive me to Houston."

"Not happening." She picked her target. All she had to do was wait for the right time.

"You may want to rethink that."

"Take my Jeep. Go. But leave me out of it."

"You don't even understand, do you?"

"Understand what?"

"I don't know exactly who you are, little lady, but I sure as hell know—"

Gracie stomped the accelerator.

The high-performance engine jumped to life. She aimed straight for the black Chevy Tahoe parked in front of the Torch of Friendship on the mural. And hoped she cleared the silver Honda at the end of the next row.

Nobody told her this part would be in slow-motion. Outside, the parked cars flew by, but in her mind, an hour had passed and they were still moving through molasses. Behind her, a thud and the huff of air expelled from Truitt's lungs when the G-force slammed him into the seatback. They had to reach the Tahoe before he overcame it.

What if the air bag doesn't work?

CHAPTER 75

Gracie opened her eyes. Where was she? Blood. She touched her face. Blood on her fingers. Again. Nosebleed. *Crap! Truitt!*

She sat up, pinching her nose with her left hand to stop the bleeding and unhooking her seatbelt with her right.

An unconscious Truitt sprawled half across the console. She didn't see his gun.

Someone banged on the driver's window. She reached into her thigh holster and pulled out her cuffs. After setting them on the dash, she worked one of Truitt's hands behind his back and attached a cuff. She reached across him for the other arm. A drop of blood fell from her nose and landed on the back of his shirt.

Banging on the window continued. Truitt stirred. She tried pulling on his other arm, but from the position she was in, she couldn't move it from under his body. He moved again.

She abandoned her efforts and pulled her Glock, pressing it to Truitt's neck as he'd done to hers just minutes before. "Don't even try it."

He stilled. A second drop of her blood joined the first. She pinched her nose again.

The driver's door opened.

"Gun!" Gracie hoped whoever had opened her door wasn't an idiot. "Get back. Gun!"

"Gracie, it's me. Donovan."

"Call 911. Tell them Bastion agent needs assistance. Go back to your car first."

"I'm calling now, but I'm walking back, too."

When Donovan moved away from the car, she turned her attention back to Truitt. "Truitt, can you hear me?"

"Yeah." His voice was muffled.

"You made me wreck my car."

"This hunk of metal? That's no loss."

"The insurance people will total it. I'll have to spend time looking for something else. You know anything about cars?"

"Not much."

"You're probably not going to be driving very much anyway where you'll be going."

"I have a cramp. I need to move."

She yanked his arm higher. "I don't care. Move and you're dead."

Where was a patrol unit? There should've been a dozen of them buzzing around here by now. This area bulged with tourists year-round, and SAPD kept it in a tight grip.

"Police. Drop the gun."

She hadn't heard a siren. What the hell? "Move to the passenger side where I can see you."

"I said drop the gun, ma'am."

"My name is Gracie Hofner. I'm the Bastion agent. My ID is in my thigh holster, but don't you dare touch me. This man is Webb Truitt. SAPD is looking for him. He has a gun, but his right arm is pinned beneath him on the other side. I have one cuff on his left arm." Blood dripped from her nose onto Truitt's shirt again. "Truitt, you better not have made me break my nose, too."

"Go fuck yourself."

Two seconds later, a patrol officer wearing a

bike helmet looked in the passenger window. Sirens sounded close by.

Officer Bike Helmet said, "Positive on the cuff and pinned arm."

Gracie risked a glance at him. "You have a partner standing behind me?"

"Yes, ma'am. He called it in. We got an affirmative on Truitt."

"You hear all that, Webb? You're going down."

The back driver-side door opened. "Gun's on the floorboard back here." The officer's voice was strained.

"Good news, but I can't be sure he has only one. Can the two of you get in here and free his arm?"

The previously unseen officer appeared on the front floorboard. "I'm here. My partner knows what to do. He'll be coming in the rear passenger door now."

The other officer came in head first and inspected the situation with Truitt's right arm.

"I'm snaking in under you from the floor." The officer behind her bumped her hip. "Be gentle."

"That's no fun."

He snorted. "Okay, I have hands on his arm. Raise up as far as you can."

The bike officer's gloved hand appeared right below hers. "Okay, I've got him. You can back out. I'll take his left arm."

She nodded and backed out over him. When her feet hit the pavement, she returned her Glock to her holster.

Donovan stood on the sidewalk, a look of disbelief on his face. A small crowd had gathered around him.

Two patrol cruisers pulled up. One of the officers offered her some tissues and a wrapped wipe. "Are you all right? Do you need to go to the hospital?"

"I'm fine. Just a bloody nose. It's the only thing about me that's delicate." Three officers escorted Truitt, fully cuffed, from her Jeep. "Excuse me."

She walked to the bike officers, checking on her nose—just to be sure. No pain, and everything was solid. "You guys were great. Thanks for getting here quickly."

"It's what we do. Your handbag is on the floorboard. Make sure everything's in there before they leave with the suspect. We didn't find anything on him, though, other than wallet and keys. I already told the Patrol to hold up."

"What about a gun? Did he have another one?"

"No. He was clean. Just the one. It's bagged."

"I'll check my purse. Give me a minute." It was still closed and nothing was on the floor. All the same, she unzipped it and checked. "I'm good. Thanks again."

Both officers waved. One stopped at the patrol unit holding Truitt, and a few seconds later, it pulled out.

Another officer approached. "We've called for a tow. Where do you want them to take it?"

She gave them the name of a Jeep dealer. "Will you do me a favor?"

"Sure."

"Get in touch with Detective Nicholas Rivera at SARIC. Wait." She fished out a card from her holster. "Can you write his number on here? I don't have a pen."

He nodded, and she gave him Nick's number. "Tell him we got the shooter, and I'll call him later. He's off today."

"Sure thing. I'll go do this right now and get someone over here to get your insurance information."

"Thanks. I have to call my boss."

"Gotta keep them all in the loop."

As soon as he left, Gracie called Jackson. The call rolled to his voicemail and she left a brief message. He was probably talking to his PD contact and already knew. She disconnected and searched a small crowd for Donovan.

She found him and waved for him to join her. He jogged over and placed his hands on her shoulders. "Are you all right? What were you thinking?"

"It's just a bloody nose. I get them all the time. What I was thinking was I'd be damned if I'd go out on Truitt's terms."

"You wrecked your car. And another one. You could've killed yourself." He explored her face with his eyes and his hands, brushing her hair back from her face.

"If I hadn't wrecked, Truitt would've killed me. Plain and simple. I had a much better chance at survival by doing what I did. I was buckled in, had an airbag, and knew how my engine would perform. I wasn't going to die. This is something we train for."

"Wouldn't you rather work in a bakery? Or," he smiled, "sell insurance? I couldn't believe my eyes."

She touched his cheek with her palm. "No offense, but no. I love my job."

"I can see that."

Gracie grabbed his hand. "Follow me to my Jeep and stand behind me so the officers can't see what I'm doing."

"What?"

"Just do what I tell you to do."

"Am I breaking the law?"

"Not if you stop asking questions. Good. Just stand right there. Don't move. Tell me if one of them starts over this way."

Gracie bent down by the front driver's wheel well. A few seconds later, she stood up and dropped the tracker into her purse. "Okay. Thanks."

Donovan searched her face. "What did you do?"

"Do you really want to know?"

He frowned. "Not if you don't want to tell me."

"Good. After the tow truck takes my car, I can

leave. Will you wait and take me home?"

CHAPTER 76

The officer she'd spoken with earlier returned, and Donovan stepped back. "Detective Rivera said to tell you maybe you need a refresher driving course."

Gracie laughed. "He would. Thanks."

The officer had also located and notified the owner of the Tahoe, who was on his way to the parking lot. It didn't take him long. Gracie gave him her insurance information. Even though he understood the reason she'd wrecked his vehicle, he wasn't happy about it. Gracie wouldn't have been happy, either, and she was glad her Jeep was on Bastion's policy and not a personal one.

After the tow trucks left with both vehicles, Gracie thanked the officers and walked with Donovan to his car. His earlier nervousness had passed, and she didn't worry about their safety with him behind the wheel.

He turned toward her. "Which way?"

"Left at the light, then left again at the next street so you're going south. Just keep going. It's going to turn into Lasoya and then South Alamo Street. Cross Cesar Chavez and keep going. I'll let you know when we get closer. Takes about ten minutes."

"I'll get you home safe and sound."

"Oh. This is Thursday, right?"

"Yes."

"I forgot I have to go water Fiona and Isabella."

"What?"

"My friend's on a cruise, and I'm watering her ferns. Turn at this light. To the right. I'll direct you."

Isabella had drooped a little, but she perked right up with the water. And a little pep talk. "Your mama will be back to give you your next drink, but after she's home, I'll be back to visit. So behave. I've got my eyes on you, missy."

As previously, Gracie checked Ariana's windows and doors before getting back in the car. She gave Donovan directions and retrieved her phone from her holster. Jackson still hadn't called her back. Something must be heating up with another agent someplace else. "I need to call the insurance company and my boss. Do you mind if I get started?"

"Go ahead."

The insurance company was easy. Plus, they set up the rental and told her where to go to pick it up. When she finished, they were entering her neighborhood. "Turn left at the next light."

She'd get Nick to take her to pick it up. If he was too busy, she'd ask her neighbor, Josie. Payment for all the free beer bottles.

"I can take you to pick up your rental."

They turned onto her street.

"Did you read my mind? I was just thinking I'd ask Nick or my neighbor. I need to clean up. It'll take a while, and your sister needs you."

"No, I didn't read your mind. I just listened to you talk. You need someone right now, too. I'm here, and I'm offering. Besides, I need a break from baby duty."

Gracie giggled at the real reason he was offering. "Thanks. I accept. Turn left at the next street. My house is on the corner, and the driveway is the first one on the right."

Donovan parked, and they got out.

With the first step, Gracie moaned.

"Are you okay?"

"I feel like I've been in a fight. I need a hot shower. Come on in."

They walked into the kitchen. "Make yourself at home. TV's over there. A little food's in the fridge." She waved in both directions. "Beer and water. I haven't been to the store in a couple of weeks. Take a nap if you want. The sofa sleeps good. I'm going to be about an hour by the time I make my calls and re-energize myself under the shower."

"Don't worry about me, Gracie. I'll be fine. If I don't hear from you in an hour, I'll come checking."

"Knock first."

CHAPTER 77

Gracie propped herself on her bed against the pillows and called Jackson.

"Where are you? Are you okay?"

"At home, and I'm fine."

"I got your message, and Neva Salazar called me. Good work. I've been tied up with another project."

"No problem. I'm going to have to get a new Jeep."

"My personal belief is that's a good thing."

"I loved my Jeep. Of course, the insurance company hasn't made a decision yet, but I feel certain they'll total it. I have a rental."

"It's time for you to move on."

"The real reason I called you again was to let you know Truitt called me out for not realizing he put a tracking device on my Jeep. So we don't have to wonder any more why that was on there. I took it off. Do you want me to bring it in?"

"Yeah, the DA's office will want it. Or the Feds. You can bring it Monday, and I'll hold it."

"Figured as much. Do I still report for work at the bakery tomorrow and Saturday?"

"The Rangers want to give it a couple of days to see if anyone comes looking."

"Okay. Donovan Beck saw the whole event. Good thing I'd told him earlier who I am and sort of what I do. He saw Truitt in cuffs. I haven't told him anything yet other than Truitt would've killed me if I hadn't banged him up a little. If he asks for more, I plan to stick with my standard line about not being authorized to talk about anything. Does that fly for you?"

"Yes. When you come in on Monday, you can meet with one of our attorneys. If anyone brings it up before then, you can confirm, but that's all. I've seen you handle this kind of thing before, so I'm not worried. You're a natural."

"What about the Cantus?"

"They'll remain here until Truitt's formally charged. Maybe longer, depending on his bail situation. I don't look for that until Monday morning. I changed my mind on releasing them immediately after the Rangers said they wanted to watch for a few days."

#

Gracie still had one foot in the shower when her phone rang. It was Nick. She punched the button. "Hey, you got my message."

"Why didn't you call me back?"

"I just got out of the shower. You were next on the list. You know how it is."

"Yeah, I'm razzing you. The patrol said you got the shooter and you were okay. Who was it?"

Gracie filled him in.

"Good God, girl. You could've done yourself in."

"Nah. Not a chance. But I'm going to have to get a new car."

"Poor baby. Get something that looks like it's from this century."

"I loved my car."

They talked for a few more minutes and agreed to try to meet for lunch one day next week.

She put on a little pink lip gloss and combed through her hair to let it dry naturally. If Donovan didn't like the way she presented herself ninety percent of the time, now was the time to find out.

Wanting something soft, Gracie dug through her

closet for a pair of loose gray sweatpants. She'd have to wear her hip hugger, though. Her clip-on holster would weigh down the elastic waist. Donovan would have to deal. A pair of running shoes. And a faded purple tee that read *Runs With Scissors.*

CHAPTER 78

Donovan was switching channels when she came in. He turned the television off. "You look comfortable."

"This is the real me."

"I like." He walked to her and pulled her to him, bumping against her hip hugger. "What's going on?"

She stepped back. "That's the real me, too. It's a hip hugger concealed holster. Even though Bastion isn't a law enforcement agency, our work requires me to be armed at all times. Showers and sleeping excepted. But my Glock is always close by, even then. I want to be as upfront with you as possible."

"You're much more complex than I am. I like you, but you may need to catch me up from time to time."

"Let's just see where this goes, okay?"

"Fine by me. Are you ready?"

"Would you like to go to dinner afterward? My treat. I need some real food in my belly, and I'm not cooking."

"Sure, only I'm paying. I was going to suggest dinner anyway."

"You decide where, so I don't have to think. As long as I can wear what I have on, I'm happy. But I want to pay."

#

She got her rental, a white Ford Escape. It would do. They decided Donovan would follow her home and they would go to dinner in his car.

He drove them to a little Greek café near his sister's house. Inside, eight tables, centered by cobalt blue candle holders filled the tiny space. Only two others were occupied. Framed travel posters of the Greek Islands hung on white walls. Greek folk music played in the background.

The waiter, who she assumed was the owner based on his cordiality and accent, showed them to a table in the corner and lit the candle. The setting was romantic, and Gracie relaxed right away.

Donovan ordered a bottle of white wine. She never drank white wine, but tonight it seemed like the right thing to do. While they waited for their roasted chicken and potatoes, she took his hand. "I want to thank you for not asking me about Truitt."

"I assumed he was connected to another case you're working."

"He's a bad actor. I'm not authorized to say more."

"I understand."

By the time dinner was done, she was stuffed. And so relaxed she could've floated to the ceiling—if such a thing were possible. All she wanted was to crawl under the covers and go to sleep.

Donovan drove her home and walked with her to her back door. "You've had a busy day."

"I can barely move."

He pulled her close. "Lean on me."

"I may go to sleep."

"That's okay. I'm glad I could help you and you weren't hurt."

"Thank you for everything."

"I don't think I've ever known anyone like you."

Gracie smiled against his shirt. "Is that a good thing or a bad thing?" She moved her arms to drape over his shoulders. He was soft and cuddly, but plenty strong and firm enough to lean against. She wanted to cuddle.

"It's a very good thing." Donovan kissed the top of her head, her forehead, her cheeks, working his way toward her lips.

She returned the pleasure with her own kisses to his neck, chin, and jaw. When their lips met, his kiss was firm and steady. His tongue played with hers until he changed position and drew her closer. After a second or two, she giggled. Or as much of a giggle as possible in the middle of a hot kiss.

Donovan lifted his head. "Are you laughing?"

She shook her head and giggled again.

"What?"

"I drank too much wine." She did her unsuccessful best to stifle another giggle. "I was thinking your kiss was way more jalapeno than it was cupcake." And she burst into another round of giggles.

Donovan smiled. "That sounds like a good thing."

She nodded, not trusting herself to speak again. Instead, she tightened her arms around his neck to pull his lips back to hers.

He kissed her again, but lightly, before he stepped back. "I shouldn't have ordered the wine after your trauma today."

"The wine was good. I needed to relax, and it did the trick."

His fingers played with her hair. "Yes, it did. I need to go home. Right now. So don't tempt me."

If she hadn't been too tired to think, she would have. "Okay. That's probably a good idea. Are we still on for tomorrow night?"

"Don't even try to keep me away. We'll talk about it in the morning."

"Plan."

CHAPTER 79

Gracie awoke before her alarm went off. She was a little stiff, but not bad. The aches would work themselves out during the day. She thought about Donovan and remembered his kiss. She couldn't wait to see him.

Since Donovan knew about her hip hugger, she chose jeans and her new coral blouse with the ruffled bottom. And blue Converses. It would be close quarters behind the counter at Jalapeno Cupcake. The holster would remind him she was working.

She dressed quickly. Even after doing her makeup and putting her hair in a bun, she finished with time to spare.

On the way, she stopped at Whataburger for a breakfast taco and orange juice. She ate in the car and ditched the wrappings in a trash barrel at the parking lot. By the time she got out and locked the door, the parking lot was three-quarters full.

That's when she remembered the Battle of Flowers Parade, which would begin in a few hours. This entire area would be a zoo. The parade didn't come down any of these streets, though, so the lot wouldn't be barricaded. She would be able to leave.

She was happy to see the Tahoe she ran into hadn't damaged the mural. People parking here would never know what happened. But she would always remember.

Donovan waited at the door. He kissed her on the cheek.

She kissed him back in the same manner. "What did you tell Maricelia and Natalie?"

"I moved the beer to the supply closet before they arrived. Since I didn't know how much was safe to share, I just said that Webb had been arrested and we'd have to muddle through today and tomorrow without him."

"Perfect. The story will probably be all over the news anyway. How are they doing?"

"Great! Maricelia is a go-getter and Natalie stepped right into Maricelia's old shoes. Tessa's going to decide over the weekend which positions to fill. She's planning to come in tomorrow for a few minutes. She wants to show off Emily, but she also wants to get eyes on."

"I understand that. It's what I would do."

#

On her break, Gracie called Jackson. "What's the latest?"

"I take it you haven't seen the news."

"Not all week. Did aliens land?"

"Before I tell you about that, Salazar said they found a deposit into Truitt's account at his hometown bank up in Sweetwater. It was made yesterday in the amount of fifty big ones from an account in the Bahamas."

"For getting Victor to bring a person and the diamonds across?"

"So it appears. She asked us to look into it, but it's a little out of our bailiwick."

"Here I thought we could do anything." She smiled.

"It gets sticky in some spots. Everything is double and triple encrypted with changing codes. Plus there are political issues."

"Ah, the real reason rears its ugly head."

"She said Truitt isn't talking. He's requested an attorney. But on her end, they want it as tight as possible. Everything was circumstantial until they got the gun. It's a positive ballistics match with the one that killed the Cantus. They have him. We're still keeping the Cantus until the bail hearing. Salazar is pushing to get a rush on the prints and the DNA they found. We're pressuring her, so we'll be running those in our labs starting this afternoon. The more evidence we have, the greater chance of him not receiving bail."

"Is that why you wondered if I'd seen the news?"

"No. I expected this story to take over the local stations. But it's down on the list."

"Why? What's happened?"

"Do you know who Joshua Brackett is?"

Brackett? "The name's familiar. A philanthropist? I remember reading something about him building a care facility for some group. Kids—special needs, abuse. I forget."

"That's the one. He died yesterday on his ranch— the news said it was west of Austin between Llano and Mason. It was the lead story."

"Oh. Sorry to hear that. That's north of Fredericksburg about forty or fifty miles. My dad may know him, or at least know more about him than I do. Was he sick?"

"No one knows. His housekeeper found him dead in his bed when she arrived. Speculation's rampant, so he's still the top local story. Everything from natural causes to electrocution to a bullet. The autopsy's in a couple of hours."

#

Donovan was alone at the counter when she returned. She was tying her apron when he asked, "What would you like to do tonight after dinner?"

"I'm easy—a movie?"

"Works for me. I can do better than last night."

"Last night was perfect. I have no complaints."

"All the same, it wasn't up to par for a first date."

"No problem. We'll just have a do-over."

Donovan laughed. "I like the way you think."

"What should I wear?"

"Something a little up from sweats."

The door opened and a man wearing a suit entered. Gracie knew just enough about menswear to know that his suit and shoes cost more than all the clothes in her closet combined. The suit had been tailored just for him, and even without touching it, she knew the fabric would feel soft against a woman's body. He was that kind of man, even though a gold band encircled the third finger of his left hand.

The man himself exuded charm along with a sense of power. She had no idea who he was, but he was accustomed to making decisions and being in control. Gracie made these observations before he'd taken two steps into the shop.

He took another step and smiled.

You are one handsome sucker, and you know exactly what you're doing. It's a good thing I grew up with three brothers or I'd definitely be attracted to your bad-boy ways.

Gracie returned the smile. "Welcome to Jalapeno Cupcake. What can I get for you this morning?"

"Jalapeno cupcakes. Five of them, please. Wrapped in a box for travel. Actually, I'd like the freshest ones you have, and I'd like to pick them up around two. I'm going to a meeting here in the building, and I have a lunch engagement after. Will that be possible?"

"We close at two," Donovan said.

"I'll be here before you close. My wife and four daughters will like them. I have to find ways to make them remember me."

"I have a new niece, so I understand." Donovan slid an order pad and pen across to the man. "Write

326

down your name and a phone number in case there's a problem."

"Certainly."

"We have one more baking of those cupcakes, and I'll see yours are pulled from there." He rang up the order and gave him the total.

Bad Boy paid with cash.

Donovan handed him the receipt. "The cupcakes will be boxed and waiting for you when you return."

Gracie waved. "Have a good meeting."

As soon as the customer was gone, Donovan turned to her. "I wonder where he's from. Not here. Not even Austin. We may wear a suit to a meeting, but not a suit like that one."

"Dallas. Houston. Some big city. He was right at home in those duds. Had a pricey haircut, too."

"Or he's a famous somebody, lives in the boonies, but attends a lot of events."

"And meetings. Almost everyone in town is closed today for the parade. That's a perfect time for a hush-hush meeting. Oh, I forgot to ask you. Are you going to pick me up tonight or do you want me to meet you someplace?"

"I'll pick you up. Do you mind eating early? We still have to be in here tomorrow morning."

"Not at all. In fact, maybe we can just have dinner so we can talk. Save the movie for another time. And no white wine for me."

"That's good—we have a reservation for six-thirty. I'll be there around six. Is red okay?"

CHAPTER 80

After she left the craziness of town behind, Gracie stopped at the grocery store for basics. She should've stopped for a burger or taco first—she would've bought half as much. It took her a few trips to bring everything inside. She bought a salad in the deli and ate that before she put the items away, which took longer than she thought. Now she had food for a couple of weeks at least, even if she ate every meal at home during that time. *Like that's ever gonna happen.*

It was two-thirty when she grabbed a broom to sweep off the deck and steps of Ariana's apartment. She really did need to stop thinking of it in that way. Soon it would be someone else's. Or just the apartment.

She picked up the key on her way out the back door. The steps looked really good with a new coat of paint. Or stain. Whatever they used. And the same for the deck. Things just looked tired and used after a while, especially when they were empty and not infused with someone's personality. Now they looked fresh again.

On her way up the stairs, Milo Porter called.

"Sorry, but I'm running late. I should be there by five-fifteen at the latest. Is that okay?"

"It's fine. I have a dinner date at six, but we'll have plenty of time. When you get to the neighborhood, you'll see my house is on the corner. The driveway is on the side street. Go ahead and park back there. I'll try to be on the patio when you get here. What are you driving?"

"A Jeep."

"I used to have one. Loved it."

They chatted for a minute or two before hanging up, and Gracie continued up to the deck. As she swept, the deck felt less like Ariana's. For a few weeks the scent of her herbs had lingered. Gracie sniffed. All gone. She sighed and kept sweeping. When she finished, she checked both sets of French doors to make sure they were secure.

Between them sat a tree stump she and Ariana had lugged up the steps because Ariana said it spoke to her. Across the top of the stump lay five black stones. Ariana would've had a reason for leaving them here. She would ask her when she got back.

Gracie unlocked the door and went inside to make sure there were no surprises when she showed it to Milo later. More black stones lay on the island. Gracie shook her head. Ariana must have placed them when she came back to look at the space after it was painted.

The air conditioning was on and the apartment looked good. She hoped she liked Milo and he checked out. And that he wanted to lease the apartment. She didn't have time to spend days or weeks finding a new tenant.

Back on the deck, she rechecked the door before heading down, sweeping each step along the way.

Gracie had dawdled longer than she thought. It was almost four, later than she planned, when she jumped in the shower. She still didn't know what to wear, but if they were going someplace that required reservations, she had to look decent. She finally decided on the little black dress Trinka had made her buy on sale last fall. It was barely long enough to cover her thigh holster. She added a sunflower necklace and black sandals.

A Baja Yellow Jeep Wrangler pulled into her driveway right after she stepped onto the patio. It looked good there—she could pretend it was hers. Maybe Milo wouldn't be so bad after all.

He got out, and she walked out to introduce herself. He reminded her of her youngest brother. Same straw-colored hair, and shaggy, like Axel wore his. Same chiseled face with a square jaw. *I hope we're not cousins. Where did that thought come from? Half the population of Fredericksburg looks like us, and we're not all related. Not closely, anyway.*

He smiled when he rounded the front of the Jeep. "Gracie?"

She spread her arms. "That's me. You must be Milo."

He wore a white cotton shirt, khaki shorts, and brown leather sandals. And dark, sexy sunglasses. She couldn't see his eyes, but she felt him looking at her whole body, including her dress. A tingle passed up her spine. *Don't be a slut, Grace Elizabeth—you don't even know this guy. You just went gaga over Donovan's kiss last night.* Milo took off his shades.

Mother of God! Milo's eyes were forest green—light, with dark streaks. Almost a quarter of his left iris was amber. They mesmerized her. *I can't stop looking at him. What the hell's wrong with me?*

"I think I'm underdressed." He smiled.

Wow. If I had on socks, he would've knocked them off. "Not at all. I have an early dinner date and didn't know if I'd have time to dress after I showed you the apartment. Ready?"

"Sure." He put his sunglasses back on. "I like what I see so far."

Dammit! She couldn't see his eyes when he said he liked what he saw. But she heard his voice. *Stop*

it, Gracie, right now. Do. Not. Crush. On. Your. Tenant.
    She reached for a nonexistent pocket. "Oops, hang on. I forgot the key."

CHAPTER 81

Gracie poked her arm inside the kitchen door and plucked the key from the counter. "Okay, let's go. You lead the way."

"I want to look at the deck first."

"Go for it. I'll unlock the door and turn on the lights."

She went inside and turned on all the lights. Each room offered recessed lighting, plus vanity lights in the bathrooms and task lighting in the kitchen.

When she walked back to the living room, she spied him through the French doors. She opened the nearest set and joined him on the deck. "Are you lost in thought?"

"Sort of. It's nice out here—like a treehouse. Feels great."

"Cool! Want to see inside?"

"I suppose I should." He stopped at the tree stump and picked up the stones Ariana had left, spreading them around his palm. "Obsidian. Are you getting rid of negative energy?"

Gracie spun around. "What?"

"Obsidian."

She shook her head. "The former tenant. She's into all that."

"My sister, too. I've picked up a little from her. Not sure I'm a firm believer, though."

"I'm not sure I'm any kind of believer in it." Then

she remembered her two recent episodes. "But I haven't totally written it off. Anything is possible."

"People use obsidian to clear out stagnant or negative energy. So it makes sense the previous tenant wanted to clear the space for someone new. Maybe that's why it feels so good out here." He stepped inside.

Gracie moved back to watch his reaction to the space.

He walked around the living room, discovered the high ceiling. She could almost see him placing his furniture. He walked to the island.

"Great space. I really like this kitchen. The layout's perfect. Okay if I go on to the back?"

"Sure." Gracie followed.

He smiled when he saw the office and gave a soft whistle at the master suite.

She walked back to the living room to give him a little privacy.

He joined her a couple of minutes later. "I turned off the lights back there. This is an amazing find."

"You can thank my aunt for that. This is her baby. And my mother."

He laughed. "I can see that. What is she asking for rent?"

"A one-year lease is twenty-four hundred a month. Two years, twenty-two. Three, two thousand. She also wants a twenty-five hundred dollar deposit. No pets."

"I don't have time for a pet."

"She's ideally looking for a long-term tenant like the previous one, and she's allowing for that. Oh, I almost forgot. You get the right-hand side in the garage, and the right-hand storage area. It's about ten by ten."

Milo thought about it. He spotted the rocks Ariana had left on the island. "How can I say no? The place is perfect. Including the light and energy. Where do we go from here?"

"Down to the patio, and I'll give you all the stuff you need to fill out. Let me lock the French door before we leave."

"I'll get the lights."

Milo went out first. She followed and locked the door.

"Well, hello!"

CHAPTER 82

Gracie jumped at the sound of Donovan's voice. "Hi. Is it six already?" She'd been so caught up with Milo, she'd forgotten about her date.

"I'm a few minutes early."

"It's five-fifty." Behind her, Milo's voice was soft.

Gracie gave him a quick nod of thanks and went down the stairs first. "See, I'm dressed."

"You're beautiful." But he only glanced at her. His gaze remained on Milo.

Was Donovan jealous? Or controlling? She'd picked up on little clues, but now it showed up in dark black clouds.

"Y'all come on over and find seats on the patio." Their footsteps echoed behind her. "I have to go inside to get the papers. I'll be right back."

Gracie pulled three beers from the fridge, picked up the envelope from the table, and shouldered her way out the door. "Okay, guys. I come with beer." She passed them out.

Two mumbled *thanks* came in return.

"Donovan, this is Milo Porter. He's going to be my new tenant. Assuming he passes muster. Milo, Donovan Beck. You may see him around."

This time, she got some muttered words and a couple of nods. Her unsettled feeling remained. Donovan's behavior concerned her, but she had a job to do.

She opened her beer and turned her attention to Milo. "All the forms you need to complete are inside. They're also available online at a secure site. The URL is inside, too. I'd prefer you complete them online because it saves me a little time, but if paper's your thing, that works fine. Just so you know, my uncle is a banker. And you already know I'm in law enforcement. Between us, we will check you out. So if out of the blue you feel like you're getting a colonoscopy, it's probably just one of us."

Milo laughed. "Thanks for the warning."

"No problem."

"I have my iPad, and I'll fill these out either tonight or in the morning. Do you want me to text you when they're done?"

"The program notifies us." She picked up the envelope and pulled out a sheet of paper and a pen. "This is the one I need you to fill out now and sign. It's the one that authorizes us to search using your Social Security Number. There's one of these online, too. It also needs to be filled out. The program won't let you close out until it's completed."

While he filled out the short form, Gracie went to stand next to Donovan, not knowing what to expect. "You look nice, too. And you don't smell like sugar."

He smiled. "Some days I wonder if I'll ever like cake again."

"Sure you will. Did that guy come back for his cupcakes?"

"He did. Happy as could be."

"Must've had a good meeting."

"He asked about you."

Gracie's insides stood at full alert. "What about me?"

"He just said you were 'cute as could be' and 'a real asset' to the shop."

"What did you say?"

336

"That I agreed completely, but that you were a temp and we hoped we got as lucky the next time we needed someone extra. I didn't tell him anything else."

Gracie relaxed a little. "Did he ask my name?"

"No."

She felt better.

"Did anyone ask about the beer?"

"No. Well, Maricelia and Natalie did—they saw it in the closet."

"Bastion's picking it up tomorrow."

Milo stood up and handed Gracie the form and the pen. "Okay, done. I'm going to take these with me in case I have problems online. Hopefully, I won't need them and can drop them off on Sunday on my way out of town."

"That's fine. If I'm not here, just leave them on the table out here. They'll be good. Great meeting you." She held out her hand.

"Same here." They shook. The tingle returned. She wondered if he felt it, too. "Have a great weekend."

"You, too." He held her hand an extra moment longer than necessary, but not so long that Donovan would notice. Maybe he did feel what she felt. A minute after letting go, he backed out of the driveway. She turned.

Donovan stood two steps behind her. He placed his hands on her shoulders. "Now I have you all to myself. I like the sunflowers."

There's no tingle. "Thanks. I bought it at an arts and crafts festival last summer. It makes me smile."

Donovan wasn't smiling. "Do you think you'll rent to that guy?"

She didn't care for Donovan's attitude, and if it continued, she would bring it up. Right now, she shrugged. "Depends. We're thorough. If he checks out, probably yes."

Her phone rang with a call from Jackson. "I have to take this."

Donovan nodded and released her shoulders.

She walked out to the driveway. "Hi, what's up?"

"We've got them."

"Got who? What?"

"SAPD sent us all the prints and DNA to run against Truitt's."

"Yes!" She pumped the air.

"Our lab knows it's a priority rush. We'll have everything possible to the DA's office before Truitt's court date on Monday."

"I'm glad they decided to let Bastion labs work for them."

"This case has set a good example. I'm confident they have the right man in custody and that our labs will find the forensic proof to ensure he stays there. He's too dangerous to risk being out on bail."

"I agree."

"Another bit of news arrived that you may be interested in. About the rancher."

"Joshua Brackett. I heard on the news they were waiting for toxicology results."

"Yeah. What I'm about to share is confidential."

"I understand."

"Based on the condition of the body, they think he had a stroke. Besides the tox screen, they're waiting on a few other items, too before determining the cause of death."

"Okay." Gracie had seen deceased stroke victims. Most had contracted hands and partially severed tongues.

"Then some of the trace evidence showed up that indicates there may have been foul play."

"What was it? Do you know?"

"I only know about one—a sample taken from a table top in Brackett's living room. It tested positive for venom from a Dendroaspis Polylepsis."

"You're reading that from your computer. What is it?"

Jackson laughed. "You got me. A black mamba. That's an African snake. As poisonous as they come. Paulina called me. They were notified because it's a signature kill by a high-value target they've been hunting for a long time."

"The man Victor brought across the border?"

"A good possibility, given his point of entry and the timing of Brackett's death."

"People never cease to amaze me."

"Now you know why the Rangers are investigating. House locked up tighter than a drum. Alarm set."

"Wow."

They said goodbye, and Gracie walked back to Donovan. "We won't know for sure until Truitt's bail hearing on Monday, but it's looking up for our side."

"He's no longer employed at Jalapeno Cupcake, no matter what. Surely he wouldn't try to hurt Tessa if he's out on bail. That's like pointing an arrow at himself."

Gracie snorted. "People are capable of anything. It's important he's not released. Everyone thinks so except him and his attorney. We have to make sure it doesn't happen."

"Whatever. No offense, but sometimes the police go a little overboard."

"Don't go there until you've walked in my shoes. You saw what happened yesterday."

"I'm curious about something. Did you check me out like you're doing with this Milo guy?"

Why was he asking? Did he have something to hide? She obviously hadn't seen the full report, but they would've notified her if there was anything she should be aware of. "Bastion did as part of the assignment. I read your background. When we met, you seemed nice." *So don't spoil it now.*

He was a good kisser, but so were other men. Some without attitudes.

As if he read her mind, he placed his hand against her cheek and lifted her chin with his thumb. "I don't want to fight." He lowered his lips to hers. The kiss was long and slow and sensual. She wrapped her arms around his neck and tried to block out the fact there was no tingle. Not even a tiny one.

He ended the kiss and stepped back. "Still want to go to dinner?"

"Sure. I'm not mad at you."

But her hackles had been raised. And she did wonder what it would feel like to kiss Milo.

THE END

Dear Reader:

Thank you for purchasing this copy of *Jalapeno Cupcake Wench*, the first book in The Amazing Gracie Trilogy. I hope you enjoyed meeting Gracie and will want to find out what happens next.

Please help spread the word by leaving a review on Amazon, Goodreads, and/or the site of your favorite online bookshop. Reviews help more than you can imagine. Just a line or two saying you loved it or want to read more by the author. That's all it takes.

There's a magic place awaiting for those of you who take this extra step in helping writers develop a strong readership. We all thank you.

Carol

Author Acknowledgments

A huge thank you for help in the writing of this trilogy to Joseph F. Vinas, M.D., for sharing his expert medical knowledge, to H.R. Sinclair for her insight and wisdom into the powers and properties of stones and crystals, and to Vanna Crocker for having her finger on the heartbeat of the Texas Hill Country and answering my many questions. If anything in the story is incorrect, the fault is mine for adapting their suggestions to fit the story.

Thanks also to the wonderful people involved in the production of Gracie's story for publication, starting with my awesome editor, Susan Helene Gottfried. She made my words so much better—and I have none left to express my gratitude, except *she's the best*. Cover designer Ada Frost made you drool over the cover, and L. Diane Wolfe worked her magic to make this book work properly on your reader and look like a book instead of a bunch of pages glued together in print.

No book is written and published in a vacuum. It takes a team, and I think mine is the best. Thank you all!

Carol

About the Author

Carol Kilgore is the author of *The Amazing Gracie Trilogy*. She is also the author of *In Name Only*, *Solomon's Compass*, and *Secrets of Honor*, three standalone romantic suspense novels set along the Texas Gulf Coast. With her first published fiction, Carol won the Derringer Award for Best Short-Short Mystery Story for "Just a Man on the Sidewalk."

She and her husband live in San Antonio, the setting for the *Amazing Gracie* books, with two quirky dogs who still require help opening the food bin and the door.

Carol is a member of Romance Writers of America, Mystery Writers of America, and Sisters in Crime.

You can learn more about Gracie and be the first to know when the second book in the Amazing Gracie Trilogy will be released by subscribing to Carol's newsletter at her website: www.carolkilgore.net or connect with her on Facebook and Twitter.

Facebook:
www.facebook.com/carolkilgore.author/
Twitter: www.twitter.com/carol_kilgore

Made in the USA
Monee, IL
31 July 2021